Tom Pitts is a Melbourne-based writer, teacher, sound designer and musician. *Electric and Mad and Brave* is his first novel.

Electric
and
Mad
and
Brave

Electric and Mad and Brave

TOM PITTS

PICADOR

Pan Macmillan Australia

Pan Macmillan acknowledges the Traditional Custodians of country throughout Australia and their connections to lands, waters and communities. We pay our respect to Elders past and present and extend that respect to all Aboriginal and Torres Strait Islander peoples today. We honour more than sixty thousand years of storytelling, art and culture.

This is a work of fiction. Characters, institutions and organisations mentioned in this novel are either the product of the author's imagination or, if real, used fictitiously without any intent to describe actual conduct.

First published 2022 in Picador by Pan Macmillan Australia Pty Ltd
1 Market Street, Sydney, New South Wales, Australia, 2000

A catalogue record for this book is available from the National Library of Australia

Typeset in 11.9/16 pt Adobe Garamond Pro by Post Pre-press Group, Brisbane
Printed by IVE

The author and the publisher have made every effort to contact copyright holders for material used in this book. Any person or organisation that may have been overlooked should contact the publisher.

The paper in this book is FSC® certified. FSC® promotes environmentally responsible, socially beneficial and economically viable management of the world's forests.

For Kate

2015

Thursday, 26 November

I'M SITTING AT a desk in front of a square window in this little hospital room. Looking about, I've got everything I need: single bed, TV, air-conditioning, cards and flowers – my parents gifted a miniature ficus with a label that says, 'You are stronger than you know . . . Don't forget that.'

It's a shared bathroom, which isn't my thing, but the second bed is empty so it hasn't been a problem. Apparently, they can swing the curtain around and divide the room; they're very accommodating. I watch into the halls, the nurses and clinicians moving back and forth. They wink and I wink and it's as if I'm involved. This morning feels a little tense actually; around 2 am last night, one of the residents became hysterical and we all awoke to a pandemonium of rushing and clattering – a restraining on the floor.

Today things are quiet and I sit gazing at the lemon trees along the paving, the hedging cut square over the back fence, twigs and leaves on the grass. It's a quaint picture: boughs dipping and blowing about as if I'm at some gorgeous country retreat.

Which of course I'm not.

I am in the psychiatric facility of the South Yarra Clinic for Emotional Health and Wellbeing. It's now been three weeks with my days spent in a repetition of therapy and prescription pills. Bedtime is 10 pm and at night you hear the sound of revellers drifting in and out of the bars along Chapel Street. Most evenings I lie awake, listening to the cars and the laughter, and thinking what a fabulous location this would be – if only I was allowed past the foyer without a chaperone.

So this is the first entry in what is to become my *Mental Health Journal*.

Gloria, my current psychologist, wants me to start writing all my thoughts and feelings into a biography of sorts. According to Wikipedia, it will force me to 'delve into singular moments of my past and help to unpack issues that are yet to be confronted'. To be honest, I'm quite sceptical – but then, I figure Gloria's not made a surgical mess of her bathroom, so who am I to judge?

It's part of the Creative Arts Therapy Initiative that's been introduced here at Yarra Clinic. Since arriving, I've spent my Wednesdays in the cafeteria, drawing and painting and creating collages, using art to 'communicate thoughts and feelings that are too painful or complex to put into words'. Last week we were asked to draw our 'lines of feeling'. I drew a thatchwork of orange and green that filled the entire page. Devon said the work was 'significant'. I told him I didn't understand the activity, it had all been a bluff. He said, 'This is also significant.' I can think of no better summary of the Creative Arts Therapy Initiative.

Nevertheless, I draw and paint and collage. I participate to the best of my ability and don't ask questions. I do anything and everything Gloria suggests because I trust her and I want to get better.

'And you've never considered the benefits of journalling?'

This was our conversation on Tuesday. Gloria's a large woman with prestigious degrees and an extra crease on her lower eyelids that reveals itself whenever she smiles or looks down. Twice a week she sits opposite me, listening with a maternal aspect that makes me want to curl into her breast and take confession.

'You see, I think you might gravitate to a less abstract form of expressive therapy, one that can be done privately and in your own time.'

I told her if it meant getting better, I was willing to do anything she wanted; art therapy, behaviour therapy, journals, drugs, whatever it took. I didn't tell her that I actually have kept a diary before – after Year 7 cross-country, when I spent that week describing how Shelly Bick seemed to glide through the air like spring gossamer.

'Try starting with three pages a day,' she suggested, 'about yourself, your daily life and routines; anything that comes to mind. Just keep the pen going, even if you think it's gibberish – even if it doesn't make any sense at all. The main thing is getting it out.'

I said I'd give it my best and she smiled. It was Tuesday.

Fast forward two days, and my parents arrived this morning with a Moleskine, three pens and a miniature ficus.

My name is Matt Lacey and I'm a twenty-eight-year-old former primary teacher who worked for eighteen months, until 17 June 2010, when I was discovered weeping in a room full of students. I was awarded mental health leave and everyone was very understanding of the pressures placed on the shoulders of young teachers. At that point, I was living alone and the consequences were disastrous: I've been admitted to Yarra Clinic three times.

More recently, I've lived with my best friend and his fiancée. Sam doesn't question; he's always been supportive. He got me a job at a cafe called Globe on Chapel. In fact, had I not been admitted, I'd be there this very second, making coffee and washing dishes; visiting the endless rotation of people on their phones or sitting in clusters and speaking with fanatical concern about Indoor Plants and Carol's Biopsy and whatever else, arriving and leaving as we scuttle in a mad rush.

By lunch I probably would have begun to panic. It would be busy and impossible for me to leave and I would be aware of this and the idea would become oppressive. It would cause my hands to become light and disembodied. I would drop things and begin to think in circles, to 'catastrophise'. My chest would tighten and I would feel something like hunger, a dull pressure on the solar plexus, then vertigo – hyperventilating and rushing to the bathroom, bright lights swindling; a customer bent over the basin wanting to know if I 'need anything, mate?', the face suddenly overexposed and warped in the mirror. 'Mate? You right?' Me slamming the cubicle door and shuddering against the gaudy posters of the comedy festival.

I've been assured by anyone and everyone that this behaviour is perfectly understandable. No one has ever told me it's irrational. (I'm aware that it's irrational.) Instead, people sympathise and tell me not to worry. They congratulate me for achieving day-to-day tasks such as eating and showering.

They have no idea they're being condescending. In fact, they mean every word – only it's clear my behaviour makes no sense to them. My parents visit and inquire tentatively, desperate to be encouraging. They try to empathise and fail. I watch them standing at the bedside, nodding thoughtfully and agreeing that under the circumstances one might . . . that they can imagine how I could want to . . .

It is easier to agree than to tell the truth.

What I would give for them to say I've behaved irrationally, to slap my face and for me to suddenly snap out of it. I want to snap out of it. I want to awaken with a switch flicked, to no longer be oppressed by rooms full of people, by trains and elevators. I want to stand in a classroom and hold myself together.

If this journal is the answer, then I'll give it my all.

So GLORIA WANTS me to write about Christina.

I suppose I should have expected it.

A lot of things became clear today, actually: she wants me to write about Christina, and she wants me to write about Connie, and she wants me to write about everything that happened at Wychwood Farm. In fact, she was so desperate to broach the topic that I'm now convinced it's the entire reason she wants me to keep a journal.

You see, Gloria believes Christina is my biggest knot to unravel. She believes that if you peeled back my skull and looked over the edge, you'd find Christina pulling strings and wreaking havoc. My evidence? Only how she manages to steer every conversation we have towards Christina, or to Connie, or to Wychwood. Last week – having brought it up herself – she had the nerve to say, 'Oh, here we are again!' and give a look that was perplexed and suggestive. When I explained it was her own doing, she nodded and wrote a sentence including the word 'refusal'.

To be clear: I'm not refusing anything. Trust me, no one knows better than I the particular ways in which Christina and I managed to ruin one another. No one knows better than I that it was a clusterfuck from the beginning, and that it was always going to end in disaster. What Gloria doesn't realise, however, is that I've had time to mull over the disaster and to deal with it – several years, in fact. So it's not that I'm refusing; I've just put it behind me.

'But if it's not an issue then what's the harm in writing about it?' was Gloria's response to this, crossing her arms like she'd put me in check.

'There's no *harm*,' I said. 'I'm happy to *do* it; I just don't see a *reason*.'

She nodded and wrote something else down – I couldn't see what. When she looked up though, she had one of her pleasant smiles that reminds me how she can sleep in the dark and drink coffee without becoming hysterical.

'I'd like you to try,' she said, 'if you don't mind.'

'. . .'

Anyway, so here I am, thinking about Christina again, going over the whole mess – again – dredging it up start to finish, so I can 'delve into singular moments and unpack issues that are yet to be confronted'. I even called Christina earlier to fill in some of the blanks, ask what she remembers. Of course she had no time to talk. (It's now been a week since she's visited and I have three messages that remain unanswered. I know for a fact she isn't busy.)

Gloria wants me to begin regardless.

'You can always add things later,' she says. 'The important thing is getting it out, seeing where it takes you.'

Which is funny, because both of us know where it 'takes me'.

Where it takes me is this hospital room.

The end is easy. It's the beginning that's tricky; hence spending the afternoon going over dates and timelines, what came after what, trying to remember as much as I can.

I'll shoot Christina another message later.

In the meantime, though:

*

When I met Christina, I was eleven. She was twelve. I remember watching the landscape fly across the window and being intensely pissed off – the first memory – pissed off and eleven years old, plummeting down the Frankston Freeway towards Hastings. Christina's family had moved from interstate that year, trading city New South Wales for the sprawling wilderness of Wychwood, where I was currently being delivered because Mum had guessed the Fox FM secret sound and won a trip to Hamilton Island. She'd shrieked to the sound of glittery music. Now I was to be abandoned so she could summer with Dad in the waters of Catseye Beach. Pissed off and indignant – it had been my idea, hadn't it? a video tape sliding into its case – forcing my parents to play I-spy, then losing and becoming upset, punishing them with deathly silence as Dad explained how defeat was a part of life; the landscape a wash of eucalypt and bracken and the kinds of places that only exist in the middle of nowhere: Antique Barnhouse and Karingal's Earthenware. All of it exhausted. 'Defeat is a part of life, Matthew.' Dad becoming silent then as David Bowie's voice warped in the blustering wind, a new-age church passing with crazy triangular buttresses splayed like a fennel, Mum humming out the window. All the time, Christina was drawing closer, the frame becoming small that encompassed us both – not that I cared, closing my eyes and seeing colours flit in the dark, listening to the hum of the wheels, and Mum's tune becoming smooth and ghostly; drifting away as the car rolled on and on, and wondering remotely, why I couldn't have stayed somewhere else . . .

'That is *not* her!'

I know I slept because I remember waking as the car slowed into the driveway. Mum was tapping my leg and winding her window down. I looked out to see a girl sitting on the fence. Apparently we'd met before, but I didn't recognise her. Her face was sharp and deliberate, somehow like a bird.

'Six years does that,' Dad commenting as if he wasn't surprised, turning onto the gravel as Mum leaned out the window.

'Hi Christina! My God, you're *big*!'

Christina lifted her hand in a half-wave. Her green socks had strange pink sploshes that seemed to be there on purpose. She twirled her feet around.

'Do Mum and Dad want us to drive in?' Mum asked.

Christina pointed up the long driveway.

'Thanks, sweetie!'

We pulled away and she slid across the window, disappearing into my sleeping bag. I didn't know what to make of her. She didn't look at all excited – but she'd been waiting. The sploshes were weird.

Now she re-emerged in the back window, jumping off the fence and sprinting after the car. In the paddock beside us, two horses looked on with vague interest. I wondered if they were bored, or not smart enough to be bored. One of them stomped for no reason and Christina shot by my window, towards Aleksei, who was stepping out of the house.

To this day, I've never shifted from my first impression of Alek. I watched him realise the sun was too bright, fumble for glasses that weren't there, then shield his eyes. It was like a military salute. I thought: this is a more impressive father than my own father. Christina was buried against his leg as he pointed to where the driveway ballooned. His arm was massive and definite; a monolith warding us triumphantly into the car park. As we reversed in, I looked at my own father's hand on the gearstick, his fingers curled like the pincer of a crab.

Suddenly, there was a barking and I turned to see Connie walking down from the workshed with Mr Harvey. He was yapping and circling and generally enthusiastic. Mum was out of the car.

'Wow! This place is *incredible*!'

Connie stuck out her tongue and made a face that seemed to say, 'Tell you what's *incredible* is this bloody farm work! But I s'pose when you buy a farm . . .' She clomped towards us in a tattered singlet, denim cut-offs and a pair of dusty work boots, arriving and sliding an arm around Aleksei. For a second, they became a family portrait: Connie, Christina, Aleksei – together and delighted. They looked glorious, somehow carved in stone. If we'd been told in that moment that Aleksei was about to die and everything was going to unravel, I'm sure we'd all have laughed at such an absurd prediction.

And yet he was – about to die.

Christina still peeked from behind his leg. There was something about her I didn't like. It might have been everything. She was shy and weird. I thought: we will have to be friends because our parents have decided, but if the choice were mine . . . She looked at me with a scowl. I scowled back. If I'd been told in that moment that the two of us would grow up to ruin each other . . . I might have believed it.

Connie always reminded me of a lifestyle television host. She never quite had the gravity of an adult, instead possessing a kind of overt enthusiasm that people found either refreshing or a little much. She didn't consider personal space, and would pat and prod your shoulder unconsciously as she spoke. Then there was her laugh, a high bleat that shot abruptly before anyone else got the joke – and often when there was no joke. In conversation though, she became an 'active listener', nodding and maintaining feverish eye contact, finding things more interesting than they actually were.

The afternoon we met, she was sitting saucer-eyed across the table, listening to Mum explain how it didn't matter that our backyard had no grass because she'd developed a make-shift garden across the verandah using a series of earthenware pots.

'And besides,' Mum was on a roll, 'when it's mostly succu-lents, you're keeping watering down to a minimum!'

Connie slammed a palm on the table.

'That's it. I'm doing it. We were actually *just* saying the other day, we need something across the back verandah. Right now it's completely – anyway, we'll show you after . . .' She was tapping Alek's arm. 'Weren't we?'

'What are we doing?' He turned, derailed.

'Lynette's potted plants all along their balcony, made a herb garden. And tomatoes?'

'Cherry,' Mum beamed.

'I was saying we've got nothing across the back verandah so we should do it.'

Alek raised his eyebrows in a way that said, 'How about that!' and nothing more. He pointed to Connie's plate.

'You finished?'

The contents of her pie had oozed into a repulsive fan. He turned to Mum. 'Perhaps bring cold ones next time?'

Connie gave a laugh that was ironic, exaggerated and silent. 'Isn't he hilarious?' Aleksei grinning as he took her plate.

I watched him stride to the bench and dump the dishes on the counter – the large room cramped somehow with a thick herbish smell; rugs and weird jars and garlic strung from the beams. Beside me, Christina seemed to be conducting an experiment with her sausage roll. She raised a morsel into the light, examining how the middle was pink and the end was charred. I wondered what the hell I was doing with these people.

'Well, what do we think?' Alek turned. 'Time for a tour?'

'Ooh, I don't know,' Dad frowning at his watch.

'Just a quick one. When's the flight?'

'Three-thirty.'

'Oh, you're fine!' Connie said.

'Really? With check-in?'

Alek assured us there was heaps of time, and that there was no traffic anyway because it was the holidays, and that while he understood the function of roundabouts, he felt they were a dispensable cause of peak hour congestion.

I looked over to see Christina skipping through the sliding door and into the sun. She flew off the verandah in a pirouette, cartwheeling over the grass.

14

'Okay great,' Dad's voice behind me, 'quick tour.'

I watched her spin and spin, feeling my heart sink further.

Mr Harvey led us around the property, rushing away and bounding back. He was a mix of blue heeler, golden retriever and something else – Alek 'wouldn't have been surprised if it was staffy!' As a pup he'd been exactly half black and half grey, and the colours had inspired the name 'Halfhalf' – though this had changed after the family discovered it was annoying to pronounce.

Spiralling the grounds, Mum and Alek walked ahead in polite conversation. He was tour guide ('They told us 3.2 acres, but I measured 3.6.'), while she gushed and found things ideal and picturesque. Connie and Dad walked to one side. They'd known each other forever, it seemed. She held his arm with both of hers and he called her 'Con'. No one else called her Con. I could see Mum felt a little odd, though she never said. Christina was in front, throwing balls for Mr Harvey, skipping and cartwheeling. As we crossed alongside the eastern paddock, she dropped and tumbled like a ragdoll to the bottom of the hill.

'Wrong way, sister!' Connie called, before turning to Dad and lowering her voice. 'I think we've got an audience.' She nodded towards me; he smiled.

'Why don't you show Matt the chickens?' Alek asked.

'Oh, Matt!' Mum exclaimed – then, to no one in particular: 'Matthew loves chickens.'

This is true; I enjoy how their necks are like kaleidoscopes. But it didn't mean I wanted people to know. I shrugged as if I couldn't care less; Christina walking back up the hill, staring daggers at her mother.

'Honey?' Connie had her eyebrows raised. 'Matt wants to see the chickens?'

Christina turned on me. Somehow the chickens had become my idea. Without responding, she walked off towards the coop.

When we arrived, she said: 'Here they are,' and held out a hand. Three hens pecked into the dust. Christina was bored and insolent.

'Why do you like chickens so much?' she asked.

'I don't.'

'Your mum said you do.'

'She doesn't know me.'

We watched them cluck and nod in silence, then we made our way back.

Mum and Dad were already getting in the car. They kissed me goodbye and told me to be good, then waved as they sped up the drive. I watched them disappear onto the road, the barred gates drawing slowly shut behind them.

Saturday, 28 November

THREE WEEKS AGO, I tried to end my life by gassing myself in a car.

It looks odd written out like that.

Yesterday, it came up again, out of the blue. Gloria and I were discussing job seeking, moving forward.

She asked: 'Have you considered going back to teaching?'

I said: 'What, and have a collapse in front of a bunch of eight-year-olds? Hard to find work when . . .'

And there it was, sitting between us.

On Friday, November 6th, I gaffer taped a garden hose to my exhaust pipe, stretched it around the car and fed it through the window so it spilled into the back seat. I turned on the car and 'Jean Genie' erupted from the speakers. I turned it down, looked around to make sure I was still alone, and noticed a haze beginning to rise behind me. I sat silently as the car filled with exhaust fumes and wondered if music would still be playing when they found my body. I thought: how poignant if it were 'Rock 'n' Roll Suicide'.

*

Do I mind talking about it? Not really. Do I want to? Not particularly. Nor do I particularly *not* want to. It is what it is.

In the middle of unconsciousness, Sam's figure rose into view beneath the garage door. The car door flung open and I was saved. Later, in the hospital, I had fever dreams of him running around and around the bed. He would lean in and become enormous and I would reach out to push him away but my hand would uselessly extend into infinity. When I woke up, my parents were standing at the foot of the bed, watching cautiously with flowers and jelly – my grandma telling me I was selfish. Then three days convalescence and a weird final evening where I hardly slept, having spun out my body clock; the television flickering across the room as I watched doctors hurry past in the hallway.

This night I consider a non-reality. I remember looking at my hand and seeing a tube going into a bag. None of it seemed completely real. Even the act itself had not solidified. I thought: tomorrow I will wake up and it will have happened or it will have not happened. Then I was asleep.

*

The first night at Wychwood is another non-reality.

I lay curled in a sleeping bag, on a futon beside Christina's bed. Her room was a mystical grotto. She hoarded trinkets and knick-knacks and had a purple lampshade that threw enchanting light over everything. I peered at the mishmash of stuffed toys and wigs and stones and posters and sachets and advent calendars and ornaments and magazines and whatever else. My parents had left hours before and now Alek's laugh bellowed in the lounge room. He loved *Keeping Up Appearances* – the silly English woman. Connie was playing the piano and the sounds meshed together as if they were scoring a nightmare. Above me, Christina was on her bed either reading a book or pretending to read a book. Earlier on, we'd watched *Forrest Gump* and I'd secretly cried and she'd seen. This hadn't been addressed.

The music stopped and then Connie's footsteps were in the hall.

'Lights out, you guys!'

She entered the room and kissed Christina. Then she kissed me and stood by the door, flicking off the lights. Suddenly, the room was luminous. Spread over the walls and the ceiling were hundreds of invisible stars I hadn't noticed. Now they began to glow, and a galaxy emerged around us.

'Night, team.'

Connie closed the door and I lay with my eyes open, looking for constellations.

'You cried in the movie.' Christina's voice came in the dark.

'No, I didn't,' I said.

'You did.'

'So what?'

There was a rustling above me. I looked up and she was leaning over the bed, her teeth bewitching and phosphorescent.

'You're here because my mum and your dad love each other.'

There was a pause. I wasn't aware of this.

'What do you mean?'

'Don't you know?'

'I do.'

'No you don't.'

She fell back down on her pillow and was gone. My eyes rested on a pair of fairy wings that would hang for years in that exact spot, neither worn nor moved. How did she know about our parents? What did she even mean? I thought how Mum looked sad in her wedding photos. But it was absurd – she never smiled for the camera anyway.

'You're only here because they want it,' Christina said. Her voice was far away. 'I didn't ask for you to come.'

'I didn't ask to come.'

I heard her roll over. Then I was asleep.

*

Christina and I spent the holidays in this manner, forced together like cousin dogs; board games and impossible jigsaw puzzles; evening films and awkward family dinners where I was interrogated: Was I enjoying school? Which parts exactly? Oh *really?* When *we* were at school, they didn't even *have* digital cameras . . .

The house was set on the western side of Wychwood, an enormously quaint hobby farm, complete with stables, gardens, and several paddocks for agistment that sprawled their way eastward from the gravel drive that bisected the property. Lined with plane trees, the driveway ran up to the house, continuing on to Aleksei's workshed and then further still, finally ending in a clearing at the back of the property that was used to burn offcuts and felled branches. Early on, Connie had adopted the most southern paddock for a citrus orchard and it was here that she spent all of her time, staking and pruning and pattering. Alek's eternal project was the chicken coop, which sat beside the clearing and became massive as he adorned it with hatches and elaborate fortifications. He would spend hours in the workshed, constructing battlements in an endless war against Mr Harvey (who also loved chickens – more specifically, eviscerating them), a war which usually ended with Alek padding morosely through the orchard to throw a butchered carcass into the foliage over the back fence.

Christina and I pottered and lounged with nothing to do, shadowing Connie and helping to spin wire about the saplings. Alek always needed you to hold something, so we avoided him. We threw balls for Mr Harvey. Christina rode the horses and I stood away, petrified. We skirted the perimeter and imagined what lay beyond the fencing.

The paddock owned by Tom Davies intrigued us most. Standing over the eastern fence, it was entirely untouched – a mess of scrub and foliage stretching back I don't know how far, until you finally hit a river that was too wide and dangerous to cross. Originally, Alek had wanted to buy the land and turn it into 'something more constructive'. But Davies refused. He liked it au naturel. We liked it because it was a graveyard. Mr Harvey made sport of killing rabbits and would pile them in butchered clumps that were thrown over the fence to fester with the chickens. Then there were foxes and possums, nondescript flesh, tiny ribcages. From one corner, you could see the hind legs of a Clydesdale that lacerated its tendon on a cyclone fence. Davies had shot and buried it, forgetting the paddock was a marsh. By summer, the rain had dug it up. Christina and I spent whole afternoons peering through the wire at the skin curled back like a pair of stockings, the way the abdomen swelled with larvae in a grotesque mockery of respiration.

'Touch it,' she'd dared me eventually; the heat and the jigsaw puzzles and endless ballgames with Mr Harvey finally sending us into wild criminality.

'*You* touch it,' I said.

'I have already.'

'When?'

'Before.'

I nodded, studying the fence: a decent climb, but nothing I hadn't done before. The wiring seemed flimsy but it was easy landing on the other side.

'I'll do it if you do it.'

'Deal,' she said. 'You first though.'

'Flip for it.'

'No.'

'Fine.'

I peered at the mangled corpse. It seemed dead, but there was always a chance it could reanimate into a puppet of festering skin.

'What'll you give me if I do it?'

'Look, if you don't want to . . .'

She gave a smirk. Earlier that day, I'd claimed numerous superhuman abilities, including the power to crush bricks into sand. Fearing a dead animal would obviously do my reputation a disservice.

'Fine,' I said, tossing my hat and rubbing my hands together. 'I guess sometimes what needs to be done just . . . needs to be done.'

I paused a moment, delighting in what I thought had been a rather cool and nonchalant statement. Then I took a breath, winked at Christina, grabbed the fence, and was immediately electrocuted.

It's debatable whether my wailing or Christina's laughter were louder. I remember racing back through the trees as Connie and Alek rushed out of the house in alarm. Later,

Christina had spun a tale of innocence that caused me to weep a second time. Alek forced her to apologise and she spent the evening leering at me from the farthest couch. I spent the time withering with self-pity – my true character revealed – wincing theatrically and clutching an icepack that was neither cold nor of any use.

But the event was an anomaly. Mostly, Christina and I were bored; slouching about the house, about the grounds and in front of the television as time stretched itself endless. Those days mingle now in a vague image of thick heat, plodding and unremarkable. In fact, if Christina hadn't drowned, I doubt I would have remembered any of it.

It was this incident that I mark as the beginning of things unravelling – Christina flopping in the water; the incident that fooled us all into believing Alek was superhuman, and that made it so absurd for him to then find blood in his handkerchief.

On my final day at Wychwood, he was standing on the shoreline, a silhouette hurling Christina out of the water. We'd driven out to the Sorrento Bay of Islands and now the sun was sinking towards the ocean to spell the end of my incarceration. I was on a towel, separating categories of sand (not a beach person), watching them splash about in the water. Everywhere, people were lounging and bobbing like buoys in the water; the sound of drifting laughter.

'Not coming in, buddy?' Alek had jogged back up the sand and was hovering over me. 'It's beautiful in there.'

Christina was at the shoreline, standing imperiously with her hands on her hips. I shrugged and began to dig a hole.

'We're heading for the island, if you want?' he said, taking a bottle of water, his bicep eclipsing the sun.

A hundred metres out, the waves sloshed against the side of a huge jutting rock.

'I'm fine,' I said.

'Suit yourself.'

The bottle flew across and he winked and jogged back to the shore.

'It's okay, I hate the water too.' Connie was sitting beside me, buried in a novel.

I watched Christina dash back into the breakers, the water flicking up like tinsel about her feet. There was an explosion of surf and the two began to splash in twin lanes out towards the island, growing small and distant as the sun turned everything bronze. I knew I could easily have made the swim if I'd wanted; it wasn't that far.

Now a plane was flying overhead. I watched its slow arc, the white lines emerging behind, straight and curved. It was writing something in the sky – a 'D', it seemed. Now an 'A' and an 'N'. Someone's name; Daniel! No – a new line was beginning. 'DANI'. Who was Dani? I wondered. And could she see? 'MAR', the new line was saying. Mark, perhaps?

Another shout from the water.

Christina and Alek were playing again, showing off beside the huge rock island. She was in his arms, about to be thrown up into a backflip – only there was something odd about her, I thought; the way her head was flopping over, as though she was imitating the Raggedy Ann doll at the end of her bed.

There was a sting as sand flicked in my eye.

Wiping it away, I realised that Connie had rushed past me. She was in her clothes still – a yellow dress with flowers winding around – sprinting madly through the shallows and crashing into the waves, shouting something inaudible as her sunhat caught the wind and flew into the sky. 'MARRY ME,' the plane had written. 'DANI, MARRY ME.'

'Oh my God, it's a girl.'

Now a woman was beside me, cradling an infant and peering with an appalled look. People were standing in alarm, a man tearing off a Hawaiian shirt. They were all looking at Christina and Alek showing off; him paddling with one hand, lifting her as she bobbed and flopped, and Connie screaming, 'WAIT ON!' so unnaturally in the wonderful sunset. And it occurred to me suddenly that Christina was drowning. (Her head disappearing for a second.) She was drowning and Alek was trying to lift her out of the water. 'WAIT ON!' Connie's dress still sloshing against her figure. Now the crowd was lined on the shore in a panic, shouting and shielding their children – peering desperately at Alek tearing the water aside, trying to stand, trying to save his daughter – and Christina flopping weirdly, suddenly resurfacing as if her soul were trying to ascend into the sky that was now the most spectacular blazing orange. Connie arriving, and the shirtless man taking her under the arms and helping to lift. 'Oh Jesus, Jesus,' the woman crooning beside me as the baby wailed in her arms – someone else calling an ambulance. They were on their feet now – people rushing towards them – stringing Christina up like a marionette; hauling her out of the water. 'Get a towel!' Alek crashing from the waves. 'Is she alright!?' the mother with the howling infant. 'Towel! Now, now!' Then Connie sprinting by me, whipping the towel with her fingers shaking. 'Put her down, put her down . . .' Bystanders rushing about, crowding around, shrieking advice. 'Give him space!' 'Put her on her side!' Christina rolling over with a gash on her head, drizzling into the sand; Connie spearing into a mobile, 'I don't know – four, five minutes?!' 'Oh Jesus, oh Jesus.' The mother shielding her daughter's eyes as Alek pressed a towel over the wound; 'Bay of Islands! No, ISLANDS!' Connie's voice screaming over the bellowing infant. 'Oh Jesus! Jesus!'

From my hole I watched the pandemonium; Christina lolling and Alek peeling her fringe away, leaning forward to kiss her forehead, whispering softly, 'Christina,' and stroking her hair as Connie yelled at the paramedic and the crowd hovered awfully with nothing to do.

'Christina. Hey.'

Somehow the word seemed to bring life.

There was a gasp as Christina suddenly convulsed, lurching forward and spewing water in a fountain.

Connie dropped the phone and fell to her knees, clawing at her daughter's hair; Alek rolling her into the safety position to vomit again, clear liquid gushing into the sand.

'You're right, sweetie.' He drew her in.

Everyone was silent now, the infant calm in its mother's arms. Only the sound of waves and a tiny voice still twittering in the receiver.

'You're alright.'

I still hadn't moved, watching from my hole as the scene played out like a pantomime. Now I looked back over the water, at the huge rock jutting out, indifferent to the havoc. Waves were slapping against it, rising up and becoming annihilated. I looked at Christina.

Next time I would swim out.

Sunday, 29 November

I KNOW IT sounds absurd, but I'm convinced the incidents are connected; in my head Christina awakens and then Alek becomes ill. They happened almost a year apart, yet somehow, I'm certain one led to the other.

It was eight months later that Alek discovered blood in his handkerchief. Two months after that, he received his diagnosis – to everyone's surprise.

'Never touched a bloody cigarette in his life!'

I remember my parents' voices in the kitchen, Mum desperate for something to be indignant about. I was on the computer in the back room, conquering Spain.

'It just doesn't make any sense!'

She said the sentence two or three times with increasing profundity. Then there were footsteps and Dad came into the back room. He smiled and nodded to the screen.

'Is this, um . . .'

'*Civilization.*'

'Ahh, yes. That's right. I've been meaning to try this. Meant to be pretty addictive?'

I nodded. He had no interest in gaming and was never

going to try it. There was an uncomfortable silence as he watched a few moves, then he drew a breath sharply, like he'd been reminded of something.

'Actually, while I've got you: me and your mum are going to drive out to see Connie and Alek.'

'At the farm?'

There was a pause.

'No actually, they're at the Alfred. They think Alek's . . . well, he's been quite unwell. We're just saying hello, seeing how he is.'

'Can I come?'

'It's just adults.'

He rocked on his toes. Andrew Schilling's father had died of cancer earlier that year. News spread all over the school about how his body had withered like an old leaf.

'We'll only be an hour or two. There's pasta in the fridge.' He smiled and closed the door; opened it again.

'You might want to take the olives out.'

*

Christina had found Alek collapsed on the kitchen floor. He'd been mashing banana and banana had sprayed all over the room. It also emerged that he'd seen a doctor weeks before regarding a bloody handkerchief. I thought it was strange: a man like him with a handkerchief.

In the beginning, he remained at home. It was terrifying, but doctors had plans and actions and everything was positive: 'People beat worse things than this, *trust* me . . .' (Dad imitating Connie imitating an oncologist.) The family went on as normal. Alek continued to master the stock market. His hair thinned and he shaved his head. He wore a fedora to cover his baldness – then riding gloves to complement the fedora. He developed the funereal aspect of a rich and sinister businessman. But he was still sharp, forever cheerful. He laughed more than ever, began to wink at strangers. He developed a wry shrug that seemed to mean, 'and after all, isn't this life?' and he would shrug and laugh and wink as if we were all conspirators in a great circus.

As you'd imagine, with the cheer, and the doctors' anecdotes, and the beatable odds, a confidence began to grow among the family; first a budding hope, then a belief, then faith. Finally, it was irrefutable knowledge: remission was inevitable and soon we'd all be awake and be cheerful again, like the foyer after a horror film.

Remission came.

Soon after, we had them over for dinner – it would have been June/July 2000 – in the dining room with Alek waving his fork at the head of the table. He seemed to believe in his own invincibility and at that point none of us saw any reason to refute.

'*Good, good,*' he said. 'No, they've still got me hooked up – but feeling good, aren't we? We certainly *look* good.' And doffing his hat, he revealed a head that was now a polished bowl. I stared in fascination.

'I know, I know; I look like a villain.'

A thick vein was running along his temple, disappearing behind his ear.

'*Matthew!*' Mum spat with her eyebrows raised, face like a dagger. She apologised and I turned away; Aleksei laughing.

'It's fine. Don't worry, I get it all the time. I have a *beautiful* head. We all laugh about it. Why not? You have to anyway.

In fact . . .' He became solemn. 'They say: laughter is the best medicine. Yes?' He nodded sagely, then considered. 'Obviously though, if it's cancer . . .' cocking his head, 'chemotherapy seems to be more effective.'

There was deathly silence for a moment, all of us averting our eyes from the brutality of the joke; no one daring to look at anyone else.

But only a moment.

Suddenly we began to laugh – all of us at once. For perhaps a minute, we laughed and laughed, raucously, setting one another off over and over again, holding our stomachs. The tension was annihilated and we were unbridled; our laughter was gratitude. Alek turned to me and winked, and I winked back, realising that illness would bow to a man such as this, whose head shone like an award. We were foolish to have worried, I realised, because there was nothing to worry about. And at that thought, I began to giggle again, setting the table off again – all except Connie, that is, who kept to a smile, having witnessed Superman being wheeled into an ambulance. Now she linked his arm and grinned.

Later, on the stoop, as we hugged and said our goodbyes, Aleksei pointed at me.

'When are you coming to stay with us then?'

'Oh . . .' Mum made to object, but he threw up his hands.

'Stop. No . . . It's no burden; we love to have him. Don't we?' He elbowed Christina. 'Huh?'

She was standing beside him. They'd shaved their heads together and now hers was a light fuzz. She'd never looked more like his child.

'Yeah,' she said, as if existing was lame.

Connie rolled her eyes and the adults chuckled.

Then we stood in the driveway, watching them disappear. And everyone felt good.

But of course, it was a hoax.

Before November, an oncologist was explaining how the cancer had returned unexpectedly and spread elsewhere. Now it attacked with great elan. Alek had to concede defeat. He retired from work, vowing to fight and return. He fought but did not return. He grew horribly ill. He was forced into a private room, surrounded by complicated equipment that made the process take a long time. Connie also retired, pulling a chair beside his bed and never leaving it. She held his hand and watched him wilt. She saw his skin lose colour and pull taut on his neck. His mouth became an incision and drew back from his nose. Then he was like a bird. She watched it happen; every cough and sputter.

All the while, doctors and nurses came and went. They had warm smiles and clipboards and various procedures and eventually, no idea what to do. They offered cups of tea and coffee. They avoided the room.

But Connie never missed a moment. She sat watching Alek gasp wretchedly through the night, not really alive and not really dead. She sat through cruel moments when he would suddenly awaken, when he would recognise her and smile and, for a brief moment, be her husband. She would watch him close his eyes again.

I don't know how long she stayed at his bedside, with nothing to do but watch. It was long enough to become withered herself, though. Perhaps all those evenings, wilting in the fluorescent light; somehow she joined in, became

31

just like him, and what emerged after was a pale and sickly version of herself.

We visited once, towards the end, me and Dad. Connie was wiry and sleepless, desperately eager; her helplessness all-pervasive. She thanked us for our support again and again. She sat us down and ran for more chairs. Then we told light stories and she laughed as if she was insane. She allowed no silence. She offered us drinks and I wanted hot chocolate but Dad's secret look told me I didn't.

The whole time, Alek was asleep with tubes in his nose, Christina beside him, holding his hand. Her head was shaved again, this time with a razor – two bandaids stuck where she'd cut her scalp.

'What are you looking at?' she'd asked when the adults were out of the room. We'd been sitting in blistering silence.

'Did you do it yourself?'

'Why?'

'No reason,' I said. 'It looks really good.'

'Thanks.'

Aleksei coughed and the sound was a broth of fluid.

There was nothing else to say.

Meanwhile, at Wychwood the grounds had become wild and overgrown. The trees were stripped and leaves blew all across the paddocks. The rain fell and the horses trudged everything into sludge; they broke through the fencing.

Soon Dad offered to help. He began driving out on weekends, mowing and raking and weeding and pruning, coming home after dark. Once, he stayed three days. When he returned, Mum was cold; she said he was giving too much. He said it was only time. 'What's a bit of time when someone's dying?'

Then it was money.

It turned out Alek had made money, but not as much as everyone thought. It began drizzling away. Connie had stopped working to keep vigil at the bedside, convinced it was all a hurdle. There were disputes over insurance and she didn't hire a lawyer; she kept vigil instead. Then months stretched out and bills continued to arrive. They piled up and Dad paid them. Mum was furious. I remember their fight in the kitchen: 'It's not our responsibility!' 'What, so we just let it *happen?*' 'What's going to happen?' 'Not every conversation includes you, Matthew!'

Finally, the day came.

We received a call and Dad sat me down to explain how 'it's better for everyone in the end'. He meant well and gave me a hug. He didn't consider that Connie's entire investment had been in hope, and now hope was gone. He only meant well. It slipped his mind that Christina would grow up fatherless, and he forgot that Alek was dead. He'd somehow managed to forget everyone involved and mean well at the same time.

It had happened the evening before: Connie waking to the sound of a passing car and immense silence. For all his vigour and panache, Alek had slipped away without a sound. She'd looked to the bed and found he no longer existed, that he'd been replaced with a body. For her, it had been a moment of non-reality. In those early hours, somehow his death was not solidified. She looked at the corpse without emotion, thinking: 'I will wake tomorrow and it will have happened or it will not have happened. Tomorrow he may enter the room with coffee' – then a more peculiar thought, something detached: how much his gym membership had cost over the years. All for nothing now, she'd thought. It was this idea that had caused the snap, the sudden waves of sorrow – her moan drifting into the hospital wing; nurses rushing to quieten her, putting their hands on her shoulder. But to no avail: the wails ringing out into the night, waking the patients long before sunrise, asking terrible questions that no one wanted to hear. Until finally she became exhausted, and slept again.

*

Of course, that last paragraph was invented . . .

I have no idea what happened in the hospital the night Alek died. No one does.

I've tried to imagine though: Connie at the bedside after he was gone, before anyone knew. I can't help but wonder if there was a moment of disinterest. He was a stocks man, after all; I wonder if she considered the investment, just for a second – all that time and love – thinking for a moment that it was for nothing; perhaps recalling some other life that might have happened, some daydream, if she hadn't chosen this one. Perhaps. Then suddenly crashing out of it, admonishing herself for ungrateful thoughts, remembering how many years they were happy – then driving home to make the best arrangements for awful things.

I REALISE THIS journal has become a narrative. Reading back this morning, it occurred to me that I'm writing an autobiography. In my defence, life at Yarra Clinic is so repetitive and unremarkable that I have little to say about it. Art therapy continues; I watch an incredible amount of television; I speak to Gloria. This is a comprehensive summary. On Friday I learned that post-traumatic stress can often be accompanied by dissociative symptoms, and that Gloria is excited for the Tom Roberts exhibition at the National Gallery. The rest is time split between Netflix and the cafeteria.

On Wednesday, Christina made me rearrange my entire room because she felt it was 'too medical'. She arrived unannounced, explaining that she'd been a 'busy busy bumble bee' and giving no more information. Nor did she apologise – but then I understand hospitals hold a far greater significance for her.

Instead, she peered about as though I were responsible for the décor and she was disappointed.

'But it's a hospital,' I pointed out.

Nevertheless, she made me display my get-well cards and move the ficus into the sunlight. I had to unpack everything in my suitcase. Christina knows she can ask me to do anything at all and I'll do it. She knows she can say whatever she wants and I won't be upset or object. Centuries of academics expounding the brain as driver of thought and action – all proven wrong: Christina simply grips my heart and my limbs move in whatever manner she designs. In this way, I suppose I'm a prisoner. She's aware of this, and knows I don't mind.

As I redecorated, I broached the topic of my journal, recounting what I had so far. She was inspired, recalling a few details I'd left out: there were three horses at Wychwood, not two; and it was *The Vicar of Dibley* that Alek used to watch. I told her I was about to write his funeral. That was the end of the conversation.

*

During the service, Christina seemed indignant more than anything else, grinding her incisors. I was sitting across the pew and couldn't help glancing over to see her reactions. It was at Baxter Uniting, and Aleksei lay in a polished coffin beneath an abundance of flowers and a picture of himself grinning broadly as the minister said lovely things about him and about the earth and about the afterlife.

Connie was beside Christina, dressed in black. She held a tissue that remained dry throughout the service, watching absently as people read prayers and eulogies. We learned that Alek had been the salt of the earth, that there was no such thing as fairness, and that a special place had been set aside for him in heaven. There was an exclusive joke about a set of car seats that no one understood, save three men who laughed then wept.

When it was over, Connie stood and everyone flocked to clutch her hands and clutch her shoulders. Mum and I stayed behind as Dad clutched her shoulder. I saw her smile. She was grateful and perfunctory. Then a boy played 'Hallelujah' on the piano and we crept out of the nave.

Passing rows of pews, we found the minister in the vestibule. As he shook my hand, he leaned forward, obscuring my vision.

'Thanks, little man.'

'Thank you, Matthew?' Dad prompted, raising his eyebrows.

I said, 'Thanks,' and the minister winked and then they shared a wordless joke about how adolescents lack social decorum. I didn't know why we were saying thanks.

Outside, it had become hot. The clouds had parted during the service and now we stood in brilliant sunlight. I watched a lady rummaging for her glasses. Then six people I didn't know brought the coffin out of the church and slid it into a hearse. Everyone was silent. Somewhere far off, a man was having an unpleasant phone conversation. His voice sailed back with distant urgency. The piano boy was standing with his back against the church, waiting for people to tell him he'd performed well. The car door slammed and the sound rang through the air. It hung poignantly in the silence. Someone coughed. The man was no longer on the phone. The pallbearers had stepped back from the car and stood with their hands clasped before them.

'Well . . .' Dad said quietly. 'That's the end of it.'

The engine started up and we watched the car pull slowly out of the driveway. The hush remained as it crept up the street, and even when it had disappeared, still no one spoke. Finally, from the silence, a young child yelled out, loud and unaffected by the reverence. Her mother picked her up so she could see over the crowd. Then another voice – an old man had spoken and a woman was bringing her hand across his shoulder. Suddenly, as if pulled out of a doze, voices began to churn everywhere, bubbling into conversation: someone commenting on the minister, a man throwing his hands apart in mock gesture, people laughing good-naturedly. The service was over. Alek had been put to rest.

Scanning the crowd, I found Christina standing at the roadside. She was alone, with her eyes on the vanishing hearse. I watched her a moment, feeling a thought arise, feeling it strike suddenly, with immense brutality: Aleksei was dead. He was gone. Forever. And yes, he'd been valorous and yes, the fight had been superhuman – but in the end, effort was irrelevant. He was driving off to be slid into a furnace and sprinkled over the lapping breakers of Sorrento Beach.

Now there was a space beside Christina.

'Did you want to say something, Matt?'

Here was Dad, with a hand on my shoulder, trespassing on my intimacy.

And of course, he was right, I did want to say something, some flake of wisdom that would cause her to turn away from the hearse, from the tremendous weight of the space beside her. But what though?

'Go on,' he said, nudging me forward.

I stumbled through the crowd to Christina, who was still looking up the road. She turned and saw it was me, her eyes hardening.

'Hey,' I said.

'Hi.'

But for all my intentions, I could think of nothing to say. Somehow in the bright sun, she seemed adorned by grief, as though tragedy itself were a fascinator draped across her brow. There were two colours in her irises, I realised: green and hazel. Searing colour. How had I never noticed?

'I'm so sorry,' I said.

She nodded and looked back to the road. The hearse was gone now; the last moments of her father disappearing and she'd looked away so I could tell her that I was so sorry. I studied her face, sharp in profile, powerful almost.

'Hi, Christina.'

It was Dad again, saving us from terrible silence; arriving and reaching out, taking her in his arms.

'I just wanted to let you know . . .' he said, speaking into her hair, 'if you or your mum need anything – anything at all. You know where to come, don't you?'

I watched her nod, closing her eyes, softening in his embrace.

Then he stood again, releasing her.

'Come on, Matt. We'd better go.' He shot one last smile, a summary of his compassion: 'Anything at all, yeah? I mean it,' then walked away.

I turned to Christina. Her eyes were back on mine. They seemed to be asking a question: 'And you . . . ?'

'See you soon,' I said.

She nodded, as if the answer were clear as day.

Tuesday, 1 December

IT TOOK ALEK twenty-one months to die. He became sick and turned corners, then got sick again. It was a whirlwind and sometimes there was dark and other times there was light – but he fought regardless, so courageously that people shook their heads and claimed he was superhuman. It never occurred to me that he'd simply been dying the whole time.

This realisation came crashing when I saw Christina at the roadside.

In the days after, I began to view things differently, my memories becoming distorted. I would think of Alek at the dining table with his shiny head, only to suddenly recall that his eyebrows had been skin too – that he'd sat upright in hospital only because he was too weak to stand, and that he'd refused coffee because he'd not been able to keep it down. Christina at the roadside had debased the narrative – his Glorious Fight had become his Sad Wilting – and when I thought of it now, I could no longer recall his photograph on the casket, but only a withering man with tubes in his nose.

Once it was there, I couldn't shake the thought – and of

course the other, more confusing question that would rise inevitably afterwards: 'And you?'

It kept surfacing, in the dark when I was trying to sleep, warped into an accusation, keeping me up in grim self-loathing, recalling my impotence at the roadside; at Sorrento when Alek had crashed out of the waves.

And *me*?

By this point I was entering Year 9, 'When things get serious,' as Dad loved to remind me. But school seemed oddly pointless now. There'd be a change, blown in with the repeating image: Christina alone – and what were inference and geometry against that? Against the lure of the inevitable question? No – suddenly there was something greater, a purpose, a space to fill at the roadside.

Now other memories began to take on fresh significance: Christina banning me from her clubhouse – one of my bitterest memories – that late afternoon three summers before, when we'd seen Alek disappear into the kitchen to make surprise plates. 'Come on,' she'd said, sneaking under the garage door, into *his* space. I'd followed her into that treasureland of chicken wire and fencing and gardening implements, to the back of the room, where an old couch was sitting against the wall, conspicuously ajar. Christina had pulled it away to reveal a thin straw mat, dipped in the centre. Drawing this back revealed a hole in the cement full of Arnott's Tic Tocs, a copy of *Bridge to Terabithia*, and beneath – my eyes widening – a crumpled pack of Marlboro Lights. She'd slammed the rug down.

'This is my clubhouse. No one knows about it. Not even my parents know. Yeah? Not even God. Not even my best friend in the entire world.'

'What do you do here?'

'That's not for you to ask.'

She'd glared at me.

'You're never allowed to come here again. Is that clear?'

It was.

'Good. I want you to forget this; forget everything you're looking at right now – everything you *think* you've seen. Do you forget?'

'I do.'

'Good. Now get out.'

I'd left the shed with a lump in my throat, confused and disappointed at being so brutally rejected from a place I a) hadn't known existed and b) hadn't actually asked to see.

But why even tell me!? I'd thought later, the question causing me to fling myself out of bed and pace the room. *Why not keep the secret?* And reviewing the memory, I suddenly realised it made no sense at all. How could I possibly forget? Surely it would have been better if she'd just said nothing to begin with? Unless . . . (*gasp!*) Of course!

And from that moment, I would think of her club-house not with dejection but with a thin smile of delicious conspiracy. It was a secret. Ours. And one not even Christ was privy to. I would recall the memory, feeling elation at being included. Forbidden – sure – but included.

Yes, a change had come, and with it the shattering disarray of self-awareness. Suddenly I began to see myself in the mirror – really see myself, as though through someone else's eyes. I would sweep my hair to the side and peer at my reflection. There was something heroic, I thought, with the hair swept over, and I would gaze in satisfaction, having conversations with myself, fictional meetings at the

42

roadside: Christina yelling into the breeze, 'I just don't know how we'll cope alone!', and my Spartan reply: 'You don't have to . . .' (I extend a hand; she takes it . . .) The fantasy suddenly relocating to the bay of islands: crashing from the surf and cradling her on the sand, her face peering, sputtering, thankful, green and hazel in her eyes as she whispers something – the beach deserted – a secret conversation: confessions and sweet nothings. All of it happening in the mirror; all in preparation.

And as if by providence: that October I received a letter.

It was a night Dad had visited Wychwood. He came home and threw his briefcase on the bed, sighing loudly so we knew he was frustrated.

'Should be selling,' he yelled. Then a pause. 'It's madness!'

Neither of us responded. He stepped into the lounge room.

'Utter madness,' he said again and waited. He was jittering, desperate to wax indignant – you could see he'd been having a discussion with himself in the car. Mum refused to indulge him though; her grieving had ceased after the funeral. Now she looked with disinterest, nodding and turning back to the television. There was tense silence as the reporter explained how the structural make-up of the towers had caused them to collapse. Then Dad sighed and went into the kitchen.

To be fair, Mum had not known the family as well. For her, the funeral had put the incident to bed. But there was something distasteful in the way she tried to avoid it now, speaking in broad platitudes. 'Yes, nature can be cruel,' she would say, then leave to do something else. I could tell Dad found it heartless, as though she lacked some inner mechanism allowing her to empathise.

She can be like that though, Mum – even now; dismissive of the fact that Dad's life might continue when she's out of the room. To Mum, any past not involving the two of them is something distasteful and irrelevant. Attempts to question her – and believe me, I've tried – always end up provoking the same baffled derision she saves for science-fiction movies, as though she herself only manifested once they were together.

But then perhaps this is a little harsh. After all, at that point I had no idea why Dad was driving out to Wychwood.

'By the way, Matthew,' he called from the kitchen. 'Mail for you.'

He returned with an envelope. Sure enough, my name was written above two dots and a swirly line. Now Mum did stir, I noticed, suddenly showing real interest, peering from Dad to the letter, then to herself somewhere. There was a pause, and for a moment the fire seemed to add a grim foreboding to her expression, as though witnessing a premonition. Or maybe I only imagined it.

Either way, I took the letter to my room and lay on the bed: (These next words are verbatim – I have the letter.)

Hi Matt,

How are you? I hope you're well. I'm writing because Mum is watching daytime TV and she wants me to go and do something else. It's very quiet here. The last few weeks there's been nothing to do. For months we had people coming and going. People from the church bringing food and moving furniture. Mr Timmer-Arends, my year level coordinator, came and it was weird. We have this lady

Genevieve who helps Mum with everything. I guess she's a counsellor. They go into Mum's room. Then Genevieve comes out and we pretend I didn't hear anything. I had one called Steph. She's twenty-five and she was pretty cool. She had good music. Do you know The Strokes? I haven't seen her much though coz I'm back at school. I started last week. I'm totally behind but they say I can do as much as I want.

Nothing else has happened really. Aunty Carol's been here a lot, cooking and cleaning, taking me to school. She stayed for a month but that was two weeks ago. Now she comes after work. Everyone's back at work, like nothing ever happened. Only Mum isn't doing anything. I'm worried about her. Aunty Carol says she needs to grieve and that's why she stopped staying over. She said Mum needs space and time to grieve. I'm not sure though. I've discovered that grief changes size. It expands and shrinks. It takes up whatever room it can. If you give it no space, it becomes tiny. Maybe it even goes away, I don't know. I only know that if you give it room, it becomes massive. Right now it feels massive. We cleaned out the house and moved Dad's stuff. We put it all in the workshed coz it was hard for Mum having it around. She's made room for grief. The house has never seemed so empty. I want it to be full. I've been going to the workshed. I like to sit among his things. It's weird that I'm telling you this. I think it's because you're not actually here. I'm talking to you and you can't say anything. I don't have to look at you. Maybe I won't even send this letter, who knows? Anyway, it's just stuff I've been thinking about.

Are you going to visit here again sometime? Maybe in the holidays? Tell your parents I want you to. Say I said.

No one will offer and they'll probably say 'no' because everyone's worried and thinks it's better to leave us alone. But tell them I said, 'I want you to come.' Say those words. That I'm bored to death and if you don't come, I'll kill myself. That's a joke. I don't think things like that. But please ask them though. It would be great to see you.

Anyway, I hope you're good.

Lots of love, Christina

xo

p.s. Write back. I'm bored.

My instinct was to fold the letter away, as if intimacy could ring like an alarm. Reading over it, something had risen inside me, a prickling. She could have written to anyone, and yet she'd chosen me; she'd been alone and I'd come to mind. So . . . a change had occurred for her too, then. Right. But when? I thought of our strained relationship; the blistering silence in the hospital when Dad had left the room and there'd been nothing to say. Now she was explaining the nature of grief. When had we bonded? At the roadside? When I'd commented on her shaved head? Or was it my absence – I was a sounding post and she could confide without looking me in the eye. Either way, she'd wanted to tell someone and she'd thought of me. (The prickling again.) I read over the end: 'Write back. I'm bored.'

Yes. I would. Of course.

I found a school book and opened a fresh page. To say what though? To validate her concept of grief? To disagree? To give any opinion at all? The page seemed more blank than usual. I took a pen and began to write about school, about how my subjects were dull and my parents were fine. I told her Sam had bought cigarettes and we'd smoked them and my head had spun like a top. And what else? I tried to think. Her father had tubes up his nose. What could you write when her father had tubes up his nose?

A noise in the kitchen pulled my attention: a colander hitting the floor. Mum howled and there was silence.

I looked at what I'd written, thinking of the tubes, then tore up the paper and threw it in the bin. I would reply later. Yes – sometime. But right now, I couldn't think. I put the letter in my desk and shut the drawer. I opened it again. The page stared with its 'x' and its 'o' and its 'lots of love'. This was code-red security. I covered it with a binder.

In the kitchen, Dad was on his knees with a tea towel and a plastic bag of rigatoni.

'Matt! I was just ordering fish and chips,' he said. I could hear Mum in the bedroom, thumping and crashing. He acted as if there was no noise at all. 'Did you want something?'

'Can I go see Christina these holidays?'

He paused and stood up, brushing himself off. He looked to the bedroom.

'I don't know if that's appropriate.'

'Why not? She wants me to go.'

'Did she say that?'

'Yes.'

'What did she say exactly?'

'She said, "I want you to come."'

'Right.'

There was rigatoni in his fingernails. He'd rolled a piece into a worm and it dropped onto the laminate.

'Look, I'm not sure it's a good idea, to be honest.' He was nodding, trying to think why it wasn't a good idea. 'I just think they probably want space.'

'It's not until January.'

'I know. But people need time. When something like this happens, when people band together . . . which is what *we* did – which is fantastic. We showed our support. You want to make things easier for people when it's . . . at a time like this.' He paused, considering. 'You need to know when to step back. Everyone needs time to breathe. Space.'

'To grieve.'

'Exactly.'

'You were there today.'

'I was gardening. Don't be smart.'

The front door opened and slammed. The noise appeared to slap him in the face.

'Is Mum getting food?'

'No.' He was strained. 'No, she's had to head out for the night.'

There was a pause.

I said: 'Grief expands and shrinks. It fills whatever space it's given. If you have too much time and space, it means you can never move on.'

He narrowed his eyes. 'Who told you that?'

'Andrew Schilling's dad had cancer.'

'Is he the one who lives on South Road?'

'No. That's Eugene.'

I heard the car door slam and the engine start. He sighed again and looked at his fingernails.

'Look, let me think about it.'

Wednesday, 2 December

IT WAS THREE days before Mum came home. I remember Dad rushing to open the door. For a month, he became a strange, polite version of himself. In December, she left again. She returned with new hair and a smoking habit. Nothing was explained. I found horrible pamphlets in their bedside drawers. I found a book called *Stepping Stones to Intimacy*. One evening, Mum came into my room, gripped my shoulders and whispered, 'You mean more to me than anything in the world. *Anything*.' To prove it, she bought me a PlayStation and watched me play *GTA* for hours and hours. She smoked on the balcony. Dad retaliated by enforcing a rule that dinner was to be eaten at the kitchen table. He bought a tablecloth and prepared gorgeous meals that we ate in silence. He did the washing up. Then TV. Endless police dramas. In the ad breaks they wouldn't speak though, seated apart on separate couches; waiting for separate bedtimes.

Eventually, Dad took a stand – arriving home one afternoon with tickets to South-East Asia, slapping them on the table like a return serve. I recall their excruciating words in the living room; my name being thrown about. When the fight was over, Mum emerged with a glass smile and went to the balcony to smoke and smoke. Dad called me in to explain the 'great news!'. Connie had just called to ask if I'd stay for a couple of weeks in January.

'So guess what?' he said, his eyes screwed in a weird simulation of delight. 'Looks like you *are* going to Wychwood.'

'Is everything okay?'

'What? Yeah, of course . . . Timing's perfect actually, coz we're thinking of getting away ourselves then too.' He looked over at Mum, pacing behind the glass like a ghost in a prison cell. 'Y'know – bit of sun, bit of sand,' narrowing his eyes, 'really just . . . *get away.*'

By January, they were pretending to be in love. They touched each other's arms and found things especially interesting. They laughed out loud. They practised all the behaviours of love in the hope that the behaviours would eventually become instinctual and it would be as if they were real lovers. On the first Monday, we drove to Wychwood – the sun inching over the horizon. They were sitting easily in the front seats, listening to *Ziggy Stardust*, Mum singing aloud as Dad tapped the steering wheel. In fifteen hours, they would be on the shores of Ha Long Bay, rekindling whatever needed to be rekindled. For now though, they turned to pat my knee, winking in the mirror and assuring me that I was loved and that there was no need to be affected psychologically by their emotional distance from one another.

I sat in the back seat, watching the landscape shoot by and feeling my stomach turn. Having spent the entire drive wondering if Christina would be waiting on the fence, I'd reached the conclusion that I didn't know if I wanted her to be or not. Both scenarios were disturbing, resulting in the same paroxysm of anxiety. My parents could see I was nervous and figured they were responsible – Mum turning to rest a hand on my knee. She had no idea that I hadn't replied to Christina's letter. She didn't know that for months, it had sat in my desk and every time I'd entered my room, I'd felt its presence – that over time, it had become imperious, the idea of it sitting under the binder with its 'xo' and its 'lots of love'. I began taking it out. I would be awake at night and would have to read it again. I would read the 'lots of love' again, over and over. One night, I read it and masturbated. When I was finished, I thought of Alek's tubes and was disgraced and couldn't sleep. A week later, I did it again and slept great. I had a dream that Alek wanted to speak to me before he died. He leaned in and said, 'Lots of love,' and I awoke in great shame, swearing abstinence. All the while, I was unable to write back. So many times, I sat with a pen and tried to write. I would think of Christina and begin. Then I would think of Alek and have nothing to say. I would scrunch up the paper.

Now I was in the back seat, having still not replied, and my hands were sweating. I looked outside and the landscape was enchanting and warped. Somehow the morning dusk was causing the landmarks to become strange imitations of themselves. At Karingal's Earthenware, all the statues cast weird shadows on the concrete. I watched their lidless eyes, convinced that if I kept looking, they would move. *Would she be on the fence?* We passed the church, where a group of revellers stood idly. Behind, the building loomed with its bizarre triangles. A man nodded. I nodded back and my throat had become thick. We were flying towards the estate and the pine trees seemed to close in behind the car.

Finally, the house appeared. There was no one on the fence.

*

Dad parked the car and tilted the mirror so his eyes appeared. They were stern. He reminded me that Alek was dead, and that the lingering memory of his death meant I had to clean up after myself and be an easy guest. Mum agreed: his death meant I couldn't wear the same clothes for days in a row.

A door slammed and Christina and Connie were on the balcony. They stood side by side, waving together as if attached to the same string. Connie was wearing a yellow dress of winding flowers that wrapped her body like a magic-eye. She seemed aglow – porcelain, somehow.

'Sorry we're so bloody late!' Dad said, fossicking in the boot. 'The morning sort of . . .' He wrenched my suitcase onto the ground. '. . . got away from us.'

He looked at Mum, who performed the shrill imitation of a laugh. For a moment we stood like an ensemble of porters.

'Mattttyyyyy!'

Connie rushed forward to crush me in a hug, bathing me in perfume and annihilating my hair. 'So good to srrr yrrrrr.' She stepped back.

'Jeez, he's shot up, hasn't he?'

'That's the broccoli,' Dad said, spearing a wink. 'You better not eat these guys out of house and home.'

Mum laughed another performance.

'Hopefully he does!' Connie said. 'The garden – honestly, we've got that much. I hope you like veggies.'

52

'Haha, no.' Dad laughing as well. 'Matt likes anything! He's actually a really easy guest and won't be a hassle at all while he's here.'

They all grinned and chuckled, then fell silent. Connie's husband was dead.

Dad took a sharp breath. 'So have you um . . .'

'Great!' Connie jumping in. 'Great. Yeah, this one's back at school; I'm back at work – pushing the oldies about, you know . . . catching up – and we've had the carpenters in . . .' Her hand flung at a tarpaulin sheet that used to be the wall of the rumpus room. 'Remember we were going to extend that verandah around? Anyway, we've started that – God forbid . . . But *good*, y'know? *Good*. It's really just the orchard. Chris and I are down there at least once a day, aren't we, gorge? Pruning, chopping . . .'

Christina smiled at the introduction, offering a half-wave. I returned it, still brooding over the disgrace of having my hair crushed by Connie's hug. Twenty minutes in front of the mirror and now I stood with idiot flat hair. Still, it was good to see her; she looked well; her father was dead.

'. . . in summer, though,' Connie was saying now. 'It's just keeping those bloody whiteflies away.'

'Really, whiteflies?' Dad turning to Mum, 'Didn't you have – when you tried to grow those snow peas?'

'What?'

'Remember – and you had the dish-soap spray.'

'You're thinking of aphids.'

'*Oh*, riiiight.'

'No, aphids are slightly . . .'

'Right *right*.'

'Yes, aphids can be tricky.'

'Oh but *white*flies . . . no yeah, they can *really* be a pest . . .'

Another silence. In the roadside paddock, a horse whinnied and rushed back along the fence. Why the hell were they talking about whiteflies?

'So, did you want to stay for a coffee?' Connie venturing.

Dad looked at his shoes.

'Aw no, sorry,' Mum said. 'Didn't we say? Yeah no, we've got to run.' Her expression was kind, but not the expression she wore when she was being genuinely kind. 'Thanks again for taking him.'

'Not a problem at all,' Connie said. 'You'll have a great trip; trust me. It's *gorgeous* there, just *gorgeous*.'

Her grin seemed pained. It really was the most bizarre exchange – as though they'd been asked to imitate a conversation rather than have one. And not one mention of Alek . . .

Nonetheless, my parents said goodbye and jumped in the car, waving their arms like a birdman rally. Connie watched them go, then turned to Christina and me, still with that same big smile – though somehow it had become shattering glass.

'Well, what do we reckon? Brunch?'

Thursday, 3 December

JUST A NOTE:

Reading this last section, I feel I've added qualities that weren't there. A day later, I would find Connie weeping on the floor of the workshed. Later still, she would become insane and do something I've never quite forgiven her for.

The trouble is, you can't unsee an image. Now, when I think of Connie smiling in the driveway, I see shattered glass. I see latent madness. But perhaps she was only smiling?

It makes me think: Am I telling the truth here?

Something to keep in mind, I suppose . . .

Nevertheless, that first morning, I was confused to discover the vegetable garden was actually a wasteland. We took a walk before it was hot, and behind the house I found the garden beds sun-bleached and withering; there were no vegetables, only weeds and wiry remnants, creeping up stakes and splayed into nothing. Moving about, it occurred to me it wasn't only the gardens – in the distance the fencing along the paddocks seemed to drape, with bowed planks falling loose, gates bent at the hinges. All over, the property appeared to be sick somehow – sick and yet neat, as though cleaned in a rush: the grass hurriedly mown, only to reveal rabbit warrens undermining the paddocks, the little holes dotting almost up to the drive. Then the chicken coop: overrun with creeping vine that had been chopped in a kind of installation. But there were no chickens. Even the trees somehow appeared to hang in disillusion.

Of course, no one mentioned anything, Connie leading us about with the enthusiasm of an air hostess, explaining and pointing out all the work to be done.

'I'm thinking a few more natives to screen the neighbours – these ones here . . . No, you're right; gums *are* evergreen! Just let me know if I'm boring you, won't you?'

'You're boring him.'

'Thanks, Chris – I'm sure Matt would say if I was *boring* him . . .'

Coming back past the rumpus room, she'd paused a moment, narrowing her eyes at the flap of tarpaulin where the outer wall had once been. I watched it billow softly in the breeze, becoming swollen and revealing behind it the jagged hollows of a window frame.

'Bloody carpenters aren't here till Thursday.' Connie spoke under her breath.

'So!' She spun around. 'Rule number one, Matthew: rumpus room's out of action. Yeah? Really sorry, but you're going to have to bunk up with this one.' She winced and cocked her head towards Christina. Then striding away: 'Now *these* are the conifers. I was actually thinking–'

But I'd stopped listening, a thick humidity having suddenly descended, chafing my wrists and collar. *Bunking with this one.* I looked at Christina. She was listening to

Connie chitchat, nodding and agreeing, looking everywhere but into my eyes. In a few short hours we would be side by side in pyjamas, cleaning our teeth in front of the mirror. How thin were the boundaries of intimacy, I thought, imagining her mouth foamy with toothpaste.

xo, lots of love . . .

Nothing was said though; there were no glances, no secret communication. Instead, Christina went inside to start lunch, leaving me to her mother's infinite descriptions of Australian natives.

Once we were alone, Connie linked my arm and pulled me close. There were one or two more things to show me – if I didn't mind, of course. It was just the far paddocks; she had plans for the back fence and wanted my opinion, seeing as I was interested and all. And besides (squeezing into my shoulder), it was just *so* good to see me.

She'd kept the orchard for last, sprawled at the back of the property. And as we approached, I saw to my surprise that it was nothing like the rest of the grounds. Instead, the trees stood in lush, colourful rows, flittering their leaves and sagging under the weight of huge fruits; ripe peaches and apricots filling the branches and catching the sun. I strode among them, feeling the instant relief of heat falling away, trapped with the sun high above the canopies. Sound, too, seemed to disappear, so that soon I heard only the distant rustle of trees swishing elsewhere – and of course Connie's girlish laugh that echoed all around as she flew among the trees like mother earth: 'I call it my palace!'

I strode on, marvelling at the plums and nectarines strewn in clusters across the grounds, taking in the bright scent, sickly sweet, and enjoying the tempered sun. Only there was something strange, I noticed, pausing to inspect one of the trees – something not quite right. A plum was hanging from a bough before me, so engorged its skin had split, the flesh bruised inside. Stepping back to look at the trunk, I discovered it was the same: bloated and tumorous, swollen with some repulsive disease.

'Hey Matt.'

I turned to find Connie behind me, holding a peach the size of her palm.

'Tell me,' she said, lifting it up, 'have you *ever* seen anything like *this* straight off the vine?'

Her eyes dazzled.

She was lonely, of course, it's as simple as that – and this I *did* notice: the aching cheer that hangs about people who used to be fabulous; the way she never left my side, as if her goal was to prevent any moment of intimacy between Christina and I – sitting beside us with a plate of fruit and crackers, watching us eat and thinking of activities for three: 'The games are all in the shed – quite a few good ones actually . . . a couple of puzzles. You like puzzles, don't you, Matt?'

At first, I was concerned – in my anxiety, I convinced myself that she somehow knew about Christina's letter and my activities in the dark; that she was staying close by, lest Christina become defiled. But I soon realised this wasn't the case. Deciding on a puzzle, she'd jumped up and rushed to the shed. It was the same way she'd rushed for chairs in the hospital – 'You two sit tight now!' – fleeing silence like a child avoiding bedtime.

Christina had watched her go, then looked up from her sandwich.

'Sorry,' she said. 'We haven't had that many visitors.'

When Connie returned, we set to work on a two-thousand-piece jigsaw of sky and grass. But after the edges it became impossible, so we abandoned the empty rectangle for *Mario Kart*. Connie had never played and thought it was a riot. She screamed when she crashed and didn't know which screen she was supposed to be looking at. She found it amusing to drive in the wrong direction and then we had to wait for her to finish.

In the evening, she took us to *Lord of the Rings*, sitting between us with a bag of Maltesers. She'd read the novels, and gasped whenever the film didn't align. She anticipated one-liners and laughed much harder at Gimli than I thought the portrayal deserved. On the drive home, she explained a character called Tom Bombadil who – in her opinion – was vital to the books and should never have been cut from the film. Not once did she seem to pause, seem to even breathe, her words flowing together one after the other, as if at the first moment of silence one of us might lean forward to ask: 'And how are you coping with the death of your husband?'

I remember sitting with my head against the window and feeling my heart sink lower; the enchantment of my expectations slowly dissolving in her flurry of words. So this was to be my holiday, was it? I listened to her natter natter all the way home, recalling that evening in the hospital, and how she'd laughed at the bedside like a woman possessed.

Later, we'd brushed our teeth and climbed into our beds. Christina's room was the same as it ever was, knick-knacks and bric-a-brac. Beside my head, her valance towered like a huge wall. Connie kissed her goodnight, then knelt and kissed me too, taking my head in her hands and pressing into my cheek. Who the hell kisses someone else's kid, I'd thought, wiping at the cold half-moon where her lips had been. She stood and flicked off the light.

Instantly, the room ignited in an explosion of stars.

'Night, team,' Connie said, closing the door.

I lay awake with everything blue and luminous, peering from trinket to trinket, the shadows stretched like the statues in Karingal's. Christina had rolled away and I could see a steady rise and fall in the blankets. It had been an exhausting day, after all. Now she was asleep and I was alone, listening to Connie tread about the enormous house. The sound brought a vague swimming remorse as I wondered what on earth she did of an evening, alone in the dark, with nothing to distract her save the buzzing television. Then the thought dissolved, my mind drifting away to the orchard: Connie floating among the rotting fruit; 'I call it my palace!'; how the trunk had swollen with its revolting growths; raising the peach with her bright eyes; kissing my cheek–

'Why didn't you write to me?'

I was hurled back into the room, back onto the futon where I hadn't moved. Christina's words hung thickly in the dark. Somehow they were clear, as though still reverberating. Or maybe I'd imagined them?

'Matt?'

'Yeah?'

So they had been real. Now there was silence, the words disappearing as she waited for an answer. Except I had none. Only that her father had tubes up his nose.

'Write to me next time,' she said.

'I will.'

I would.

Another silence. Her silhouette looking up into the stars.

'Don't worry,' she said. 'It's not going to be like this the whole time.'

'Like what?'

'You know.'

Her face appeared above me, smooshed into the pillow.

'I've got a plan.'

'For what?'

'Escaping. I have to show you something.'

'Escaping?'

'You have to promise to come, though. You can't bitch out.'

'Why would I bitch out?'

'Promise.'

'I promise.'

'Okay.'

She turned onto her back.

'Where are we going?' I said.

'Get some sleep. I'll tell you tomorrow.'

'Why can't you say now?'

Silence.

'Why would I bitch out?'

'Shh. I'm trying to sleep.'

I watched her silhouette. She was still looking at the ceiling, the white of her left eye catching the gloom.

'Matt?'

'Yeah?'

She took a breath to say something else, then paused. I waited. She breathed out.

'See you in the morning.'

Then the sound of sheets as she rolled away.

I lay still, waiting for her to turn around again, to say something else. But the conversation seemed to be over.

Was it?

See you in the morning?

No – that can't have been what she'd meant to say. There'd been something else on her lips. Hadn't there? Yes. In that pause, she'd almost said it: something mad and terrifying. Although maybe she couldn't say. Maybe to say meant stepping off a ledge into . . .

–Alright then, fair enough. Either way, I knew what she'd meant. She'd meant now we had to lie for hours, barely an arm's length apart, with the starlight glancing off the walls, illuminating her neck, which I could see clearly, turned away – or perhaps displayed. And of course, it all meant I wouldn't sleep now. Damn her.

I looked up at the ceiling, peering into the constellations and smiling to myself.

I said: 'See you in the morning.'

*

In the morning, Connie emerged in a uniform with her hair tied away. Her lipstick was bright and she was a professional, tossing things into a handbag.

'Morning guys! I'm back around four-ish yeah? – unless the traffic's the traffic . . . don't worry, I'll do the horses when I get back . . .' She harried about the kitchen. 'There's a bit of stuff for sandwiches – cheese and tomato . . .'

She pulled a Tupperware container out of the fridge and pointed it at Christina.

'You're in charge, yeah? Number's on the fridge. I don't

want to come back and find the place is burned to the ground.'
She turned to me. 'Keep an eye on this one; I don't trust her.'

'I'll do my best.'

She laughed a bleat and took her handbag, skipping out
to the car. As the engine hummed to life, a thick plume of
smoke spilled from the exhaust pipe. Connie reversed into it,
then sped off down the driveway, leaving a noxious trail that
looked like it could kill you.

'You done?' Christina was nodding at my Weet-Bix.

I was done.

'Good,' she said. 'We're going.'

As soon as the gates were closed, we were over the fence and
crossing the eastern paddock, Christina rushing forward like
a dog off the leash.

'Where are we going?' I called after.

'I said I wanna show you something,' she yelled back.
'Mind the snakes!'

I didn't know if she was serious. It was hot and dry as
she raced down into the shade of the trees at the edge of
the property. The easternmost paddock was filled with enormous gums that twisted in disfigured shapes – *Eucalyptus
obliqua* – reaching every way as if to string roots in the sky.
They were called widow makers because their boughs would
drop unexpectedly and kill farmers. Now I was among
them, the sun flicking on and off overhead, watching
Christina leap up onto a huge bough that had fallen at the
edge of the property. She scurried along it and turned back,
crossing her arms in triumph. The weight of the bough
had crushed everything beneath it, including the fence to
Davies' paddock.

'Are we going in?' I asked, peering at the foliage around her.

'Unless you want to finish the puzzle?'

She was biting her bottom lip and raising her eyebrows in a weird insinuating manner I've thankfully never seen since. I looked back. The house had shrunk to the size of a shoebox and become hidden in the branches. I imagined Connie's car suddenly returning, peeling up the drive; Mum answering a telephone in Vietnam; my parents' vicious words on the plane back to Melbourne; their marriage in tatters.

'Shall we?' Christina said.

When I landed in the thicket, everything disappeared: the house and the workshed, all the paddocks; even noise seemed unable to penetrate the havoc of thistle and bracken now surrounding us. The paddock truly was untamed, with enormous clumps of sedge and nettle and woody needle-like trees somehow growing in crazy entanglements; blackberries spreading a mesh of thorns. I took a step and my foot crunched something I didn't want to look at.

'Whatcha reckon?'

Christina had her arms out like she was unveiling a feature wall.

'I don't know,' I said. 'Are there snakes?'

'Not really. Only in summer.'

It was summer.

'C'mon,' she said. 'It's this way.'

It wasn't the first time Christina had been 'this way'. Moving further in, I discovered the ground already trodden. I kept behind as she burrowed forward, ducking and peeling away foliage, keeping to a path that was visible only to her. Branches were swatting my face and I had to keep one arm up as a shield as she shot ahead, almost at a sprint ('Hurry up!'

'Where are we going?' 'You'll see!'), jumping a felled trunk, now a rusted oil drum, now skipping over beds of little blue flowers; on and on, steadily downhill until soon great trunks began appearing – the swamp gums – rising enormously with their ribbons of bark, shooting straight and high and reaching together until the sky was entirely gone.

I paused a moment to peer up at the canopy, feeling all at once the keen sense that we were alone in the middle of nowhere.

'How far?' I yelled.

'Close now!' Christina's reply sailing from somewhere ahead, causing me to lift my pace.

The temperature had dropped under the canopy and now, as the ground began to dip even further, I heard the sound of rushing water; the surge rising suddenly from somewhere in front. Overhead, birds were appearing and disappearing, darting and chirping gaily over the churning sound and I pushed on in the vague direction of Christina's voice ('Matt! Hurry up!'), wondering what on earth she was so desperate to show me; what could be all the way out here, far from anything.

Finally I tripped through a dense wall of sedge, slicing my wrists and hands as I tumbled over. Then, standing to brush myself off, I parted a last veil of foliage and found that the thicket suddenly ended – strangely, in a perfect line, as if it had been cut deliberately. Christina was waving down beneath me, and I realised now what the rushing sound had been. She was at the bottom of a steep hill, standing on the rocky banks of a river. Having heard it from the thicket, it seemed oddly quiet now, so much flowing water, but I could see it was too wide to cross – spreading grandly along with the trees before bending and disappearing out of sight. It occurred to me that neither of us had brought bathers.

'What are we doing here?' I said, and at the question, her eyes flashed in a way that made my throat feel just a little tight.

'Didn't I say last night?'

'Say what?'

She grinned and turned away, flying up the bank.

'Don't worry, we're almost there!'

'Fucking where?' I yelled, peering up into the sun – high now, almost in the middle of the sky. When had Connie said she'd be back? I figured we'd been gone about half an hour; maybe a little longer.

I followed Christina up the bank, passing scrub and yellow wattle and keeping an eye ahead as she disappeared around the bend, trying to recall what she'd said last night, before she'd rolled away and left me awake for God knows how long.

'Well?'

Now she called again, and rounding the bend, I found her standing out over the river, high on an ancient footbridge, waving her arms. It really was the oddest thing, the bridge, seeming to appear out nowhere, apropos of nothing – and far taller than it needed to be too, rearing metres above the water. But then, I guessed the river had once been a highway for lumber trade; wide barges needing clearance, drifting with their loads of great trunks.

'Come on!'

She was pointing over at the far bank, then scurrying down the steps towards what I realised was some kind of house, squatting just back from the river. I crossed over, noting how quiet the water seemed now, and followed her back into the trees.

It was a bizarre little shack, as ancient as the bridge, and once blue, though now decrepit and half-devoured in a mess of graffiti. When I arrived, Christina was already prying at a board fixed to one of the windows.

'Have you been inside?' I asked.

'Nah, usually I just stand and look at it.'

She grinned and yanked a gap wide enough for me to fit through, the nails creaking as dust billowed in a hail of flaking paint. She brushed it aside then swept her arm in an aristocratic gesture of permission.

Falling inside, the scent of stale damp hit first, the walls seeming to groan under their own dilapidation, and perhaps the sheer mass of spider webbing that laced every crevice. I brushed myself down, dust curling in the bands of light under the boarded windows. I wondered how long it had been abandoned – and in a hurry, it seemed, judging by the table on one side, full of strange equipment: an ancient radio and a lamp perched over a scattering of documents. A radio tower perhaps, left over from a time when it wasn't quite the middle of nowhere.

Christina slid in beside me, landing on her feet and pulling the board into place so the light dimmed and sound sucked away in a vacuum.

'What are you doing?' I whispered for some reason.

'In case anyone comes by,' she whispered back, moving to the desk and running a hand across the radio.

'Who?' I said.

'No one.'

She grinned and a strip of light dazzled against her jaw. It made me think of the previous night: her rolled away with her neck displayed.

'What is this place?'

'Found it last year,' she said. 'Don't worry; nobody comes here. It's probably abandoned.'

'Someone has to own it.'

'Sure. We do.'

I would have laughed, only her eyes had taken on a strange look, sharp and brilliantly alive. There was a pause as the wind swept outside, rumbling beyond the walls.

'So is this what you wanted to show me?' I asked.

She shook her head.

'Then what?'

For a moment she didn't answer. I felt my throat thicken again, recalling at once the shameful nights I'd spent clutching her letter. There was something in her expression – one of domination, I realised. It made me wonder if maybe, wildly, there'd been corresponding nights here at Wychwood.

'You promised, yeah?' she said.

I had, of course, though exactly what, I didn't know. I waited for something to happen, for her to step towards me. But instead, she crouched down and began to pry at one of the floorboards, tearing it aside with a clunk.

'What are you doing?'

She tore another, clunking it away, then another; then she reached down and fossicked for something, drawing up an old backpack that was bursting at the seams. It fell with a thud on the floor beside her and she unzipped it, grinning as my eyes grew wide.

'Holy shit.'

Inside was the rough inventory of a doomsday sympathiser: cans and dried food, two-minute noodles, nuts and fruit, towels and old clothes, torch, batteries, books and magazines, bandaids, et cetera, all hoarded and packed together.

'Is it yours?' I said.

'In case I ever need to leave.' Still she had that vividness in her eyes. 'Whenever I want; it's all here, everything I need. I leave in the middle of the night and no one'd have any idea. By the time they start searching, I'm on a train. They're lined up back in the trees, searching. Can you imagine how long that'd take? And I'd already be far away.'

I held a weathered can of chickpeas. 'When did you bring this down?'

'Last few months. Bits here and there. Don't worry, Mum's got no idea. No one knows but you.'

'*Why* though?'

Suddenly, I could hear the sound of the water, flowing loudly just outside the walls, as though a tide had come to fill the silence. Christina narrowed her eyes, her entire manner seeming to change.

'You don't want to be here, do you?' she said.

'What? Yes, I do.'

'You're afraid.'

'I just want to know why you're running away.'

'No – either you don't want to be here or you're afraid.'

'. . .'

Now she grinned. Not with humour, though – it was the grin of a sceptic, like she'd discovered the workings of a magic trick and confirmed everything was an illusion.

'I knew you'd bitch out.'

'I'm not bitching out,' I said.

'Yes, you are. Why do you keep looking at your watch? You're worried about getting home.'

'No, I'm not.'

'You are.'

'I'm not – I just don't want to make things worse, alright?'

That grin again. 'Worse than what?'

'You know what I mean.'

'Do I? I bet you can't say it.'

'Say what?'

'Don't you worry about making things worse for me too?'

'What? I – no.'

'Then stop walking on eggshells around me.'

'I'm not.'

'Yes, you are!' Suddenly she jumped up, her entire face darting towards me, red seeping into her cheeks. 'Look at you – you don't know what to say. You're worried about upsetting me. You're worried about things hitting close to home. I bet it's why you didn't write to me. Isn't it? Coz you think I'm fragile. Well, listen very carefully. I'm the only person in the world who isn't fragile. Yeah? At school, people avoid me because they think I'm fragile. But it's them. Miss Henriette, my geography teacher, cried when she saw me. She told me I was so brave because I'd come back. Right? Now everything I say is correct. She's terrified of me. She tiptoes around. And I'm acing geography. I don't know anything about geography. It's fucking hilarious. Except then I think about it and it isn't funny – because she doesn't respect me enough to treat me like everyone else. Do you respect me?'

'Yes.'

'Good. Then if you're afraid, fucking tell me.'

'Okay, fine; I'm afraid.'

A pause. She nodded.

'Thanks for saying. It's okay to be afraid. Sometimes I'm afraid.'

She knelt down and started stuffing things back into the bag. I watched, unsure if I believed her or not. All the bravado, wielding her father's death like a dangerous weapon she had no fear to swing. She paused.

'Look, I'm not saying I'm doing anything. This is all just in case. Who knows, maybe I *never* will. But at least–'

Her head flung up.

'What is it?'

'Shh!'

But now I'd heard it too, from outside: voices murmuring, the sound of crunching footsteps. Christina ducked and I followed her lead, peeking above the windowsill.

'Fuck!' she hissed, rezipping her bag. 'We have to go.'

In the thicket, two men were treading down from the trees, zigzagging vaguely in our direction. They paused and one of them demonstrated an invisible line along the tree-tops, pointing back to where they'd come from.

'Wait,' I said. 'I don't think they're coming this way.'

'They are.'

'How do you know?'

She sucked air through her teeth. 'Because I was lying. I've seen people come here before.'

'What!?'

'Well, I've seen *this* guy sometimes.'

'Are you fucking serious?'

'It's okay – shh!'

She stuffed the bag in the hole, forcing the floorboards into place, then beckoning me over, pushing at the boarded window. I stuck my leg through the gap and shimmied down as quietly as I could, flopping onto the dirt below. Now the voices were loud, words intelligible as the men drew closer.

'Quick!' I hissed as Christina's leg appeared in the gap.

I grabbed the board, pulling it to give her more room but grossly miscalculating the force required. There was a huge crack and I fell backwards, brandishing the board as Christina fell from the sill and thudded on the ground beside me.

The voices stopped.

'Fuck!' Christina was clutching her arm, blood drizzling from a gash on her wrist.

'Holy shit,' I hissed. 'Are you alright?'

'It's fine; it's just a graze.'

She brushed at the wound, causing blood to fan over her wrist – obviously not just a graze, but there was no time.

'Oi!'

The shout came from just behind the house, then heavy footsteps as the men clambered downhill towards us.

'Go! Go! Go!' Christina scrambled to her feet, pulling me up as her wrist flicked blood like a sprinkler.

We flew back to the bridge with the men behind us cursing and shouting; Christina still clutching my arm, smearing blood across my wrist and shirt as we stumbled up the stairs and back down, tripping and collapsing onto the grass, then stumbling up again. 'Get back here!' Their voices were right behind us, it seemed, hurling obscenities as we raced along the banks and back into the thicket.

Friday, 4 December

I JUST WANT to pause a moment, because it was around this time that the boy jumped under the train I was on. I want to say April 2002, possibly May – anyway, it was around the same time.

It was an extraordinary experience, surreal: the train screaming to a halt, the driver making the announcement. Gasping and reacting. When we got off, a conductor was shining a torch on a clump under the last carriage. I remember everyone trying to console one another, drawn together in mutual devastation. Then we were being told to walk back to the station, to not look behind the police officer.

I never thought I'd been psychologically affected by the incident – I still don't think I was. Yet for some reason, it has a habit of making its way into my dreams. It has a tendency to hijack them, arriving midway through and seeping in, as though to remind me that it's still there, beneath everything.

Last night was no exception. I think recounting the river caused things to stir. It's a dream I've had before – until halfway through, the boy and the train seeping in, same as always:

I'm running through Davies' paddock and it's pelting with rain. I can barely see, ferns and boughs swatting my face, until I arrive at the edge and step out to the river. Suddenly everything's bright under the moon, night-time but still bright, and as I look out, I can see the river thrashing about and raging like I've never seen in my life; the rain having caused it to swell and break its banks so that now the water, always so calm, is flying leftways in a torrent of churning rapids, crashing over jagged rocks. And I can see things skittling by, twigs and branches and detritus and then, just a little further up, Christina.

I look and see her standing out over the water on a felled trunk – the same as the one over Davies' fence, only it's stretching over the water. She's wearing a dress of winding flowers and peering straight ahead. And I say, 'What are you doing?' because it's clear she's about to jump.

But she doesn't hear. She doesn't look over. She's peering straight ahead and doesn't seem to realise I'm there. And so I look to where she's looking and I notice a light on the water – only thin, but getting brighter – creeping along from upstream, kind of like a sunrise. And things are glowing into focus: rocks and churning rapids, only it's going too fast to be a sunrise; it's something else. And I realise then that any second, a train is going to come out of the trees.

And it will be going too fast.

The thought pops into my head; I'm not sure why. But suddenly it's there, clear as day: *It's going too fast; she won't be able to get out in time.* I think without dread or anticipation; I simply know.

And so I yell again: 'What are you doing?', but Christina doesn't hear me because now the train crashes into view;

not a metro train but an old freight with a single bobbing headlight, crashing in from behind the trees. And it seems to be speeding up. So I turn back to Christina, and I'm yelling and jumping and waving my arms as the train plummets towards her, closer and closer; light reaching her bare feet, ankles, shins, knees; now her winding flower dress suddenly illuminated. And I wonder how a train can be speeding along so fast without tracks?

But of course, it's not; because that's when I notice the body of water behind the train. And I realise the train was never on tracks; it was being pushed along in the current, lifted and tossed by a great hurtling river that has come to life – and the train that seemed to crash so wildly has suddenly become like a plastic toy, bobbing at the front of the massive wave that's surging towards Christina. And she won't be able to get out in time, I think, because it's going too fast. But she doesn't even try. She just watches it approach, keeping her eyes on the lamp until the last second. And in that second, she looks at me. And I realise she's known all along that I've been watching. She's just chosen not to look. And as I realise this, she's swallowed. The river sweeps across and she disappears. All except for her hand. As the torrent comes over, I notice that she's raised her left hand. And I see her middle finger is touching her ring finger. And I wonder if perhaps she's trying to communicate somehow.

But I can't see her in the water.

I HAVE TO be careful, having spent the last two days somewhat anaesthetised, swimming about in my dream . . .

Now I return to Christina and I, running back to the house – through Davies' paddock after almost being caught, the two men hurling expletives and falling behind.

It was one of her episodes, I'm certain: her elation, sprinting forward with her hand bleeding all over the thicket, bloodied leaves trekking a path; 'It's fine, I don't feel a thing! Like, *nothing*!' Throwing her hand back for me to see, not bothering to wipe it away. Yelling behind, 'There's no way they'd find us! Look how much space there is to cover – we'd be miles away before anyone even knew!' Then flinging her bloodied hands as if to emphasise the point; running and cackling – all the signs her mania was rearing its head again in that hysterical upswing before things would inevitably dip the other way.

Now that I'm aware – here and now, in this hospital room – it's easy to identify, to diagnose even: her slurring words, the speech; the certainty her ludicrous plan was infallible, that she was invincible, and somehow impervious to pain – sure, *now* it's clear. And if people viewed her now, I'm sure it would be with that same bemused smile; my father's smile: standing at the window, terrified I'll do something embarrassing; his anxious desperation to leave the room—

But of course, I need to be careful. Because all this is telling the end before the middle, isn't it? Or at least letting the end skew the truth.

It's the trick of memory: it's imbuing my fifteen-year-old self with knowledge I never possessed. Because in truth, at fifteen I had no inkling. At fifteen, Christina was simply fantastic. Crazy? Sure. Insane – why not? But wonderful crazy, electric and mad and brave in a way I could only admire from afar. And in truth, at that moment, I was just as mad as she; my adrenaline charged at the proximity of our pursuers. How long did they follow us for? – two minutes? half an hour? – scampering about the trees with their voices behind, becoming ghostly and finally disappearing; fear causing my pupils to dilate as I swiped at branches and followed the sound of Christina giggling, the echoing laughter of a wood nymph: behind me, it seemed, now in front, now to the side. I chased after her, watching blood fling as she swatted aside branches that seemed to obscure her view into the future; peering at crimson drops like ornaments on a Christmas tree, peering at my own bloodied hands and imagining us on a train somewhere, having disappeared overnight, huddled in the intimacy of a luggage compartment – as parents and friends scoured Davies' paddock for any trace, shouting voices and torches swivelling across the surface of the river, a height of noise and panic as we crouched together beneath it all.

My fear had gone now, my concerns about the time. Instead, as I chased her through the trees, a balmy euphoria seemed to have pooled about me, drawn by the warmth of the sun, and by this fabulous morning in which she'd confirmed me as a conspirator.

And coming out of the thicket, everything seemed vindicated, for there she was, standing on the bough with her hands on her hips, gazing like an explorer, an astronaut and a deep-sea diver; the image of her meek at the roadside seeming as distant as it was preposterous. Yes, I thought, I would follow her on a train or wherever it was – just as the French did Joan of Arc (who was schizophrenic – wasn't she? Surely . . .). Thoughts of time and Connie discovering us had disappeared. I didn't even find it strange that Christina had fallen silent, mid-sentence; I was too caught up. I certainly didn't notice the police car in the driveway.

The house was deathly quiet when we arrived. As it turned out, Connie had revised her morning commute, popping by the service station to buy pies and Big Ms and delivering them to the house – which of course had been deserted. Now it was an hour later and she was pale and caustic and two police officers were sitting at the table with cups of tea – both earl grey.

Christina slid open the door and Connie spun in a fury. We stood in tattered shame as the officers looked at one another, confirming things were just as they'd suspected: a huge waste of time.

'Well well well.'

The officer who liked it black stood and extended a hand.

'The lost have retur–' he began to say, before realising Christina was covered in blood. 'Jesus!' He shot into action, throwing the shirt aside and inspecting her wound, turning the wrist, turning it again, realising his urgency was unnecessary; committing anyway.

'Bandaids,' he spat as though requesting a defibrillator.

Connie made to move.

'Stay there. Where?'

'Kitchen, third drawer down.'

'Got it. You sit tight.' This was to Christina as he rushed to the drawers, fumbling about and returning with a bandage.

'There we go,' he said, wrapping her hand. 'All better now, eh?'

'Thanks.'

He paused, peering at her wrist, pulling the sleeve up further.

'How'd you do this?'

'Fence over the back,' Christina said. 'Cut it climbing over.'

I caught her split-second glance. The officer frowned, then took a breath as if to say something – looked at her arm again.

'Back fence, eh?'

This came from his partner, who to this point had chosen neither to help nor move. Now he stretched.

'What you going out there for?'

'Just a look around,' Christina said.

'"Juz' a look around."' He gave a buffoon's imitation. '"Juz' a look around." What, without water? Without bandaids? Sunscreen too, I bet. No? Sounds like a pretty good idea then – heading out in thirty-two degrees into bloody snake land out there. Reeeal good idea. Oh, and *especially* . . .' Now he stood. '*Especially* sounds like a good idea to go gallivanting about the neighbourhood without Telling. Your. Mum.'

His last words were emphasised with steps towards us. He leaned in menacingly, then suddenly winked, as if we were secret conspirators.

'See, love . . .' Now he turned to Connie, pausing to consider just how he was going to put this. 'Ninety-nine per cent of cases like these the kids just skip off and don't tell anyone. Right, kids?' He winked again. 'I mean, I've got two at home myself and trust me, they're out and about like a yoyo. Let me give you a word of advice.' He flumped a muggy hand on Connie's shoulder. 'Next time this happens, just take a couple of breaths and wait an hour. Just one hour. I guarantee you, they'll be back. After all, kids will be kids.'

Connie was standing in proud humiliation. She mumbled an apology.

'Heyeyeyeyey,' the policeman threw his hands up in defence. 'It's what we're here for, isn't it?'

He gave a reassuring smile, then flashed his partner a wink that suggested it was completely normal in this situation for a woman to lack reason and become hysterical. He hoisted his pants and downed his tea.

Connie had apologised again and again as the police left the house, supplicating against the glass as the officer wound up the window. As soon as they were gone though, she became deranged. For half an hour, she paced the room, spinning towards us and baring her shame and disgust as if they were weapons to fling. 'How am I supposed to trust you? I don't know how I'm supposed to leave you here . . . Jesus! The *one time* . . .' Her thoughts flowing together: 'How long though . . . a couple of hours? *A couple of hours!* and your shirt – Matt, do you . . . it doesn't wash off – blood on white – you can't just . . . Jesus!' And she shook her head and turned away, saying, 'It doesn't wash off . . .' again to herself, as if the phrase were a summary of everything.

I stood beside Christina with my head hung, not speaking and not looking, but attempting to dissolve, believing that if I could somehow dissolve then everything would be fine. Connie sensed it. She bent towards me, whimpering, 'Matt . . .', craning her neck so that I could see how she was wretched and pitiable. 'I thought . . .' then pausing to sigh, flapping her hands, 'I guess I don't know what I thought . . . but whatever it was, I must have been wrong . . .'

Each word was a dagger massaged into the skin. What *had* she thought? I wondered. Whatever it was, it didn't matter. (She was turning to Christina.) She'd been made a fool of. *We'd* made a fool of her. Alone in her enormous house! And for what? For an idiot plan to escape? Suddenly the whole idea seemed absurd; the bravado of children dressed as super-heroes. Two of us on a train? Christ! *We* were fools!

'. . . and do you know what's in the paddock!?' Connie was close to Christina's face now, '. . . coz *I* don't. Yeah? But I *do* know that number four has a Rottweiler and no back fence – and *summer* too, are you friggin *serious!?* We've had snakes on the *verandah*, let alone . . .'

Spittle was flying between them, showering Christina. Somehow, it seemed to pass through her though. Her face was estranged, looking elsewhere to the window, as if she were still on the bridge, peering out over the river.

'. . . and if something *does* happen?' Connie was ragged, the words not cutting like she wanted. 'Whose fault is *that*, huh? Huh!? That's a *question*!'

'Ours.'

'*Wrong! Mine.* Yeah? Coz *you're* not in charge – *I'm* in charge. As much as you might like . . . *Hey!*' Christina had gone again. Connie snapped her fingers in her face. '*Look* at me when I'm talking to you.'

Christina looked. She waited, unaffected, as though watching a conversation between two people that didn't include her.

'We're sorry,' she said. 'Is there a punishment?'

Connie faltered, suddenly disarmed.

'I don't know how to make sure you won't do it again,' she said. It was a plea. 'What if you're bitten? You don't even have a phone . . . does *Matt* know what to do? Do *you*? Do you know what happens if it's a brown snake?'

Christina shrugged. 'You get cancer?'

Connie sent us out with a wheelbarrow and a Dutch hoe and told us to clean the roadside paddock, where they kept the horses. We trudged about slowly, scooping piles of manure. Neither of us felt like talking. Connie wasn't going to call my parents, but she'd been surprised and disappointed and somehow that was worse. Now I heard her piano in the lounge room. She was playing something sad that crept over the paddock and caused everything to become poignant and forlorn. The plane trees swaying over the fence; a horse approaching to sniff the wheelbarrow. A gust of wind blew its mane to the other side. Ahead, Christina flung the hoe into the soil. There was still something distant about her, as if she were adrift somewhere, far away – perhaps on the bridge, fleeing over the river. I watched her peering into a pile of shit like it was something to unravel and understand.

When we'd finished, I offered to take the wheelbarrow back, Christina accepting vaguely. I watched her totter off to the house, then made my way towards the workshed. By this time, the piano had stopped and Connie was nowhere to be seen. The garage door was open and I walked in, looking for a spot to put the wheelbarrow. The room was quiet – only the sound of the tumble dryer – and somehow oppressive.

It had once been Alek's pride and joy, the workshed, his cluttered treasureland of power tools and gardening equipment. But now, stepping in, I was confronted with piles of boxes and photo albums, bags of clothes and books and documents. It was like I was peering straight into the soul of the man, the inner mechanism behind the blazing personality whose head shone like an award. Everything had been removed from the house in a tragic exorcism, and now sat amassed like an enormous beating heart in the place he'd loved most.

Peering about, I found everything had been ransacked, boxes torn open and books and paper flung about. I knelt and picked up a photograph: Alek standing majestically with Christina atop his shoulders, saluting the camera. I grinned at her expression, then paused. There was an odd sound, beneath the spin of the tumble dryer; a kind of jolting. Sharp breaths – was it? I peeked around the corner.

Connie was sitting against a pile of boxes with her face buried in a photo album. On the page was a picture of a man standing beside a Kombi with his arm around her. She was sobbing into the image, choking and jolting, and I watched in fascination as her mouth contorted. I'd never seen an adult cry.

Suddenly she looked up, straight into my eyes, as though she knew I'd been there all along. Her cheeks were flushed, her eyes swollen and red, and with perhaps the hint of a challenge in them. Because she knew I could see the album. She was looking at a picture of my father. There he was – perhaps eighteen, nineteen – beside the van in the bright sun with his arm around Connie.

'I'm sorry,' I said, shuffling back.

But she didn't answer. She looked at me with deep rings about her eyes, still heaving and jolting, unable to stop – but without attempting to stop. She didn't jump to her feet or attempt to wipe her eyes. She didn't even close the album. She only looked in bold defiance, as if there were no longer any circumstance to hide behind.

The look said: 'Here I am.'

BUT IT DOESN'T warrant pity. It doesn't deserve it. Connie was an adult and she'd cried and, yes, in that moment I'd felt pity – finding her on the floor. In that moment, I was concerned and wanted to help and didn't know what to do. But over time, my feelings began to change. After all, I thought, children cry and children are brought up to learn that crying leads nowhere; that it begets nothing but more tears. No – over the years, I began to detest the image of Connie with that photo album, weeping for some other life that might have been. There was something childish, something indulgent about it – and self-inflicted: the house was too large; it was obvious. The grounds were too vast; the plants and gardens all withering faster than anyone could keep up with. And yet, there she stayed in her enormous house, defeated on the workshed floor.

I suppose it seems callous. But Connie must have known; it must have crossed her mind, sitting beside Alek in the hospital bed. She would have known the property was too big. She would have come home and heard her voice echo in the lounge room and known it then and there: Wychwood was a dream for two. It was a crazy idea they probably fantasised over red wine before she was pregnant: a tree-change into the gorgeous eucalypts, away from the madding crowd. 'Somewhere far out,' she would have said. 'I want grass and trees – somewhere to raise a kid!' Then one weekend, years after, when things were no longer enchanting, driving by Wychwood, Connie would have seen the plane trees swishing behind the gates and had shivers at the incredible sound. The farm was as she'd imagined. And it had been like providence because they'd got it for a steal. And in the evening, unpacking boxes, she would have looked out the window and seen Alek chopping wood under the weeping boughs or wheeling bins into the darkness, and she would have pinched herself. Because Wychwood was the romantic dream of a young couple. It was not one to be lived out by a woman mourning into her middle age.

I couldn't understand why she stayed. She must have loathed it; the echoes on the tiles and the endless driveway, the endless grass to mow. How long can it have possibly taken to discover that she was no longer enchanted by the swish of the trees? Sitting on the verandah with her porridge before another day bathing the elderly, and realising all of a sudden that she felt no illusion, that the trees and the cicadas no longer seemed to hum wistfully together, they simply droned and she felt nothing – realising that it was all a ruse and that she had fallen for it: the trees had never swished enchantingly, they'd only swished. It had always been white noise and it meant nothing other than soon they would drop their leaves; and soon she would have to sweep the driveway; and the driveway was endless.

And yet, there she stayed, for years, growing tired. I can see her clearly: drunk in the living room, lifting her hands. 'The heart cannot retreat,' she says, as though fate spins its thread and who are we to intervene?

—Only she could have sold! She could have escaped; the answer's obvious. She wasn't even old: mid-forties – still half a life. And still youthful; always seeming younger than she was. Yet she chose to live alone in that enormous house. She *chose* it: year after year, drinking and wallowing and living out the dream, letting it fester and become defiled.

—Actually no, it's not even a choice; it's a *non*-choice. Moving Through would be a choice, succumbing to grief and letting it wash her away to some other beginning, perhaps not ahead but to the side, a light appearing somewhere; walking towards it – there's a choice. Killing herself would have been a choice. Taping a hose into the exhaust and bending it round into the window. I survived and I'm glad, but it's a choice all the same. Hiding things in the workshed is not a choice. It's nothing.

I've been writing for two weeks now. Today I don't want to write. Yesterday I didn't want to write, because I didn't feel like it. Today I don't feel like it either. Today I see no reason, I find no positivity. And yet here I am at a desk, having written. I've made the choice when it would be far easier not to. And perhaps I am cruel; perhaps I'm an arsehole and everything I'm saying is unwarranted. But nevertheless, today I think of Connie in the workshed and I think: There are people who act and there are people who don't. There are people who are scared of action because action is terrifying and it's easier to look away, to move things into the workshed, to deny evidence of your own son's self-destruction, to ignore signs and let him skim towards disaster as your heart screams for you to intervene.

–Does no one realise things rot when they are left alone? Thoughts, memories, people; they fester and are corrupted – And I know better than anyone! – Things grow monstrous when we stow them away, when we shut them out, when we pop out for some air, for 'just a quick coffee', for 'just a stroll!' – 'C'mon, Matt! Just to get away; what's half an hour? How are you going to let yourself heal if you never give yourself a break?'

–Easy words. Easy to moralise when there's no stake; coming up with principles to justify inaction. Well, you know what's fucking hard? Looking things in the eye. Acting. Making a decision. *That's* how I feel today – right? Today the principled among us have no fucking balls. They're the people who find themselves on floors, weeping at the cruelty of the world, weeping at the horror show of their son's volatility. Oh, and what – I'm supposed to feel sympathy now? Tell me *that* isn't cruel!

*

Connie is currently at the assisted living facility on Sable Road. She is fifty-three years old – their youngest resident by fifteen years.

She does nothing with her life but wait for Christina and I to visit, which happens rarely because her deranged view of the past makes conversation unbearable; her inability to listen. Each time, I sit quietly, Christina between us, jittering my knee as she weeps over better times.

If I seem callous, it's because I refuse to become this. I simply refuse.

Is THIS A joke!?–

Five minutes, I want. *Two* minutes. That's all I ask. Stand outside the door, set a timer, I don't care; just allow me two minutes.

Honestly, what am I possibly going to do with a pair of nail clippers?

PRIVACY. IT'S ALL I ask . . .
 Do I have to yell and scream?

Sunday, 13 December

Apparently, I must.

2016

Friday, 1 January

HAPPY NEW YEAR.

I've been unfaithful to this journal and I apologise. How long now? We'll call it a month or so – mostly spent in bed, mind you: Netflix and iView etc. Last night, I woke to the sound of fireworks. In my dream, they'd become explosions and as I opened my eyes, I thought there was a war. On TV, SBS had programmed André Rieu – live in Maastricht to bring in the New Year. I watched him skip about the stage for a half-hour, then fell asleep making the same resolution I make every year.

My birthday came and went without much fuss, as usual, sucked into the end-of-year festivities. My parents took me for a meal at Patee Thai and it was the first time I'd been out in weeks. A day or two earlier, I'd felt the turn and knew I was healing. Even so, it was a shock to the senses. Out on Chapel Street, the holiday atmosphere seemed charged, the footpaths teeming with revellers – same as it ever was, I suppose – bustling inner Melbourne. I watched from across the tables with my wristband explaining that I am from a psychiatric facility, watching them laugh and drink and smoke and be desperately close. It's all therapy though, isn't it? In the end? The free man's sanitorium.

Still, they were free. And here we can't spin the curtain around to lie like spoons for a moment . . .

Reading back, I've been harsh on Connie; those last entries in particular. I suppose they reveal my own headspace more than anything else. Nonetheless, I've been an unfair judge.

After all, it wasn't helplessness that caused Connie to weep – as I would come to understand. Nor was it a common occurrence. No, it was not in Connie's nature to wallow. Rather, in the face of adversity, she was always staunch, refusing to bow down. I think of the encroaching wilderness of Wychwood: her endless pruning and weeding, renovations against an aging property. And against the memory of her husband: wasn't moving his remnants an action? Stealing him away so he could only haunt the workshed?

As for the photo album: it was a single moment, 'a moment of weakness,' she might have said – one she well deserved – but a moment all the same.

And we would never mention it again.

The morning after, Connie was herself again, charged and reassembled. I recall waking to the sound of bright clangs and peering out the curtain to see her driving stakes along the fencing, nattering to Mr Harvey in a sprightly monologue that would last the week until I was picked up. And action, action – refusing to dwell on our little incident in the shed, she'd emerged that morning with a list of accomplishments: it was the fencing and the chicken coop; it was the nasturtiums beside the house, then the rabbit warrens – not to mention that bloody bough across Davies' fence. A list of work to take her mind away and bring her to life again.

I viewed it as an opportunity to redeem myself.

See, after finding Connie in the workshed, I was plunged into a crisis of remorse; the police and her tears – I became racked with guilt and desperate for atonement. I started helping her around the grounds and with the garden. I did the sweeping and the mowing, offered to chop firewood. I raked horse shit from the paddocks and piled it in high clumps along the back fence – all that old work of her husband. I spent entire afternoons in the glaring sun, sweat pouring as I slung new wire about the fence posts; meanwhile, Connie flew about with her shears, grinning and pruning and seeming to regain vitality as the grounds became lush again. I could see she appreciated it. On one occasion, I caught her watching, gazing from the orchard and not registering that I'd seen. For a moment, she'd been still, then something had clicked and she seemed to awaken, mouthing a 'Thank you'. I'd nodded back, feeling good, pleased at the nourishing effect of my work.

But if Connie was brought to life then over the coin, things seemed to fall the other way. Christina understood what I was doing, I think. She took my lead without objecting, sweeping when I swept and digging when I dug. But as the week progressed, I noticed her growing vacant in the most eerie way, as though something were causing her to retract into herself–

(And once again, I can't help envisaging Gloria's prognosis, or Colin's or Anita's; all the other ones – something domestic and unmagical probably, barely raising an eyebrow:

anhedonia, dysphoria, a fall from the hypomanic. I can see them in rooms prescribing Zoloft and Prazosin, worksheets for emotional regulation, flittering their hands in front of her eyes and telling her to think about trains . . .)

–But of course, to me emotions were not chemical then but ethereal. I'd never heard of anhedonia; and so the blankness draping over Christina that week struck me as something far more mystical; Persephone living half her life in the underworld. To me, it was as though Christina had stayed behind that day at the river; leaping from the bridge and leaving behind an imposter, one unable to feel excitement or anticipation; one that saw a leaf and swept it away, digging slowly with no goal but to feel soil clutched in its fingers.

One afternoon, planting ironbarks along Davies' fence, I caught her gazing at the bandage on her wrist, mesmerised by the stains, fingering them with her thumb.

'What are you doing?' I'd asked. 'Is it alright?'

She'd snapped awake, looked at me like I'd never heard of the Beatles.

'You need to turn the soil . . .'

Then she was gone again, back to middle distance where I wasn't allowed, peering the same way she'd peered into the horse shit – only there seemed to be shit all around now, and she was watching it pass by like a diver in a deep-sea cage.

Next it was her clothes: the same clothes for days in a row. In her room, she had a pile that went onto the chair, then the floor, back onto the chair again. Then it was only the floor and she lived in a dressing gown. I couldn't remember her showering, doing her hair, looking in a mirror – it all seemed irrelevant – and with the bandage loose at the edge, soon she was Raggedy Ann again, floating and flopping about the house.

'That's not how we dress at the dinner table!' Connie had snapped one evening as Christina emerged in her dressing gown.

There'd been a horrible silence as she looked up and discovered an entire world all about her, then nodding passively, 'Sorry . . . I forgot,' returning to her room as though Connie had reminded her of something else.

I remember creeping in later and trying not to wake her, trying not to make a sound, sliding under the covers – only her wakefulness had been tangible; her eyes awake, rolled over and staring at the wall.

'Christina,' I'd whispered, and she'd been silent. 'I'm sorry.'

Then turning onto my back and peering at the stars, feeling the distance between us as if it were light years – certain that if I stretched out my hand, it would extend into infinity before ever reaching her.

Of course, it wasn't only dysphoria though. There was another side to things I wasn't aware of: the fact that ever since we'd run from the river, Christina had been consumed with an idea, something turning in her mind and eating away at her.

It was my last night when I finally learned what it was, that strange night I'd woken and she'd not been in bed; her mattress empty above me, sheets tossed about. There were sounds, I remember: a clinking in the bathroom, under the noise of rain – it had been raining hard.

I'd sat up in bed, thinking perhaps it was morning but finding the windows still dark. Outside, the paddock had been grey and colourless and I'd listened a moment to the sound under the rain. Clink clink. I'd got up and stepped into the hall, peering at the light under the door, and whispered her name.

'Christina.'

No answer though. Only a rustling behind the door and so I'd tiptoed forward, slowly creaking it open.

She was in the bath, clothed, with her arm on the ledge and piles of bright tissues on the floor about her. As her head shot up in surprise, I'd noticed the dirty bandage half unwound, her hair and T-shirt all wet.

'Jesus!' she hissed. 'Do you knock?'

'Sorry – what's going on?'

'You scared the shit out of me is what. Why are you up?'

'Can't sleep. Are you alright?'

'Fine.' A pause. 'I had to redo this.'

'Is it still bleeding?' I asked.

'Yeah. No. I just did it again.'

'How?'

Her eyes darting about.

'You can't tell – I went to check on the stuff.'

'What stuff?'

'Shh! The bag. I wanted to check if it was still there, if those guys found it.'

'And did they?'

'Stop talking so loud – it's fine.'

'Why didn't you say? I would have gone–'

But then her eyes were wide. I could hear the sound of footsteps now, pacing the lounge. Connie was awake, coming closer. Christina grabbed my shoulder.

'You can't say anything. Yeah? I'll kill you. Please.'

'Why would I say anything?'

'Just don't.'

'Here – let me do this,' I said, taking the bandage.

She offered her wrist and I began to wind it around. But the blood wasn't dry and the fabric, still brown with old blood, seemed to squelch as it pressed into itself.

I paused a moment, looking at the stains.

'What?' she hissed.

'How is there so much blood?'

'. . .'

–Because she'd fallen, of course, as I later found out. The real story. She never even made it to the shack.

See, that entire week she'd spent peering at the ceiling, imagining the men pulling up the planks and finding the bag; tossing and turning and wondering if there was anything in there that could lead them to her; imagining police cars arriving at the house, all her plans to escape in tatters. She hadn't wanted to involve me though, figuring she'd caused enough trouble, and so that night she'd left me asleep, skipping over the futon and taking a torch and a jumper.

It had started raining halfway through Davies' paddock. Hard rain. The thicket became impassable as boughs swatted her face and the rain turned everything into static; the torch rendered useless as she staggered slowly, drenched through and wanting to turn back but having gone too far for that. Then along the banks it had been equally dark; the river swollen and rushing in torrents. There'd been no moon either, only the weak torch beam as she fumbled to the bridge, using the water as a guide, keeping close to the edge. At some point she'd tripped.

To be honest, the outcome was better than it might have been: a few cuts and bruises – she didn't go in at least. But she reopened the wound on her arm.

Somehow she'd made it home, refusing to look at the blood covering her wrist and hand like a rubber glove; thin diluted blood drizzling everywhere in the rain. She'd crept into the bathroom, turned on the water to hide the noise and tried to pressure it closed, until I'd come in.

–Now though, footsteps were pattering down the hall, the two of us flurrying whispers as they drew close; the handle clattering and the door flying open.

'What's going on?!' Connie hissed, tottering and bleary-eyed. 'It's three-thirty!'

But neither of us replied. She was looking down at Christina's bloody bandage, the tissues on the floor, sleep disappearing as her eyes grew slowly wide. Christina looked at the wound then to her mother, shrugging without surprise or concern.

'It won't heal,' she said. 'I think it's infected.'

Connie had rushed Christina into the kitchen, leaving me to stand awkwardly in the hall as their voices pierced the rain: Connie pleading, Christina sullen. I tried to hear words but couldn't. After a time, Christina had appeared again, passing by me without a word.

'Hey.' I'd touched her arm. 'Is it alright?'

She didn't respond though, instead appearing to fade down the hall into her room.

I'd found Connie in the kitchen, staring out the window, with those same red rings I'd seen in the workshed.

'Is she okay?' I asked.

'Pardon? Oh.' She seemed to realise who I was. 'Sorry – yes. She's fine. She's a little under the weather.'

'Is she sick?'

Connie's smile seemed to half-dismantle. It reassembled.

'Can you hear that?' she said, nodding to the window.

The rain had stopped. Now outside it had become windy and I could hear the trees swishing in the garden, waving their arms as though glad to be free of the downpour.

'I love that sound.'

She tossed the towel in the sink, turning with a wan smile.

'Thanks for your help this week,' she said. 'It's been so nice having a man around here.'

That was the tightest she ever hugged me. And not like I was a child either, but like it was something she desperately needed. Her lips were on my collarbone, leaving a cold half-moon.

After she left for bed, I stood for a moment in the bathroom, peering in the mirror, at my chin that was fuzzy with new stubble; acne rippling about. I was taller too, I thought, scratching at a pimple. I took a tissue and wiped it clean. Paused.

The bin was entirely filled with tissues. Sitting on the floor beside the sink, packed to the brim in a white mound, some slipping down onto the floor. The whole arrangement was so starkly clinical – like strawberries and cream, I thought – with the brightness soaking away in the deep red of Christina's blood.

I hadn't been able to sleep then; lying awake, sensing Christina rolled over a trillion miles away. Above me, the sheets rose and fell. I would reply to her letter, I thought.

As soon as I was home, I would write, 'Your mother cried in the workshed,' and everything would make sense. She would understand and forgive me. It would be different next time.

The thought was consolation and I closed my eyes and began to drift, thinking of next time: the two of us on the bridge again, skipping to the far bank and sneaking into the abandoned shack, pulling the board closed behind us – then suddenly intimate; finding ourselves alone in thin bands of light, the sound disappearing beyond the walls–

'Are you awake?'

The fantasy disappeared. I opened my eyes to find Christina kneeling above me, teetering on the mattress like a gargoyle on a wall, the whites of her eyes glowing phosphorescent.

'What are you doing?' I asked.

'Can I come in?'

The words issued from a space where her mouth should have been. They hung in the gulf between us. I had the sudden feeling of standing on a cliff.

'Okay,' I said, wondering what was at the bottom.

A silhouette flapped as Christina arched a leg off the bed – the futon capitulating beside my ankle. I could hear the sound of my loud heart as another foot swung blackly. Now she was above me, the stars peeking behind the outline of her shorts, making a pool of her belly; the sheet pulling off my shoulder. I was trying to breathe slowly, holding in thick gasps to calm the adrenaline. But my skin was electric. The room was electric. She slid a foot under and it sparked like flint. Then turning away, she was pulling my arm under her neck, shuffling back and pressing into my crotch. The pressure made everything flex and I held my breath, knowing she could feel.

For a moment we lay tessellated, with my nose pressed in her hair and the room pulsing about us. Her breathing was hypnotic and I waited, mind flittering – not to sleep of course; there was no possibility of that – but scattering, swooping about the room, viewing us from above, if the sheets pulled away – a couple on a tandem bicycle perhaps. But my heart beating so loud. Could she feel it? Could she feel lower? Christ! I imagined Connie stumbling through the house. Had Christina made a noise climbing off the bed? I wondered. How loud was it beating? And I could see the doorhandle turning, the sheets torn away. We would be in so much trouble. But somehow the thought brought no fear. No – fear was a non-reality, a distant trivia only serving to make the room pulse. Christina had shuffled again, reminding me that she was there.

Now I brought across my left hand. It had been sitting at my hip and I dropped it around her waist. Below the T-shirt, her stomach was bare and she took a trembling breath as I began to brush in light strokes, stumbling over her belly button, feeling skin that was smooth and dry. I didn't know what I was doing; I had no goal, no hope of anything else – I only stroked, believing that somehow the gesture proved my devotion. I realise it sounds absurd, but at that moment in the dark, I believed it bravely and fiercely. And I was convinced she understood. I was with her, the strokes crooned. Here I was, a passenger on a motorcycle, clutching as tight as I could. And yes, I hadn't written and January had been a disappointment, but still, I was devoted – and if she needed proof then she only needed to look around. Please look around. And as I swept, I felt that surging electricity again, causing my hand to shake. Her bravado at the creek, those things we'd said, they were here in the room, adding to the pulse, and to my strokes that were becoming broad now, rising to the shelf of her ribs – my stumbling curiosity; I'd seen the fascinating elastic behind her singlets. But now I only felt skin that was smooth and dry as I traced her ribcage, then higher still, bending my lips in the shape of a kiss, pressing them into her hair so she could feel, pressing my whole self so she could feel–

Suddenly I snatched my hand away, realising my mistake. There was no elastic. There was only the swell of a breast that appeared weirdly and unexpectedly above a stomach so like my own. Suddenly it was there, pressed against my thumb and I tore my hand away, falling back in a panic of shame, croaking an apology. There was a horrible eternity: me staring at the stars, dismayed at the violation – terrified that she would reply. But she didn't. Instead, she reached for my hand again, drawing me back around. She was trembling now, wrapping me tight like a coat, as terrified as I was – and so I slid my nose into her cheek to kiss the terror away. More proof: my lips moving up her chin. Only her cheek was damp, I realised. I felt a warm flush. Tears? I tried to pull away and she hauled me tighter around, refusing to let go, refusing to let me see. It was a blistering silence. I could feel her eyes wide open, thinking thoughts that had nothing to do with stars or electricity, but something else, something that must have been terrifying. She was still trembling – Christina: the only person in the world who wasn't fragile, suddenly clearing her throat to speak.

'If you could go anywhere in the world,' she whispered, 'where would you go?' Her voice was tiny and desperate, like I'd never heard.

'I would be here.'

There was silence as I felt her shuffle ever so slightly out of my grip.

'I'm being serious,' she said.

But so was I.

God knows how long we lay there, with me wound around her like a skin, feeling her breath jolt and tremble, terrified that loosening my grip would cause her to fall apart in my arms. When she finally stopped, still I wouldn't let go. Sleep was unthinkable. We only lay in silence, peering into the dark under the bed, where the stars couldn't reach.

Some nights, to get to sleep, I put on a film; set my laptop on the desk and put on whatever, let it play and play. The content itself is irrelevant, of course. It is merely to have the shapes move in front of my eyes; the comfort of colour and sound filling the silence, sending me off.

I have no issue with days. I don't think anyone does. Days are easy, filled with distraction: meals, activities, visitors. Days are when we all shine and everyone is fooled. Like Alek at the dinner table, with his bravado; laughing at his illness. But nights, though . . .

I can't help thinking there must have been moments in the hospital; peering at the ceiling as his body ate itself alive. Is that why Connie was there all the time? I wonder. Is it why she didn't laugh at his famous chemotherapy joke? Because she'd seen the evenings, seen his smile wipe away, waiting for the nurse to leave so she could slip behind him and they could lie like spoons: her clutching tight and whispering in his ear as he peered, wide-eyed, into the dark . . .

Nights are difficult, with nothing to do, with great silences to fill, for thoughts to seep in. It's why I set the laptop on the desk – and I'm not the only one, either; if you listen, all through the clinic there are computers pittering in the dark; scores of eyes watching shapes flit about, and waiting for morning, when there's light and the spell's gone, and we can wonder what the hell came over us.

And it was just the same that morning after Christina and I eventually fell asleep, tessellated under the stars: as though the entire episode had been a dream, a non-reality promptly forgotten. I'd opened my eyes and found the sun bright under the curtains. The stars had vanished and the room was no longer a galaxy but a room. Everything super-natural was gone, the electricity – Christina's sheets tossed in a bundle. I tried to remember falling asleep and couldn't: I recalled peering under the bed, the flush of Christina's cheeks, then blank.

Stumbling down the hall, I heard voices in the kitchen; Connie drizzling an anecdote as she hovered above the mushrooms.

'Christ, he's risen!' she exclaimed, splattering butter into the pan. 'Full English this morning, Matty! Toast or muffins?'

The rings under her eyes were gone, I noticed, her voice brand-new.

'It's multigrain,' Christina warned, tossing cutlery on the table. 'You having OJ?'

'So what it's multigrain,' Connie snapping back. 'Multigrain's not the devil.'

Christina also seemed to have risen afresh, showered and neat like she'd never spilled a tear. All about me, in fact, things seemed bright and cheery, the trees bobbing out the window as if it weren't life but an advertisement for a fun breakfast cereal, Connie sprinkling the rosemary: 'You know, Matt, this was every Sunday when I was a kid – our gran preparing the most ex*traordinary*–' et cetera et cetera. There was no trace of last night's hysteria, the desperation and Christina trembling; the entire fantasy having slipped back in the lamp as I awoke.

'–Matt?'

I turned back to the table. Here she was, still waiting for an answer.

'You want OJ?'

The query was pleasant and professional, her eyebrows raised in fresh innocence, their meaning clear: last night was to be annulled.

It was as suffocating a breakfast as I've ever experienced: Christina and I spearing glances as Connie prattled about her grandmother's legendary breakfasts, better times, and the endless scent of rosemary and marjoram: 'God, isn't it just *amazing* the link between smell and *memory*?'

We let her patter, barely speaking, deep in a conversation of glances. I would look and Christina would be looking; we would catch eyes and look away. An entire recapitulation of last night's activity shot across the table – glances so full of meaning, it's a wonder the memory didn't project onto the wall.

Then afterwards, cleaning the dishes, Christina had become sullen, peering out the window where Connie and Mr Harvey trotted up the path. She wanted me gone, I knew. It was clear I'd witnessed something I wasn't meant to see, some tragic part that was supposed to be hidden. Now she dried with the focus of a monomaniac, peering intensely as if engrossed in the task.

–Christ, and here's when I fall into those cycling thoughts, useless hypotheticals, wondering how things might have been if I'd simply never asked; if we'd left it as a confused and ghostly night at the end of a rather awkward summer holiday – perhaps to have never been repeated. Would we this? Would we that? Would Christina have ended up a full-time carer? Would I have difficulty gripping my pen? Stabilising my hand?

These sorts of questions. Trust me – you can fall down a hole.

But anyway, it's irrelevant, isn't it? Because Christina would not get her way that day. No – of all people, Connie suggested the two of us take a final walk. To this day, I don't know why she chose to stay behind, but she did, and Christina and I eventually found ourselves alone that last afternoon, walking down the driveway and past the gates.

Out in the street, everything seemed to drape in a manner reflecting the end of holidays: trees hung dreary and lethargic. Only Christina refused to adhere to the mood, striding with brisk impatience, streaming ahead as though to make space in a barrier against conversation. I'd trailed behind, my head a spiral of thoughts: blood squelching up from the bandage, her refusal to roll around, her tears – and then this morning, pitching a tea towel as if nothing was awry–

'So are you going to say about last night?'

The question burst out of me like a blush, causing her to stop in her tracks. We'd been passing a bus shelter. She paused a moment, considering, then turned around.

'What would you like me to say?'

111

'I don't know. Are you okay?'

'I'm sensational.'

She crossed her arms, owning the boldness of the lie.

'Alright,' I said. 'Well, I'm sorry if I did anything to contribute.'

'Why do you think it has to do with you?'

'What does?'

She narrowed her eyes.

'Why are you being so nosy?'

'Because I'm worried.'

'You're *worried*?'

Up the road, a bus was approaching. She watched it a moment, then puffed a laugh. 'Well, you're going home anyway, so what does it matter?'

Now she shrugged coolly, hiding the embarrassment of her own melodrama.

'Are you upset I'm leaving?' I said.

She was watching the bus.

'Because I can–'

But now her head flung around. 'You shouldn't be worrying about me. You should be worried about yourself.'

'Wh–'

'Why are you always sorry?' Her cheeks were flushed. 'You're always worried and you're always sorry. Stop worrying about other people and worry about yourself.'

'Myself?'

'You just apologised to me and you have no idea why. Why are you sorry, Matt? Why? Do you even know? It's like you're tiptoeing around in case there's something you were s'posed to be sorry for but you never said.'

'No, you're misunderst–'

'You've been following Mum round like a dog the last week coz you felt bad – because for the first time in your life, you broke a rule.'

'That's not true.'

'Isn't it?'

'No.'

'You sure?'

'Okay, what should I do then?' I said, feeling my cheeks burn. 'Run away? Like you? Should I get on this bus right now? Should I try and get people to go looking for me? That's mature, that's brave.'

She chuckled: 'Nah, you'd bitch out.'

'Would I?'

'Definitely.'

'And how would you know?'

Now a thin smile.

'Okay then,' she said. 'Prove it.' She pointed to the house we'd stopped outside: 'Throw a stone at that window.'

'What?'

The bus slowed almost to a stop and she waved it on, then crouched to pick up a stone sitting beside my foot.

'I want you to throw this stone,' she held it up to my face, 'at that window.'

'Why?'

'Because I reckon you're full of shit.'

I scoffed.

'Don't laugh. You're sick and you need help.'

'*I'm* sick?'

'Tell me this: Have you ever had sex?'

'*What?* How does *that*–'

'Some of the girls at my school are doing it.'

'Wha . . . I–'

'It's okay,' she said. 'You don't have to answer. It was a trick question. See?' She was indicating my flushed cheeks. 'Exhibit A.'

'I'm not sick.'

'Fine, then throw the stone – that window, right there.'

'I just don't see how it proves anything.'

She turned and hurled the stone with all her might. I watched in disbelief as it flew wide, slamming into the frame and chipping the paint.

'What the fuck are you doing?!'

'I'm helping you. Do it.'

'No.'

'Do it or your life will be insignificant.'

'No!'

She threw a second stone, slamming off the awning.

'Fucking hell!'

'Do it or I'm going to keep doing it until you fucking do it!'

Now there was noise inside the house. Voices and alarm. She picked up another stone and I grabbed her arm.

'Alright, alright! Jesus!'

I sighed and took it from her, weighing it in my palm.

'Do it.' Her eyes flashed expectantly.

'Fine.' I looked at the window. 'You happy?'

I drew back my arm back and threw.

It was without exception the greatest throw I've ever made in my life. We turned just in time to see the rock sail through the trees and crash directly into the window, annihilating the glass before advancing further, into a vase of hydrangeas perched on the sill. There was a dazzling explosion as the flowers somehow launched upright, pin-dropping in a maelstrom of china and glass.

'Holy shit,' Christina said in the silence that followed. 'Good throw.'

We stood, stunned, peering through the hole now gaping in the window, a moan beginning to sound from in the house.

'What do we do?' I asked.

'I don't know,' she said. 'But I'm pretty sure you're a criminal now.'

'Really? W–'

And in a swift movement, she took my hand, swung me round and smacked a kiss on my lips. I closed my eyes in surprise, feeling the heat of the sun. Somehow it seemed to consume everything: her lips, the taste, the commotion behind the window. A woman was howling now, but I didn't care – danger was remote and irrelevant. I was a criminal, but we were kissing and so I forgot. When I opened my eyes, everything was blue and overexposed, Christina looking fixedly.

'Don't ever be sorry,' she said, her face massive and close. 'You make things bearable.'

Now a man's voice was booming and I looked away, gazing at the wreckage of the window, at the front door tearing open behind the screen door.

'Oh shit. Do you think–'

But Christina was already halfway up the street.

–Then I was calling her name, over and over, chasing her back through the streets, my head racing, my heart in my mouth, convinced for the first time that she might actually be insane, but at the same time, feeling my chest hammer like it never had before, recalling the man howling in a thick accent, shaking his fist from the porch as his wife moaned at the window. I'd run and run, my high heart pulverising, terrified, but at the same time close to something I'd never experienced, some new kind of elation; racing through the streets, howling her name as we made for Wychwood.

Then, sprinting back into the driveway, we'd found my parents, tanned and relaxed after an easy flight, holding hands in a way that seemed a little distasteful. I'd not expected them and had come shrieking in a craze, in the exhilaration of that first lure of anarchy; cackling as if to wake the dead. Mum and Dad and Connie had all looked up as we arrived, Mum raising her eyebrows: 'Yes Matt, the *whole* neighbourhood knows you're here . . .' while Christina, having arrived first, sucked in gulps and turned to wink. 'Told you I'd win.' It was all a secret, the wink confirmed, nothing to be voiced in the company of adults – and so I sealed my lips, turning to Dad who turned to Connie, regathering his thoughts. 'Ah yeah – God – that's right, the *culture* . . .' He'd been gushing over the high-end food, over sights and markets and the breathtaking accommodation of Nha Trang: 'Honestly, hand dryers like you've never seen in your *life* . . .'

There was a true absurdity to it: my heart still thumping, fingers still jittery – the memory of hurling the stone and the wild face of the man in the window, the warmth of Christina's lips still on mine – earth-shattering revelations. *(We were really going to keep it to ourselves?!)* And yet here was my father detailing the river cruise in which they'd almost fallen asleep, while Christina stood opposite, smiling gaily with shoulders abuoyed; gorgeous and light, peering about the circle – now shooting me a secret wink. *(We weren't! Madness!)* I watched in admiration, unable to keep my eyes off her: the only person in the world who wasn't fragile, my conspirator; the person who seemed to be able to suck more from life than I'd ever dared, and who could send my heart so high in my chest that still it was refusing to come down. She was laughing now at something Dad had said, giggling bright and new with her shirt bowed at the neck, revealing skin that was light-rinsed and delicate; now in shadow, now bright again – where my lips had been, I thought suddenly; *my* lips. Last night. Where they'd bent in the shape of a kiss, and she'd pulled me around, wrapping me tight and letting my hand slip across her belly – *my* hand, yes – my hand on her belly, stroking her ribcage, and rising higher to–

I realised I had an erection.

I crashed back to earth and looked about the circle. No one had noticed, thank God. They were nodding with concern. *I* was nodding with concern. Because now Dad was talking about poverty – about how it littered the sidewalks and how there were tin shacks all along the river Mekong. 'I mean, the exchange rate's great for us,' he was explaining, 'but it does make you think, doesn't it?' We were agreeing that it did – myself included, with my erection; crossing my hands in front and wondering how I could possibly be erect at a time like this, when there were tin shacks along the Mekong.

But then I wasn't alone, was I?

'We found some of it quite eye-opening actually.' Here was Mum, nodding as if she were afraid it was so, 'litter just *there* on the streets . . .'

I thought of her on the balcony with a cigarette, peering out at the endless possibilities of her own life – the seething, stifling tension that followed her about the house. Now she was clasping Dad's hand like a trophy, the man I'd found on his knees with a bag of rigatoni, after paying for his guilt with money for hospital bills. And bills for whom? For Connie, who'd wept in the workshed over his photograph, and who was now saddened by the litter in the streets. A rot had spread to all of them, I realised, like the peaches in the orchard. And even Christina, whose attempts to seize the frenzied pulse of life would soon lead to a padded bed. All of them. Yet here they were, commiserating the poverty of the Mekong as I stood with my erection – me, the worst of them all, with that terrible fault of mine: cowardice – standing there privy to everything; to cigarettes and rigatoni and shattered windows and photo albums.

Suddenly, I had the urge to speak. At that moment, I was filled with an urge to scream that all of us were in trouble! That we were in trouble and no one knew because no one was daring to speak. Because it was easier to agree that there was poverty in the Mekong–

'But don't . . .' I said, then paused.

Suddenly I could feel their eyes on me. Waiting, expectant. I cleared my throat.

'I suppose then . . . all we can be is grateful?'

Everyone raised their eyebrows, nodding, impressed at the unexpected flush of wisdom.

It was a profound silence: Christina, Connie, my mother and father – all of whom had witnessed tragedy and refused to look – they agreed with my summary.

Yes, I thought. Hiding erections is a part of life.

THERE I GO running ahead again, injecting premonitions into my fifteen-year-old brain.

I confess to being influenced this time, my parents having visited on four occasions this week.

Only a half-hour ago, Mum was swanning in unannounced, rushing to the ficus and examining the leaves, tsking in the same manner she did over the fern and the monstera before that – both of which died.

'Matthew, you can't just let it sit,' she says, explaining once again the benefits of indirect light, of damp soil and the need for constant nurture. I let her chastise me – an acknowledgment of her desire to be needed – studying her face as she speaks, the caking mascara that somehow manages to emphasise insecurity, rather than hide it.

Of course, the reason for today's visit is another update: the back room is now half-painted and they've moved Dad's gym equipment out of the spare room.

Mum's taken to detailing all renovations; the implication being that I will stay with them when I leave (with a deeper, psychoanalytic implication that I will remain curled in her breast forever).

The thought strikes me: Is my mother the kind of woman to buy a temperamental plant, in the knowledge that I will not care for it and she will have to intervene? I find myself diagnosing her: Munchausen by proxy. The way she pours her devotion into the ficus.

'So thanks for that, mate,' Dad jokes. 'Guess I'm working out in the garage . . .'

Mum scoffing: 'As if you ever use it . . .'

She has a white-knuckle way of holding his hand that I can't be sure is domination or desperation. I suppose they achieve the same result: over the years, Dad's shoulders have hunched so much that now he gives the impression of a walking apology.

'True, true.' He chuckles at his own buffoonery.

–Anyway, this was just before.

Now I sit down to journal and suddenly we're standing in the driveway fourteen years ago, and Mum's gripping Dad's hand with white knuckles and he's a buffoon. And I'm a soothsayer.

I've been telling lies again: dressing Mum in a confidence that simply wasn't there at that time, giving myself the ability of divine foresight. Did I honestly stand in the driveway with a sense of foreboding of a terrible future? Of course not. I was just hoping no one would look at my pants.

I need to stick to the facts, tell what actually happened. Otherwise what's the point? Otherwise I may as well be writing a fantasy.

*

So what are the facts then?

The facts are: fifteen minutes after my parents and I left Wychwood, the man from the house with shattered windows would pull into the driveway. Three weeks after that, Christina was at a boarding house and Connie was a spiralling mess.

And while the seeds had been growing under my nose, the truth is, I'd been too oblivious to consider them. I had no premonitions. In fact, it would be weeks before I noticed anything awry – and even then, what I noticed wasn't seeds but rather the unmissable fact that Christina managed to suddenly vanish into thin air.

See, the moment I got home – after the stones and after my parents in the driveway – I was shutting myself away and putting pen to paper, composing my long-promised reply letter. For an hour and a half I wrote and wrote, pouring my heart onto the page in a manner I believed was love in its most pure distillation. With perspective, the result was heinous and overly sentimental – but nonetheless, I'd rushed to the letterbox with my head spinning.

That next week I spent as a child the night before Christmas, lying awake with a head full of candy, twirling in a breeze of euphoria, sighing at the shimmer of the moon and the bobbing agapanthus and various other execrable behaviours of the infatuated.

But I heard nothing for almost two months; not a peep, no explanation, nothing to say where Christina was or what was happening, or why or with whom. There was only silence. Deafening radio silence. Of course I tried reaching out; calling the house again and again, leaving messages that were short and aloof, then long and mournful. I even tried calling Connie's mobile, only to hear a fluidy gurgle, followed by a rustling and a snappy voice:

'Yes, who is it?'

'It's Matt. Is Christina there?'

'Matt who?'

'Matt Lacey.'

'Lacey? Is that Irish?'

'It is.'

'Right – she isn't here.'

I'd called again, assuming a wrong number, only to suffer the same woman becoming enraged. 'She'll call when she's home!' But Christina never called. She never called and never wrote, she never visited. There was only baffling silence.

Then, on a Friday weeks later, Dad had shuffled into the computer room with a covert expression and taken a breath.

'Matt – just thought you'd want to know . . .' He'd peered about as if the room were bugged, lowering his voice. 'Christina's moved to a boarding house.'

'What?'

'A boarding house – well, she's had to move.'

'Had to?'

'It's Kewfield Secondary. She's back for the holidays – and some weekends, I think – we're not exactly sure at this point . . .'

'But why?'

'Why? *Why?* Perhaps because it's not really our business, is it?'

And he'd reversed out of the room with his eyebrows raised.

The news had thrown me into disarray. I knew *why*, of course. I understood at once what had happened: Christina had taken the fall. The man had found his windows destroyed and come to Wychwood with an axe to grind. She'd taken the whole thing on herself – I could see the incident playing out. Now she was locked in a boarding house or a nunnery or whatever it was, stripped of electricity and outside correspondence, while I, the true criminal, continued life as normal.

I'd found myself slipping seamlessly in at school again: attending form room and peeling the barcodes off textbooks, covering myself in an (ob)noxious cloud of Lynx as my face slowly pustulated in a massacre of acne. To the naked eye, I was the same as nine hundred other students flumping their way to school, flumping their way home. But of course, it was only external. Internally, anxiety had taken hold, remorse swelling grotesquely and causing everything to pale in significance. School suddenly seemed like a preposterous interruption, some monstrous joke: returning from Wychwood, from lying under the stars with Christina in my arms, suddenly I was stuffed in a classroom and instead of stars, there were whiteboards full of inverse proportions and impossible French conjugations. From scaling the footbridge over the river, suddenly teachers were handing me *The Grapes of Wrath* and demanding that I reveal how it showed the dehumanising effects of capitalism. The change was absurd; everything to do with school was absurd and overwhelming and unnecessary, as though it were no longer a place of learning but the result of some unknown rival's conspiracy against me.

So I began to dissociate. I sat in class refusing to listen, refusing to engage, refusing to do anything but draw elaborate squiggles in a misguided act of defiance; tuning out and doodling and dreaming up romantic gestures of apology; peering out windows as if the frames encased not glass, but a lens into the whimsical future.

It wasn't long before people noticed. I soon developed a reputation for laziness, and teachers began to hate me. I don't blame them either. *I* would have hated me. At this point, I'd caught up physically and surpassed most students in my year level. My chest was broad and my calves were thick and I would sit like a troll hunched into a tiny human chair, my little grey shorts and five o'clock shadow causing me to look like a grown man at a costume party. I would slump at the back of the room, oafish and stupid with cheeks like a flipped egg, drawing profanities all over my work.

Once, Mr Arakelian made me show my textbook to the entire class. I'd drawn a penis swirling from the crotch of a long-distance runner into the mouth of Harold Holt, who was making a speech over the page. Mr A said it was a masterpiece, then swooped in with a searing question about my future. I responded with the truth, a shrug, and the class laughed. I realised I'd been insolent. Mr Arakelian fumed, his face becoming swollen and red, as if he was attempting an imitation of the drawing. 'I don't know what's got into you,' he sneered, 'but my opinion of you has hit rock bottom.' I stood with no answer, wondering how to explain that I'd experienced a flake of the divine and now it was gone and all that was left was ashes. But he didn't give me the chance. He hissed the words, '*Rock. Bottom,*' again and ordered me to sit beside his desk as he wrote a scathing e-mail, titled 'mATTHEW'S bEHAVIOUR!!'.

I remember arriving home that evening to a planned intervention in the kitchen: Mum and Dad with their fingers laced over the table – Mum breaking the ice tenderly: 'What's going *on* here, Matty?' mournful and pathetic. Then for forty minutes, the two of them expressed in a variety of ways how they were 'at a loss'.

'Com*pletely* at a loss!' Dad kept chiselling from different parts of the kitchen, clearly feeling that some of Mum's points were missing the bullseye. 'I mean, last year wasn't Mr A saying you were one of his best students? Huh? What do you have to say to *that*?'

I said the death of Harold Holt was a meaningless event that served no purpose and was of no use to anyone.

'What!?'

'It's true!'

'Do you have any idea what he did for this country?'

'So what? He died; there's no moral. I don't know why we have to learn about it.'

'I don't know what's got into you.'

'It doesn't make sense!'

'Oh, but *vandalising* makes perfect sense? *Defacing* the school?'

'What . . .'

'Aah, *now* we're surprised, eh? Don't act like . . . we've found things–'

'You've been going through my stuff?'

'*Your* stuff? We *buy* you that stuff, Matthew. We pro*vide* for you.'

'Stay out of my room.'

'Don't you dare! That is not your room – we *give* you a room. If you don't want us going through it then maybe you need to work on deserving the privilege.'

'Me!? What are *you* two doing, huh? This is the first time

you've been in a room together for more than five minutes without yelling at each other.'

'What!?'

It was true; things had turned icy again. Dad had become detached and secretive – that way he had of disengaging from us: there were murky phone calls coming to the house; his low voice quivering on the other side of my bedroom wall. Twice, he'd disappeared somewhere in the middle of the night. It had caused their relationship to flare again – horribly, one afternoon in the car outside Safeway. They'd told me to go buy a Cornetto and when I'd returned, Mum had said, 'Ooh mint – yummy!' and her eyes had been red and weepy. They'd since simmered into a calloused state of agitation. They were polite; we ate at the dinner table. Only afterwards, they wouldn't want me to leave in case they were suddenly alone. It was shit to be around. Clearly though, I'd committed a far greater offence by voicing anything.

'You ungrateful . . .' Dad stood sputtering, enraged and bewildered. 'Don't you . . . that is *not*–'

'You think I don't hear?' I yelled. 'You think *I* haven't found things, huh? *Footsteps to Intimacy?*'

'How *dare* you!'

'*Stop it! Both of you!*' Mum cried. She was sitting in desolation, as if the greatest tragedy of all was the terrible effect the shouting would have on her nerves. Now she looked at me, pleading, somehow appearing to peek from under the brim of her sorrow. 'Where's that kid,' she said, 'that kid who used to mow the lawns without even being asked? Remember him?'

I remembered, but I was furious.

'Where's the mum that used to buy me PlayStations because she was upset?'

'You selfish *shit!*'

The result of the altercation was that I found myself trial-ling a seven-til-five weekend shift in the grocery department of Highett Safeway, Mum and Dad having decided a job would teach me the values of pride and fortitude and perhaps how to ignore the crippling tension suffocating every corner of the house. Safeway hired me, and so for ten hours every Saturday, I moved cardboard boxes from pallets onto trolleys and then into the store, stacking the shelves and ensuring all the labels faced out into the aisle correctly. I was given a box cutter and a name tag that for some reason said 'Aroush' and was never changed. Customers would approach with questions that were mystifying and imbecilic and I would smile and help them politely. Three weeks in, I was requested to aisle seven, where I found a splattering broth of vomit that a child had left after attempting a 720 in a shopping trolley. I mopped slowly, watching the sick spread across the laminate and attempting to find the word 'CHRISTINA' in the tiny shreds of carrot. I didn't learn the value of pride.

In fact, the only thing I managed to develop was a growing sense of resentment: towards my parents and teachers, at Christina's continuing silence, at the cruel world. I began staying at Sam's house to escape. His dad lived close to school and worked nights in rail maintenance. I would go there 'to study' and we would sit on his porch, smoking his brother's weed as I delivered exhaustive monologues on the nature of longing and despair. We never studied. Instead, I would slowly green out, watching the trees melting psychedelically into surrealist impressions of Christina's face. Or other nights spent engineering grandiose gestures of love: scurrying by the train tracks with a can of spray-paint, repeating our names in twine along the fencing between Prahran and Windsor stations. There were a lot of nights like this, actually, more than I care to admit: staggering back to peer at my blurred calligraphy and feeling like Christina was so close – *just there!* – and that I only needed to reach out and she would be in my arms; my hands stretching forward, shadow-boxing into infinity as I stumbled home with sick on my shirt; passing out eventually only to fall into the most wonderful fever dreams: rushing up and down the riverbank; Christina suddenly appearing, having emerged from the water ('This is where I've been!' she yells), unwinding her bandages to reveal her wound spouting like a fountain ('It won't heal!' she says into the wind), then taking my hand once more and falling back into the water, causing me to shudder awake into horrific reality . . .

They were the worst mornings: ghastly sunlight and Sam sidestepping nervously above me. 'You know you talk in your sleep, bro?' Everything transcendental replaced with morbid insignificance: my scrawl completely illegible along the train fencing, an exquisite pain in my temples, something duller in my chest; bumbling to school, bent dimly forward, peering out at a world more desolate than I ever remembered.

It was in this state that I finally decided to take matters into my own hands.

I left the house on a Saturday, tired of the mystery and anxiety and determined to find the cause of her silence. I told work I was ill and my parents I was working – the classic ruse – and took a train all the way down the Frankston line. It was still early morning and I remember the deceit causing me to feel unbridled somehow, my heart pumping in a way it hadn't since I'd last sprinted up the Wychwood drive with Christina flying ahead. I exited Frankston station and took a bus – the 48 winding its way by shops and houses and then finally trees and trees as the properties began spacing themselves apart. I was nowhere again, sailing along with my heart pounding, passing landmarks I knew well: the church with its triangles, the earthenware place; peering up at the boughs that swung and swayed overhead, as if to applaud my brave gesture of devotion. I was an explorer, an astronaut and a deep-sea diver, off the bus now and walking down Hartley Drive; seeing the fence, the air so clear and clean, the trees gorgeous as a wind whipped about my ears; everything appearing heightened and more alive than I ever remembered – and then chuckling to myself, aware that it wasn't the world at all, of course; but rather, like someone peering into a still ocean, enchanted by the knowledge that beneath are whales and angelfish, so was I enchanted by a world that seemed to blaze in feverish colour and sound – not for itself, but because she was somewhere within it . . .

I reached the gate and pressed the buzzer.

Nothing.

I waited.

Pressed again and waited.

Nothing.

Strange.

I peered through the gates, towards the house. Somehow it seemed to be asleep, the leaves still on the boughs of the plane trees, as though wind refused to blow beyond the gates. There was a car in the driveway I didn't recognise, and the curtains were shut. Very odd. I made to press the buzzer a third time–

'Why are you going in *there* for?!'

The voice came from behind me, high-pitched and terrified. I turned with a start to find a boy on a bicycle, holding a Paddle Pop. He was across the road, staring wide-eyed at the gates.

'What do you mean?' I asked.

He peered up the driveway, as though any second it would move, then back to me.

'That's where the insane lady lives.'

FUNNY HOW IN all that murky period, a particular memory can preserve its clarity; remaining apart in stark relief, distilled over time as everything else becomes vague.

It is me arriving home early from school, entering the house and sensing immediately a heavy silence. I hear Dad's voice murmur something from the living room; only I can't make out words, just his parched tone. I move towards the sound, treading lightly on the floorboards so they don't squeak, peering around the doorframe.

He looks so bizarre, hunched over the telephone in a bright patch of sun. 'No,' he's saying. 'I won't. Please! I won't, I won't.' He's cradling the receiver in both hands, though somehow decrepit, with his shoulder blade bulged like a wing. 'Sunday is okay,' he says. And I realise he's begging. It's some kind of plea, stammered and trembling in a way I've not seen before.

Then later in the evening, he and Mum are fighting in the kitchen. Only he's no longer decrepit. Now he's cagey and guarded, his voice caustic in a way he seldom revealed. They're talking about me.

'. . . make his own decisions – he's fifteen,' Dad says.

Mum: 'I don't care; I don't want him around her.'

Then silence. I'm peeking through a crack in the door.

'What are you afraid of?' he says. 'Honestly . . .'

And as she looks up at him, it's clear what she's afraid of – even I can see – though neither of them say.

Suddenly her eyes are welling and he's getting up to escape – or perhaps in disgust, as though she only cries to weaken his determination. He walks to the bench shaking his head; turns back.

'When did you become like this?' he says.

'Like what?'

She is pleading through her tears, but he is unmoved.

'Callous.'

Dear Matt,

I'm so sorry I haven't been in contact. It's been a crazy few weeks. I'm boarding at Kewfield Secondary College. I've been here for a month and a half.

Mum was in a car accident a week or so after you left. It's fine; she was okay. She broke her collarbone and was in a sling and everything. I had to rush over to the hospital. She lost her licence too, so Aunty Carol was staying with us and that was good, she's a great cook. Mum had to go to this clinic – she was meant to be there for a month but it was only a week and a half. We went and picked her up and they were saying rules are rules and how they're really strict about it. Anyway, Mum went out a couple of days later and took Aunty Carol's car without telling her. She wasn't supposed to leave the house, let alone drive. I told on her and she hit the roof. She went out again and didn't come back. Aunty Carol had to call the police and we walked up and down the streets, calling her name. We found her asleep in one of the yards up the street.

I've been at Kewfield since then. It's good here. My roommate's a massive bitch but it's a great school. No one knows about anything. I haven't told anyone really, except our head of house, Ms Angelides, and she's alright. I've met a few people too. I'm best friends with a girl called Alinta. She's really into acting and she made me try out for a play and I got in. It's pretty cool actually. It's called 'Midsummer 2.0' and it's kind of a new version of A Midsummer Night's Dream. Do you know the Shakespeare play? Anyway, we're rehearsing at the moment. You should come.

Thanks for writing to me too. It means a lot. I'm sorry I haven't sent anything back. It's been a little crazy. If you want to reply (and I hope you do!) then maybe don't send anything to the house. The last two letters I got had been opened already. Send them here instead:

Kewfield Secondary College
712 Greneila Road
Hastings
Victoria, 3915

Lots of love,
Christina xox

I AM SYMPATHETIC to Christina's attempts at withholding information. I understand why she did it. And that letter I received
in March 2002 – the first in a long correspondence – is a
perfect example. Not that she's lying; there's nothing false or
made up. But there's information missing, there's misleading
information, as though she's trying to show the glamour side
of things. Which is something I can relate to . . .

   –Take when I go to the cafe with Mum: I wear long sleeves
and no one takes any notice. We walk in and I could be anyone
else. I *am* anyone else, in fact; because no one has seen my
wristband.

   If people *do* see my wristband, it's like a magic trick. The
person's entire demeanour changes. I become an object of
compassion, or an object of pity – whatever; an object – they
become flighty and sycophantic. They glance across to see if
they can find any outward manifestation of the wristband.

   Of course, Mum leaps at the chance to cause a scene:
'Ex-*cuse* me?' raising her voice and raising her eyebrows,
summoning the waiter back to the table. 'Why are you
looking at him like that?'

The poor kid starts jittering. 'Like what?'

'Like you just did. Did you think we wouldn't notice?'

'I don't . . . Pardon?'

The cafe goes silent. I'm curled in the brace position. Only Mum thrives, relishing yet another opportunity to prove herself as my great defender.

'Is there a problem here?' The manager now.

'I'm not sure,' she says. '*Is* there a problem?'

'. . .'

And of course there's no problem. I'm not blaming anyone – I understand people can't help their reactions. My mother is who she is. But what's the end result? The result is: I wear long sleeves when I go to the cafe, don't I?

All of us are guilty of hiding parts we don't want people to see, of only showing the glamour side.

–Which, as I said, brings me back to Christina.

*

Kewfield Secondary is a large and resplendent government school with a website boasting the ability to turn '*any* citizen into a *Kewfield* citizen!' (though what this entails isn't revealed anywhere). The school prides itself on sweeping fields and high-tech sporting facilities and offers a lifetime of glorious memories for students who all appear to be handsome, popular and self-confident.

At the time I received her first letter, Christina had been in the boarding house for six weeks, sharing a room with Sophie Cummins: the daughter of a rich dairy farmer who had spent her childhood moonlighting as a farmhand and thus, possessed such a voracious work ethic that she'd grown to become self-righteous and impossible. Being well off,

Sophie viewed all forms of hardship as exciting hurdles to be vaulted and had little empathy for anyone battling self-doubt, insecurity or mental illness – affectations she believed were simply variations of indolence.

Given their differences, it wasn't long before the relationship strained. Sophie accused Christina of being laissez-faire, while Christina questioned a study/exercise regime that extended into infinity – both were indignant. As Christina learned though, Kewfield was populated with Sophie Cumminses; filling the dorms and clustering about the television to watch replays of athletics carnivals. They would study for hours then dress for blistering nightclubs. Christina wasn't interested – nor was she invited. They didn't like her badly hacked hair and they didn't like her T-shirts with bands that didn't seem to exist. They feared the mysterious ambience that arose from rumours she'd been expelled for lighting fires in a principal's office. Whatever the reason though, Christina soon found herself on the outskirts of popularity, and having to search further afield for acceptance. It was here, on these far branches, that she first met Alinta; that tidal wave of a human being.

Ali was a 'day-scab' (non-boarding student) who was heavily involved in the school theatre program and who moved in a number of oddish social circles. Writing back and forth, Christina's letters would often include long and passionate accounts of Alinta – painting her as a deific livewire whose optimism was so infectious that grief and negativity were extinguished wherever she went. (*'Ali is a sun; she brings us all back to life.'*) Meeting in person later, I found the portrait validated by scores of insane bracelets and coloured piercing tape. She had a wild streak and genuinely seemed to think anyone could be invincible if they simply believed it was so – with only her forearms indicating otherwise: at some point, she'd cut into them repeatedly. But cracked as she was, Ali was vital for Christina; from day one, her most loyal guardian and confidant.

They'd met in Christina's first week, Ali approaching to spruik auditions for the upcoming school play.

'Vikki said you got expelled for lighting a fire,' she'd said. 'Is it true or did you make it up?'

Christina had shrugged. 'Believe what you want.'

Ali had then accused her of faking and Christina had auditioned to prove she was a terrible actor, so how could it be fake?

In this way, the two had become friends, and Christina had been drawn into the cast of *Midsummer 2.0*, a semi-devised version of the Shakespeare classic that had been fused with original monologues about Columbine and 9/11 to create a theatrical whirlwind exploring I'm still not really sure what. Christina was given the roles of Robin Goodfellow and Woman #3, who pushed around a pram and delivered the following monologue:

> *Don't. Don't. People falling from the windows.*
> *Don't. Don't. People falling from the sky.*
> *Is it a bird?*
> *Is it a plane?*
> *Yes! It's a plane.*
> *It's raining truth today, raining life.*
> *Today won't just be another day.*
> *It will be the first day.*

As with many theatre troupes, most members of the Q-PATT [Kewfield Performing Arts Theatre Troupe] weren't interested in theatre at all, but knew their participation meant being included in a social environment that was accepting of even the least popular demographics. Also like most theatre groups, many of the friendships became confused and complicated in the euphoria of exploring their personalities in a fun and safe environment. For these reasons, Christina soon found herself sludged in a cocktail of students whom most of the school viewed with disgust, while rehearsing a play about lust with a cast of method actors who were regularly exploring the themes in the wings.

Reports of the Q-PATT were whimsical and eccentric. Every second weekend, Christina was staying in Frankston, top-to-toe with Alinta (who was more than a little in love with her), and her letters offered a glimpse into the lifestyle: drinking circles on the kitchen floor; climbing onto the school roof to smoke under the stars; midnight nudie runs across the oval. Alinta's live fast approach seemed to cause trouble for both of them. In fact, Christina's letters often read like a montage of nogoodnik clichés: smoking at train stations and defacing their uniforms, wagging school for Gloria Jean's, et cetera. In May, they'd been accused of vandalising a toilet door – both their names having been found etched into a love heart. Their mistake had been authenticating the work with signatures and a lipstick kiss. But Alinta declared it was a hoax! They'd been framed, she said, by the same cabal of students who were constantly making offensive and groundless allegations about her sexuality, and the school was only trying to hide a systemic problem with bullying and sexual harassment. Finding itself scandalised, the school withdrew its complaint and Christina had celebrated by etching a sunburst around the love heart.

Such stories, I found irresistible, addictive – rushing home to revel in escapades far more engaging than the misery of my home life, the morose shades of my parents. Soon we were writing weekly. On Thursdays I'd skip to my room, tearing the envelope and poring over the contents: from classroom politics, to the famous 'Bunsen Burner cabaret', to her descriptions of the silent janitor with his double glasses (*'I just don't see why he wears both!?'*). Even fledgling sexual experiences, I devoured in envy and captivation. (*'Deep conversation turned into spin the bottle. Mostly boys though, and the cap kept pointing to me and Ali. In fifteen minutes, everyone's mouth was covered in lipstick.'*) Her accounts were frank and never self-conscious, as if written only for herself. All the same, I would read them again and again, the same lines over and over, envisaging and imagining. Once, I read a passage so many times that the word 'massage' somehow detached from all meaning and began to sound absurd when spoken aloud. Still, I read it again, scrutinising every line, replacing myself in the narrative, poring over stories resembling the vigour I associated with Wychwood, a life that seemed far more alive and vital than my own.

But as I said, it was only the glamour side. Because for all the colourful stories of Kewfield, it soon occurred to me that Christina was leaving out a large section of her life.

Every second Friday, she was catching the train to Wychwood to stay for the weekend. But she would never speak of it. When she did, it was only trivial things. (*'Ironbark saplings died; spent Sunday replanting them along the fence.'*)

Take that first letter: the details are murky; the situation with Connie is vague – not to mention why she'd moved schools in the first place. There was something misleading, a secrecy. But whenever I brought it up, she became evasive. 'Is your mum going okay now?' I asked once in a letter. Her response was to explain that Connie had discovered *Law & Order: Special Victims Unit,* and that it was irritating because she constantly misunderstood the story and would interrupt with fundamental questions like, 'Wait, why are they arresting *this* guy?' When I accused her of being evasive, she replied there was nothing to report – that their time was spent on house upkeep, and that the only visitor they ever had was Aunty Carol, who was hardly news, and who only came in the afternoons to feed the animals and help around the house. She stopped short of explaining why all this was necessary. It was as if an embargo had been placed about Wychwood, and to mention it was sacrilege.

Though to be fair, if it hadn't been for the incident with Connie and the fruit bowl, I mightn't have given any of it a second thought. My suspicion was only aroused because I'd overheard the story about Connie drunk in a ficus, singing to a fruit bowl. Dad had been drawn into this whole bizarre situation, to both his and Mum's dismay. Christina didn't even know I knew about it. Once I heard though, it caused me to question everything she'd claimed about her life at home.

It was the night she'd mentioned in that first letter – though like everything else about Wychwood, her telling was murky and evasive, almost a comedy. What I learned later though, was that the full story was far more unsettling than Christina had made out.

Connie had been found under a tree in a neighbour's backyard – this part of Christina's telling was true. She hadn't been asleep though; she'd been crooning to a fruit bowl, cradling it in her arms like an infant. It was the end of a spate of hauntings that had been reported from Hartley Drive that evening. First, a six-year-old hadn't been able to sleep because of the 'Butterfly Woman' she'd seen wading in the pool outside her window. Soon after, Tom Davies had followed what he thought was the ghost of his dead wife all the way down to Number 28, where they were hosting a party for their son's eighteenth. To the horror of everyone, Connie had appeared in the backyard in a nightgown, soaked to the skin, asking to dance. "'Just to *dance*, just to *dance!*" over and over and over!' was Dad's perplexed re-enactment. She'd stumbled up to the sound system and begun a slow dance that caused several kids to later swear they saw her floating in the air. Unfortunately, by the time the birthday boy had rushed for his parents in the front room and they'd all returned, the 'Widow of Wychwood' (as she came to be known) was gone and all that was left were muddy streaks on the carpet and a collection of oranges. The irate father had stormed up the road to confront Aunty Carol. He'd said her sister was a trespasser and a criminal and that she'd better know a good lawyer, and that she'd better know a good steam cleaner. The police had already arrived though, having been notified earlier. This was when Christina had walked up and down the streets. It took an hour and a half, searching the properties with four policemen, Aunty Carol, and a disappointed Tom Davies. He'd been the one to carry Connie back to the house. The next day, the father wanted to press charges and Connie was forced into a thirty-day rehabilitation clinic.

It had been another of Dad's murky phone calls. He'd answered the phone with a chiming flourish, 'Llllacey residence?' Then falling dark, his voice dropping. 'W – yes? What is it?'

I'd been in my room, listening on the other side of the wall, his voice growing urgent: 'What does that mean then? Does she – Christ . . .'

He'd slammed the phone down. Then big strides into the living room. More voices now; the story coming out. I'd followed, listening from the kitchen; their argument getting louder; Mum desperate: 'Why *us* though? Why *you*?'

Then Dad: 'Because someone's in trouble; why does it matter?'

And Mum: 'The *world's* in trouble. *I'm* in trouble.'

Then the front door slamming and the car engine.

Then silence.

I'd found Mum in front of the television, stony-eyed, watching shapes flit about the screen.

'What's going on, Mum?'

'Oh!' She'd started, surprised that someone else lived in the house. 'I didn't know you were up.' She'd smiled a drawn smile, nodding at the television. 'Sorry, I was just – I wanted to watch . . .'

She narrowed her eyes. On the screen, a Replicant was being interviewed in the first scene of *Bladerunner*. She had no idea what she was watching.

'Where's Dad?'

'Your father? Oh, he's had to go help with . . .' She sucked in a breath. 'They're having a few problems at the farm.'

'Is everything alright?'

'Yes, of course. Of course . . . Connie just seems to be unable–' She stopped short, steadying her breath, as though admonishing herself. 'Sometimes people have trouble taking care of themselves.'

An image flashed of the boy on the bicycle: *The insane lady's house.*

'What about you?'

'Me?' Mum feigned an expression of indignance. 'I take care of myself just *fine*, thank you very much.'

She grinned, but I could see her eyes shining; she was trying not to blink. Instead, she laughed, making a little scene of the tear that had rolled down her cheek.

'Oop, sorry – there we go,' flicking it away. 'Sorry, it's just this . . .'

She nodded at the TV again, then sighed.

'*Bladerunner?*'

'Would you like to watch?'

'I have school.'

She drew me over anyway, pulling me close and kissing my hair.

'I can drive you in.'

We'd sat with our heads together, watching Harrison Ford rush about as Mum wept and wept; 'For those poor Replicants,' she'd said, hauling me tighter again.

To this day, I still don't understand why the Replicants had to die.

I HAVE A confession: in December I had an altercation with Devon. A physical one. It was my fault – my second offence, if we're calling it that.

Nail clippers are contraband. We have to be watched. Fair enough; it's policy. But I wanted a moment to myself. Devon was on duty. He refused. I questioned the damage I could do with such a blunt instrument. He refused again. Fair enough; it's his job. Even so, things escalated and I was restrained. My second time in seclusion.

Since last November – my first time – I've had the luxury of a room to myself. I enjoy the solitude, the privacy. I have visitors anytime. Nonetheless, as part of the 'next phase to wellness' (Gloria's words), as of yesterday, I have a roommate.

I've been showing progress these last weeks: coexisting harmoniously, presenting an even temperament, et cetera. 'Everyone's pleased at the moment,' Gloria explained on Friday. 'You're participating; you've been enthusiastic – you *look* well.' A silence. 'How would you feel about sharing a space with another resident?'

Her face took on a strange innocence. She wanted to know if I'm likely to present any more 'maladaptive behaviour' (my words).

Anyway, the long and short is I have a roommate now. Last night, Yoav moved in. As I write this, he's lying on the other side of the curtain, breathing his loud breaths through his nose. Yoav is a twenty-four-year-old Israeli war veteran who didn't speak for two years after cradling the entrails of his best friend during an incident at a Palestinian military compound. He's roughly twice my size – which I don't think is an accident – and likes to fall asleep listening to history podcasts. It's just after ten now, and all night I'll hear the tiny voice scrabbling away. In the morning, he'll trot around explaining the Tennis Court Oath or why Hannibal should have sacked Rome when he had the chance.

He's good company, I'll give him that; tells a good story – at breakfast and group therapy, his voice booming with bravado. He was in military service for nineteen weeks before being shot and discharged from the hospital with an ounce of medicinal marijuana. Then seven months he barely remembers: Goa to Ahmedabad on a motorcycle, in between the lush grass, dogs in flight, New Year's spent with a Sri Lankan milliner, rectally administering cocaine in a hotel room as England reclaimed The Ashes. He was going to play tennis, he tells us, and had a world ranking before a calf injury forced him into the war against Palestine. His stories are always fabulous, the most glorious or the most base – never in between – as if he's reached for the extreme in every direction. If the measure of life experience is grief (as we seem to believe) then he knows his wealth, and he'll drop his spoon into his cereal and sigh with a face that says,

'Such is life' – or, perhaps more accurately, 'And yet, here I am' – then he'll look into the garden and leave us amazed by his indifference.

Since he's moved in though, I've noticed something brittle in him, something weak; it's the way he sits in his dressing gown with his ankles sticking out. He has little knobbly ankles, the skin light and flaky like he's been in a bath – then the box of tissues by the bed and his bedside table all filled with medicine. I look at him closer and I think: This man is ill. He's a sick man who manages to steel himself for illustrious moments in the cafeteria when he's thrown off his dressing gown and we all marvel at his astounding life. He's a fraud.

It makes me wonder what people see when they look at me. Do people believe I'm healed when I'm not? Maybe I believe I'm ill when I'm not. Can they see something I can't? If someone else read this journal, I wonder, would it be clear to them, or would they still be unsure? Am I a fraud?

I can't help but wonder.

IT WAS JULY 5th when everything came to a head. Christina's birthday. One of her letters had included a party invitation – Ali's too, actually:

The Ali and Crisscross Sweet-6-teen Neon Extravaganza!

Obviously, it's only retrospect that confirms when things came to a head. The party was, after all, simply one event bridging other events. Still though, I always feel something in my chest at the thought of it; some desire to call out to my younger self, to fling a warning across the years.

Run away! I want to say. *Run!*

It's hard not to wonder, what if? If I was ill, if something had been on, if I'd been unable to go – useless hypotheticals; I'm aware. But I can't help wondering if I'd be where I am right now. Would I have ever seen this room? Maybe not. Would I be writing this journal?

But anyway, July 5th:

With my entire family deciding to go, I found myself in

148

the car again, passing a suburbia that slowly gave way to trees as the sun sank and everything grew luminous; Dad chatting away for all of us, explaining his desire to see how the farm had fared this winter – an obvious lie betrayed by the tan blazer he saved for occasions, by his hair slicked carefully, and by endless checks in the rear-vision mirror, touching the bags under his eyes that never seemed to go away anymore.

Mum was in the front seat, ostensibly 'just along for the ride!' though betrayed now by deep silence, and by the morbidity that seemed to have draped across her these last months. It had encroached like a season, desolating the land-scape and causing her to sweep from rooms whenever Dad arrived, spending evenings nestled beside me on the couch. She'd said nothing when Dad announced they'd tag along, tightening her lips in grim acceptance. Now she sat with her whole self turned to the window; peering without seeing as things flashed before her eyes.

Then there was me: ostensibly a friend wishing a friend a happy birthday, though with an anxiety so pervasive it was remarkable any of us were able to breathe, remarkable we could hear anything over the sound of my thumping heart. I sat in silence, in the desolation of my parents having invited themselves to an event at which I'd hoped to appear mysterious and nonchalant, gazing moodily as Dad filled the silence, and the car flew between the trees, in the direction of the insane lady's house.

Pulling in the drive, we were greeted with lights on the trees all the way to the house; fairy lights seeming to blink in time with the music that now poured through the open windows, making it seem as if Wychwood had dressed for the occasion: the fairy lights and streamers, invisible lamps placed to make the trees glow ghostly colours as they moshed their boughs in time with an oddly warm June evening. Then more balloons, red and glittering, silver and glittering – a neon extravaganza – leading the car to the house where a mirror ball inside spun colour across the window, green and red and blue; and further up, flickering at the end of the drive, the bright glow of a bonfire.

'Jeez,' was all Dad could say as we trundled up the drive, peering in admiration at a Wychwood that seemed so lavish. I looked around, feeling anxiety slip away and chuckling at myself for being concerned at what I might find. Wychwood was as it had always been. I'd been foolish to worry. And as though to emphasise the thought, now here was Connie, standing on the balcony like a headliner at a piano bar, wearing a bright sequined outfit; Connie – who was insane, it was said – here she was in a showgirl dress, waving us over and signalling to where the driveway ballooned.

Mr Harvey zhoomed down the porch towards us, prancing and leaping, half trying to say hello and half trying to shake free of the glowing antennae that had been affixed to his collar, making him somehow look like the *Book Place* worm.

'Hiii!' Connie was skipping down the stairs.

I watched her greet Mum and Dad, in fine form it seemed: flitting about, taking Mum's hand, now dabbing a kiss on Dad's cheek. It was impossible to reconcile the Butterfly Woman, everything I'd heard, the car accident and the rehabilitation clinic, swaying with a fruit bowl. None of it was anywhere to be seen; she was only Connie, with that broad smile, bleating a laugh that shot above the din of music. Now turning to me: 'Matty Matt Matt!' pecking my cheek and whizzing me round towards the house. 'The kids are up out the back if you want to throw your things in the rumpus room!'

I carried my suitcase and sleeping bag up the stairs, peering back for another glance: Connie with her arms around both my parents. 'So you're staying for a drink, yeah?'

Yes, I thought. All was well.

Inside, it seemed as adorned as out; strings of tinsel draping the ceiling and walls, catching the flailing light and causing the room to appear massive and luminous and blue and red and green. The couches had made way for a dance floor that was currently occupied by two girls in lip gloss and fairy wings, swaying to 'Ms. Jackson' and looking up from their phones as I passed through to the kitchen.

'Oi! You can chuck your shit in the rumpus room,' a voice called from the sink, and I turned to find a tall spangly girl emptying a bag of Doritos into a bowl.

'Just down the hall, first door—'

It was the first time I ever saw Alinta, pausing with her finger raised, narrowing her eyes: 'Matt?' She cut a dazzling first impression, standing in a dress made entirely of CDs so that whenever she moved, light exploded, causing everyone to squint in her presence.

'Oh my God, Matt! It's Ali!'

She'd swanned forward, shimmering with armfuls of bracelets, linking my arm and dragging me into the hall as though I'd never seen the place in my life. 'You can put your stuff in Chris's room. Do you have drinks? There's an Eski outside – Where's your neon?'

But I had no drinks, I told her, and no bright clothes – the thought having never occurred as I spent the afternoon slicking my hair and pacing in dreaded anticipation. 'It's fiiiine!' she assured nevertheless, swerving me into Christina's room and plundering a box of perhaps a thousand glow sticks, cracking a bunch and winding them about my wrists, neck and ankles until I stood decked in fabulous bondage. 'There you go – perfect.' She'd grinned and taken my arm. 'Come on, she's up by the fire!'

Out the back, fairy lights still lined the path, festooning all the way to the workshed. 'We've been here all day,' Ali calling above the music, 'doing the lights and decorations.' 'It looks awesome!' I yelled, trying to keep up and peering into the paddocks beside me, almost invisible now in the dark, the ghostly trees thrashing in silhouette behind the strings of lights. 'I swear, they're going to be finding tinsel for ten years!' She laughed and pulled me around the workshed. Now I could hear voices, bubbling laughter just ahead. I felt my throat go thick again, my heart suddenly thumping; one of those voices belonged to her, she was close.

Then we turned the corner and I had to squint a moment. For here was the fire, blinding in the dark, and a circle of revellers sitting on milk crates and folding chairs, haunted in half orange and darkness, passing around a box of cask wine, sputtering at the taste and giggling. I stood a moment, trying to make Christina out among the silhouettes – I couldn't – before Ali yanked me aside. '*Move move move!*' A squat boy was stumbling past with a massive bough of scrub, wielding it like a lance and hobbling uncontrolledly towards the fire. 'What are you doing, Jarrad?' a voice called out. 'Whaddya think? I'm making a fiiiiiiiire!' 'It's *green*, you dickhe–' Then the bough was on the fire and people were leaping off chairs, spilling drinks and shouting as flames exploded in a shower of cinders. 'You fucking idiot!' 'Jarrad,

you wanker!' And Jarrad, scuttling away, cackling under a
hail of empty cans as a lanky boy with a lightsaber leapt to
give chase; 'Fucking dead, Jarrroooooaaadd!'

I watched the ridiculous pursuit, both of them in bright
Lycra, chuckling to myself as the swishing lightsaber disappeared behind the workshed.

'Ergh herm.'

I turned back and felt my breath catch a moment.
Christina was standing before me, half her face blazing in
the light of the fire. I couldn't help but smile, she being half
as I recalled and half ethereal: her lips and cheeks covered
in fluorescent stripes and waves. They'd been scrawled in
garish colour over a layer of glitter dust, causing her face
to resemble a diagram of constellations; beneath which,
etched in brilliant orange, was the pièce de résistance: the
twirling moustache of an aristocrat. It seemed to beam out
miraculously as she peered at my neck and wrists, raising an
eyebrow.

'I see you found the glow sticks then?'

She grinned and threw her hands across my shoulders,
pulling me in for a hug.

'Thanks so much for coming!'

'Anytime,' I said.

'Yeah, we had to dress him up a bit,' Ali commented
behind me.

'Right – sorry.'

Christina pulled away and motioned like a celebrant.
'Matt. Ali.'

'Oh, we've already met,' Ali said. 'We're practically besties.'

And she stepped towards me, splaying her arms in a way
that made her bangles clatter. Seven or eight on each arm,

I noted, strings and crazy trinkets – and also . . . weird. The skin beneath seemed oddly mottled, almost folding over itself.

It took me a second to realise it was scarring.

'What – I don't get a hug?'

She was still waiting with her arms out, and with that amused expression of hers that suggested she knew every thought that had ever passed through your brain. I moved in.

'Matt doesn't have anything to drink,' she said over my shoulder. 'We'll need to fix that.'

'Oh don't, it's fine . . .'

'No, shut up. He's trying to be polite. He wants a drink. What do you drink, Matt? Anything. Actually, it doesn't matter; I'm going to get you something delicious. Wait here.'

Now she became stern, pointing at us. 'Wear a condom.' Then a wink and she disappeared behind the workshed.

Christina and I stood a moment, watching where she'd been.

'Love that girl,' she said.

I nodded.

'Her sister's a tattoo artist. She's going to do her arms when she's done with school.'

'What do you mean?'

'Oh what – you didn't notice?' Christina chuckled wryly. 'It's okay. Everyone stares.'

I nodded and we were suddenly quiet, Ali having somehow taken the conversation with her. Christina turned to the people by the fire, talking and laughing, then back to me.

'I'm really glad you could come,' she said.

Her face was half-glowing in the firelight, her bright lips grinning beneath that wonderful iridescent moustache.

'Me too.'

But the party was only warming up, I realised. Soon more and more people were arriving, the house filling with bright tank tops and tall broad boys in tutus and fairy wings, bike shorts and legwarmers and great swathes of supernatural eyeshadow. Thumping music. Ali had returned with a drink so sweet it seemed to bypass digestion entirely and simply incise itself into the stomach; 'Tropical Explosion!' she'd yelled in my ear, before slumping down and throwing an arm across my shoulder.

It was clear she was a ringleader, everyone falling silent as she spoke. There was something about her, a settled confidence perhaps. A directness. She could look into your eyes longer than you could look into hers. Then the way she spoke with her hands; you could see how she raised people up. And that night, I was grateful to her. Having detected anxiety, she made the decision to be my chaperone: rarely leaving my side and ensuring I had a drink, forcing people to involve me, forcing me to scull great gulps of rancid wine whenever the cask drew near, then cheering as it sputtered everywhere.

It didn't take long for my apprehension to dissolve in soothing euphoria, sitting at the warm fire as the party swirled about, people laughing and dancing, trees swaying overhead and Mr Harvey scuttling everywhere, entirely invisible now save his bobbing antennae. I sat talking to Ali, breezy and relaxed and watching Christina swan about the fire, laughing and chatting with friends; her lips moving beneath the sleek moustache, eyes flashing to me a moment, letting me know she knew I was there.

Soon, I felt a prickling need to piss, the wine having passed around several times already. As I stood, the ground seemed to bend strangely, taking a moment to realign, and I realised with some surprise that I was drunk. 'You right, Matt?' Ali taking my wrist. 'Fine,' I said. 'Spectacular – just gotta slash!' And I stumbled away, feeling the wind on my face, past the workshed and down to the house.

Now the party had truly amassed; and stepping indoors, I found a havoc of cups and streamers and The Strokes and maggotted kids swarming in tank tops and Lycra, flapping their arms and belting out 'Last Nite' in a circle of sploshing Woodstocks; the lanky boy dead centre now, whirling the lightsaber between his legs like some magnificent shimmering cock. I loitered a moment, scanning the wreckage as a girl slipped and shrieked, exploding UDL into the air. The mob scattered and I squeezed through a throng of bright zinc and lipstick – feeling oddly seasick – passing the lounge and into the hall by a couple of boy's boys in fluorescent tutus. 'Bathroom's full, bro.' 'Huh?' One of them throwing his arm back at the bathroom door, which stood open to reveal a girl lolling on her knees, dribbling into the toilet and a bouquet of friends waving their arms as if it was the revolution. 'Water! Get her water!' A squat girl scuttling by like an animal released, pushing me aside and powering into the lounge.

I leaned on Christina's doorframe, the house having become a fireworks display, the noise and the crowd all too much, closing my eyes to step away – but even the dark was sickly and as I took a slow breath, everything lurched and I had to throw a hand out to balance against a world that was suddenly trying to flip itself around. I opened my eyes and the bathroom righted itself in a slow bend. The lolling girl was now grasping at people and attempting to apologise with great meaning. I watched her grip, feeling the sting in my bladder, pushing off and making my way back down the hall, past the squat girl re-emerging with a glass of water, 'Here! Here!', past the rumpus room where at least three people were undulating in a cluster, into the lounge again and past the dance floor, to the door on the far side leading out to the roadside paddock; pulling my way through the crowd, grasping the door and sliding it open.

Outside, everything was turned down, the music suddenly innocuous as the door slid shut, thudding warmly without its singeing treble. I strode out onto the grass, towards the dark, away from the fairy lights festooned across the awning. They seemed to blink in time, framing wild scenes in the windows, feverish colour and people moving, their glow bracelets whirling and whizzing like fireflies. I unzipped in the safety of the dark, turning from the house and peering at the dim streetlamps far across the paddock and over the road. Then stopped.

I could hear laughter.

I paused to listen, heard it again. There were people on a bench around the side of the house, chuckling together in secret. I peered around to see, zipping up.

It was Connie and Dad. They were sharing a cigarette, passing it back and forth as the tip flared like a light signal. I was invisible to them, standing out in the dark, watching. 'Me?' I could hear Dad's voice, and strained to listen under the thud of the drum. He was chuckling. 'I . . . What? No, don't you – I've seen your serve. You playing table tennis is something every person should witness at least once in their lives.'

Now Connie was trembling with laughter, throwing her hands over her eyes. Dad chuckling, turning away, pleased with himself. He was charming, in his tan blazer, his hair slicked up; and Connie in her piano bar dress, laughing in a way Mum never laughed. 'You . . .' Her hand was on his shoulder now, '. . . are trouble.' She was shaking her head, as he exhaled an enormous plume into the air. They couldn't see me.

But I could see them. An image came suddenly – I could see Dad in a way I don't think I'd ever seen him before, his wit and his charm. It was suddenly crystal clear, like footage from the past: I could see him at sixteen. And Connie, beaming at him. I could see her at my age. I could see them both, crystal clear, with no idea what to do, knowing only what they wanted. I could see them at a party like this, with their desperation, desperate to be so experienced; finding a moment alone, away from the wild scenes, her head finding his shoulder – as it was now – still chuckling at his fantastic joke. I could see it all suddenly. And it fit so well.

'Peter?'

Here was Mum, stepping out under the fairy lights; the music swelling and disappearing as the door slid open and closed. She was returning from Connie's en suite. She couldn't see me either. I watched Dad take a final drag, blowing smoke into the air, nodding absently at something no one could see but him. Then taking a new breath:

'Here, Lyn.'

The words speared sharply out, dissolving the smoke above him, dissolving the spell. They were adults again, Connie lifting her head as he shuffled away ever so slightly. They were adults at a kid's party. And Mum was approaching with her bag. Arriving. She was ready to go. Dad: 'Yeah, I spose we . . .' et cetera et cetera. Someone had opened a door and now I couldn't hear. He was nodding though, getting up, Connie too. I was watching the end of a silent film: Connie kissing Mum's cheek like they were sisters at a departure gate, now kissing Dad's as though adhering to bureaucracy.

None of them could see me. I watched them go find me at the bonfire.

WHAT HAVE I inherited from my father, dare I ask? His appearance – definitely: his height, the forward hunch of his shoulders. When we laugh, we are twins. The way our eyebrows slant before we speak. And what else? His weakness? His inability to talk things out . . . ?

Dad and I have never spoken about Connie. I've never asked him and I never will. We will go to our graves without saying a word about it, suffering instead the intense pressure that descends whenever we are alone. We will live our lives taking refuge in conversations about football and directions. I understand this is unhealthy and wrong, but it's the way it is.

I will never know the exact details of what passed between him and Connie. I will never know what promises were made and, if so, when they were reneged. But I can sympathise that it must have been impossible for them to return to civilian life.

This I understood immediately from their cigarette beside the house; Connie laughing in that way Mum has never laughed, Dad's charming self-confidence, both of them somehow brought to life.

How do you unstrike a match? Is that the expression?

Either way, it fits – when I compare that cigarette with Dad's excruciating disinterest at home; the afternoon he'd sliced his finger chopping vegetables and Mum had fussed over the bandaid. I'll never forget his derision, watching her; derision that she could be so present in such a domestic activity, while his mind swirled with the romance of his inner life. Then the murky phone calls; his quivering lamentations, emotions he saved only for the receiver. And finally the dinners afterward, after it was over and he'd retreated into himself: peering forward at the dinner table, bereft of illusion, as though realising all of a sudden there was no other life than the one before his eyes.

How does one unstrike a match?

I of all people should know it's impossible.

And it wasn't just Dad, was it? For Connie was equally stuck. Only she never attempted to hide. No, Connie's approach was different – Connie's Way: full steam ahead, simply refusing to ever come down . . .

After my parents left the party, she'd danced in the lounge room, surrounded by kids less than half her age. Sensual dancing: raising an arm and swaying her hips with the confidence of a woman who knows that when she sways, people look – as I imagine they must have once upon a time. She had her eyes closed, writhing gently as a group of kids stood about watching, laughing and clapping. Did she realise she was the butt of a joke? Did she care? No. An elixir had been passed in that cigarette with Dad, and now she was a princess again.

I remember coming back inside to find her re-enacting the story of the fruit bowl: swaying in her piano bar dress with no idea people were giggling; swishing her hair with a glass of red wine pirouetting deftly in her hand; making a fool of herself at her daughter's birthday party – and yet in her own little world, still sixteen for a half-hour yet.

*

But it was after my parents left that the party fell steeply off an edge into chaos: everyone's make-up starting to run and a sick change sweeping in. I'd stumbled back up the path to find the fire abandoned; bottles strewn and streamers and chairs upended and everyone having migrated under the Hills hoist; standing in a ritualistic circle as two wine bladders spiralled above their heads. They'd been attached to the clothesline and Ali was spinning the bars around and around until they finally stopped and the kids below pressed the nozzles and tried to catch the splattering wine as everyone cheered. I watched them sputter and become drenched; the roaring crowd and the firelight and searing music making the whole thing resemble some dark tribal initiation.

'Hey! Where have you been?'

Christina was rushing over, flickering in the glow, arriving unsteady and thrusting a hand against my chest to balance. 'Your parents are looking for you!'

'It's okay,' I yelled, 'they've gone.'

'Right, well you have to come!' She was crawling up to my ear, clasping my shirt. 'We're playing Goon of Fortune!'

Then her lips grazed my ear as she fell back, taking my wrist and yanking me over to the game (which clearly had little to do with the television show), elbowing a space and calling for Ali to '*spin iiiiiiitt!*'. All, I noticed, without letting go of my wrist, instead sliding her hand low so that our fingers laced. I felt my heart quicken and shot a side glance at her face: eyes fixed on the clothesline, glitter dust and half that blistering moustache. But still not letting go. Now the wine bladders were spinning overhead, spinning spinning, and I looked up just in time to see them come to a sudden and impossible stop directly above me. The crowd cheered and I found Ali gripping the frame, raising her eyebrows twice in mischievous suggestion.

Christina pulled me in again, her lips at my ear. 'You have to drink!' then setting me free to reach up and press the nozzle and release a stream of hideous gushing liquid all over myself. Ali shouted my name and the people around me cheered: 'More more more more!' until liquid filled my nose and eyes and wine sprayed everywhere and the crowd went wild.

I slung hair away from my forehead, sputtering and drenched, feeling Christina's hand grasping my own again – squeezing. 'Nice one!' My heart was pounding so joyfully now and I looked up at the casks, praying for them to stop above me again so I could drink and the crowd could cheer and Christina could squeeze my hand.

As they spun though, a shriek came from behind the workshed, causing everyone to pause and look. Someone was racing around the corner towards the fire, howling a triumphant war cry. It was Jarrad the Idiot, I realised, suddenly shirtless and with his chest painted in fluorescent war stripes. He was carrying a Super Soaker and sprinting towards Christina and I, stopping directly in front of us.

'Hey Chris,' he yelled. 'Happy birthday!'

Then he winked and unloaded the water pistol – filled entirely with cask wine – point-blank into her stomach.

There was moment of stunned silence, all of us in disbelief as Christina assessed the damage. Then looking up at him: 'You fucker!'

She leapt up, snatching one of the casks from the line and racing after Jarrad, who was already fleeing with glee, leaping over the fence into the eastern paddocks.

All of us moved to watch, chuckling as they flew about the grass, Jarrad shooting behind with miraculous accuracy, drenching Christina again as she squeezed the bladder like a bagpipe, forcing a weak jet to piss lamely in his direction. 'Jarrad, you fuck!' Then running after him again.

'What a goose, huh?' Ali said, moving beside me.

'Yeah.'

'You've got to tell me how she was expelled.'

'I've got no idea,' I said.

'Bullshit. She tells you everything.'

Then we were silent a moment, watching her run about the paddock, mulling over the same question as Jarrad the Idiot cackled victoriously and Christina sprayed behind, 'Jarrad!', the word floating back under the hum of music, her bright moustache still visible somehow, all the way over there.

'Love her, won't you?'

Ali's tone took me by surprise.

'Huh?'

I turned to find all her humour suddenly gone, the amusement behind her eyes now absent. She was looking pointedly.

'Love her.'

'I do,' I said.

'Good.'

She held a moment.

'Good.' Then she nodded, turning back to Christina, who was stomping grimly towards us. 'Need a towel?'

'I'm fine!'

It was the first time I ever saw something vulnerable in Alinta. She was in love with her, of course, though I didn't know it then. But it was clear that at some point, things had gone terribly awry for her. She had scars on her wrists; from another time, sure, but perhaps one not quite gone. And all that fire behind her eyes – for the first time, I found myself wondering if perhaps it wasn't mania? The way she'd said, 'Love her.' As if there was dark knowledge behind the words.

But the thought was only a second. For it became clear at that moment that Jarrad's attack had only been an entrée for what was to come. He'd merely been the advance party.

Now I turned to see pandemonium coming from the house: high squeals and kids peeling in a throng towards us. They were rushing up the driveway, trying to escape three new boys with bright stripes and insignia scrawling their bare chests, causing havoc with water pistols they'd filled with revolting concoctions of anything they could find: beer, wine, orange juice, et cetera. They emerged in a thrilling mess, flailing their weapons and spraying anyone in their path.

Now all of us scattered, running in every direction to escape; Christina taking my wrist, 'Let's get the fuck out of here!', and pulling me down the driveway as sickly beams shot in every direction and kids howled and squealed and the trees overhead thrashed a reflection of the anarchy below.

We were flying with our heads covered, down the drive and pushing open the gates, out into the street trailing ten or so other refugees, all laughing and out of breath, drenched now but thrilled at having escaped the mayhem. I looked at Christina beside me, her make-up sploshed in a mess, glitter dust everywhere, and melting lines – all except that wonderful moustache, still twirling somehow undisturbed, still beaming out and causing her eyes to seem enigmatic, and all the more alluring in their disguise. She was Salvador Dali with short-chopped hair, drenched and sodden and staggering beside me, laughing and trying to catch her breath. 'I am so fucking sorry! Have you got other clothes?' I had, I assured her, leaning up to her ear and brushing my hand against hers in the hope she would lace our fingers again.

   –and I don't know, maybe it was my parents having gone, or maybe the cask wine or the adrenaline of the gunmen, but suddenly everything around me: the street and the moshing trees, Christina half-aglow beside me, all of it seemed to mirror the wild dreams I'd had in the dark of my room; those weeks I'd spent in desolation at her absence – those wonderful haunting dreams. Here I was, drenched and sticky and out of breath, but in them somehow, with that same euphoria having kindled about.

   Ahead of us, Christina's friends were scattered on the road, only beacons now in the dark, rings of neon binding their hands and ankles, circling their heads. I watched them: some racing in piggyback, cartwheeling, now a girl on the phone with her hair billowing like something alive; and further ahead, Jarrad the Idiot launching his Super Soaker into the air. I watched the beads fly in massive plumes like dispersing fireworks, turning red, now turning blue, now falling in a mist onto the road where suddenly all the kids were scattering. I watched them squeal and shriek and rush away, this way and that; diving into bushes, behind cars, their bracelets like fireflies, bobbing in wonderful pools of colour – all the colours and shapes searing intensely, the friendly trees over-head – and now Christina again: 'Matt!' She was at my side, wrenching my arm, 'Matt! Come on!', her voice alarmed as she tried to tear me off the road. And suddenly I understood: the red and blue light, the sharp '*wewip*' of a siren causing me to crash to earth.

I came to, rushing away and leaping into the bushes on the roadside, my heart pounding beside Christina as we peered out for the police car, the road flashing red and blue, then falling silent.

A pause.

Now there was only the sound of our breathing, slow breaths as we waited. In the corner of my eye, Christina was changing colour, red and blue igniting the constellations in her cheeks. '*Man, oh man,*' I thought, feeling her wrist on top of mine. We held our breath. Silence. The police car had appeared, slinking up the road, flaring its light like an insect. Now red. Now blue. There was no light in the bush, only her circlet. And our arms touching. We could have moved them if we'd wanted, but we didn't. We waited. I could see her peering out, see her blue halo from the corner of my eye. And her moustache, somehow iridescent. Man oh man. I was leaning across, utterly blind. I was finding half a lip. Her lips moving to find mine. We weren't breathing. We made no sound, only feeling in the dark, as the police car passed, then disappeared – maybe; I don't know. My eyes were closed.

*

Now I become the audience of a pantomime.
Run away! I say. *Run!*

I am yelling at the players, trying to fling a warning over the years.

Run home! Back down the street, to Melbourne, to anywhere else!

But of course, I don't. No matter how hard I try, the memory remains the same:

We leave the bush long after the car has gone, after everyone else is gone.

How long? Hard to say – this is where memory becomes shambolic.

Eventually though, we walk back to the house. Just Christina and I; we're giggling. Only the street is deserted, so our voices seem to fling far away. Turning down the driveway, Wychwood is deserted. The fairy lights are off and I think: 'It must be late,' or 'Everyone must be at the fire.' I can hear one or two soft voices. Soft music. But we're not going to the fire – Christina is reaching behind. She's linking my fingers and pulling me into the house. Inside, the mirror ball spins in silence, flinging colour at people asleep on couches. She's pulling me along, to her room, to the sudden comfort of carpet. She's turning to shut the door. Then we're alone. And now we've stopped laughing. We are terrified. She's holding her T-shirt down because she's self-conscious. I'm looking at the wall as she fumbles between us, holding onto me. She wants to show that she's so experienced. We're terrified though. We're kids. And through the window, I can hear other kids laughing around the fire. Music still. None of them know what's going on. I look at Christina. She's pulling her top down because she doesn't want me to see. But it's okay because I'm not looking anyway. I'm looking at her face, at her bright orange moustache that somehow I can still see. It is beaming out. And I'm thinking: Here I am, doing this now – as her eyes grow slowly wide and astonished, and she takes a sharp breath, and it all becomes very real.

Monday, 11 January

DAVID BOWIE DIED today. Just thought I'd note. We found out at lunchtime and no one's talked about anything else since. Turns out he was sick for some time – cancer, the internet's suggesting, though it's vague. Nonetheless, everyone's been taken by surprise: Facebook currently erupting with lyrics and obituaries and profile images of Ziggy Stardust. Yoav's spent the afternoon in my ear, peddling arcane conspiracies that suggest his lyrics are coded messages from beyond the grave.

He's out at the moment, thank God, and I'm enjoying a moment of peace – a rare occasion, I have to say. Since the change of living arrangements, I find myself with far less time on my hands, less space – Yoav being the kind of person who can't stand but can only loom, forever appearing behind you: 'What you writing?' A flumpy hand on your shoulder as he offers advice you never solicited.

He's out for dinner now and I've been making use of the time.

Specifically: I've spent the best part of an hour locating Alinta online. Not too difficult these days. Last night

I decided to make contact and I've just sent her a message – God forbid . . .

It's now been twelve years since either me or Christina have spoken to her. Needless to say, I'm anxious to see how she responds. It could be one of those confrontations I'd rather avoid. I think back to our last meeting outside Kewfield Hall: Ali wrenching me to my feet – I was on crutches at that point – pulling my collar and telling me I was insane and deranged. She moved to Perth the last I heard; became a doctor.

But then I figure twelve years is a long time.

Either way, it can't be undone now. The last few weeks, Gloria's been suggesting I start contacting people on the outside. To avoid isolations I'm bound to feel leaving the clinic, she says. Messaging Ali is my first attempt.

It doesn't escape me that I've chosen the person who would probably least like to hear from me in all the world. But then, I did always like Ali.

Besides, since last night I've been feeling a touch sentimental.

July 5th was, after all, the highest point of my life – and I say that without being wistful or exaggerative. It is an objective calculation; at no point before, or since, have I felt that same pooling euphoria as when I trundled beside Christina with the trees swaying above our heads; that sense of drifting invincibility, feeling our story was somehow beyond calamity.

The feeling had lingered too, into the following morning, waking in that balmy room: pale light coming through the curtains, my head aching and my mouth rancid, but with the serenity of a convalescent in a summer estate. I'd spent a moment recalibrating a long tunnel of images, starting with the fire and the Hills hoist, Connie swaying, then boys with water pistols and kids in the street, fireflies, red and blue light; and finally – the end of it all – Christina and I kneeling before one another.

She wasn't beside me. I could hear the sound of running water in the bathroom and lay listening, lingering on the thought. Then, as the taps squealed, I felt a thin pull of anxiety. We'd been so ecstatic, hadn't we? Both of us, staggering through the gates. But then something had changed when we'd knelt together. We'd lost the abandon of the road and the water pistols. In her room, something had enclosed, had become sacred – and she'd pulled her shirt down.

Now it was morning and she'd disappeared to the shower before I awoke.

I got up quickly, fossicking for clothes that had been strewn God knows where. When the door opened, I'd only found my underwear at the foot of the bed, and I stood to attention, awkward and exposed.

'Hi.'

Christina grinned when she saw me; only a small grin, but it was enough. I felt anxiety sweep away and grinned back, finding nothing to say. It was a different intimacy to the night before. A purer one somehow. She was in a towel; me in my underwear. The permission to share such vulnerabilities – now, in this bright morning, no longer drunk. And for us to grin. Somehow it spoke louder than all last night's fumbling exhilaration.

'Do you want privacy?' I said.

She half-curtsied in a parody of old-world modesty and I chuckled, taking my clothes and making for the door. But both of us went left, and then right. I made a little performance of getting in her way. Then we were in front of each other and I could feel the heat still on her from the shower. She leaned up and kissed me, causing all the comedy to fall away; then stood a moment, switching between my eyes, as though ensuring I'd not mistaken her intention, here in this bright room. She kissed me again.

'Okay, now you can go.'

I left the room.

In the lounge, I found the house still asleep. It was early – 8.30 on the microwave – and people were slumped on couches and the floor amid food scraps and empty bottles. Someone had turned off the spinning light and now the room showed a desolation of fallen streamers and cups and debris and shit and a boy curled in Mr Harvey's bed who seemed to have wet himself. Somehow though, the spectacle only managed to emphasise the tranquillity of the morning, like fog rising over the dead on a battlefield.

Taking a walk outside, I saw the same all over the grounds; the trees limp and anaesthetised. There was no movement in the paddocks. Behind the workshed, the fire had dissolved to an ashpit with milk crates strewn about; water pistols and bottles and endless glow bands that no longer glowed but had become turgid with milky cataracts. I kicked them away and strode back past the workshed, jumping the fence and wandering down among the widow makers.

At the back fence, I peered out into the mess of foliage that was Davies' paddock. The path we'd taken earlier that year was nowhere to be seen, the boughs having spent the months sewing themselves together again.

'Haaaarrrvvveeeyyyy!'

The name rang out, singsong in the stillness of the morning. Breakfast-time, obviously, I thought, peering back at the house. There it sat, hidden among trees that all seemed wintry and decrepit now without their wonderful festooning lights. How long would it take, I wondered, if it were left alone, for Wychwood to become like Davies' paddock?

'Haaarvey?'

It was Connie calling, her voice haggard in a way that matched the morning; far from the high giggling at Dad's joke behind the house. Their tender moment; her hand on his shoulder. Seeing Christina dressing in her room had reminded me of it. I watched her shadow moving behind the curtains and felt a warm shiver. Yes, it had been the same, hadn't it: the two of them giggling. Until Mum had broken the spell.

'Harvey!'

But now the thoughts stopped. Because it occurred to me at once that I'd misread the tone in Connie's voice – sharp it was, and with the unmistakable bite of urgency. What on earth had made me think it was singsong?

'Harvey!?'

People were coming out of the house now, vague and disoriented, like someone had opened a tomb. I watched them emerge, peering through spattered make-up and spent costumes, turning their heads in rising agitation, then pausing to gape.

'Harveeeeeeey!'

It really was the most spectacular vision: Connie stumbling around the side of the house, bellowing Harvey's name, completely naked save a thin nightgown that billowed and flapped like a butterfly; a Butterfly Woman, trembling and breathless and flailing a dog bowl. We stood in communal disbelief, watching her fly across the gravel, seemingly oblivious to everything around her, before coming to an abrupt halt at the head of the drive.

'Mum.'

Now there was silence. Christina had appeared on the verandah. I looked over, expecting to find an expression reflecting my own alarm. But I was mistaken. Instead, she was resolute, standing with unmistakable coldness.

'Mum, come inside, please.'

It was the strangest tone, a kind professional courtesy she'd obviously used before. Only Connie didn't seem to hear. Christina sighed and strode out towards her.

'Mum, what the—'

Then she stopped, suddenly understanding the commotion. Connie was tottering on her heels, back and forth, clutching the bowl like a rosary and staring in dismay at the gates, still flung wide open; just as we'd left them.

It was forty-five minutes before we found Harvey lying on his side, half torn apart. You could feel the collective anxiety rising as people came out of the house, their heads turning in guilty innocence. No one could remember where they'd seen him last. He'd been round the fire; his antennae – remember? Yeah! scuttling about – but that could have been anytime! He'd fled once before, from New Year's fireworks – perhaps all the neon? The Super Soakers . . .

Connie had raged and raged, the spell of last night having disappeared so utterly; howling into the receiver at Aunty Carol, who appeared minutes later, zipping up the drive in her blue Golf. (Aunty Carol, that whirlwind of a woman, capable only of zipping and zapping.) She'd picked Connie up and the two had sped off down the streets, Connie with her head out the window, crooning in a grotesque whimper that seemed more likely to summon an apparition than Mr Harvey. The rest of us were sent in groups to scour the grounds and surrounding areas; clumps of morose teenagers in fluorescent clothes and bleary make-up, trudging the streets in a miserable simulation of a steampunk apocalypse.

I'd stuck by Christina's side, circling the grounds three times, then four, finding nothing but a hole under Davies' fence that could have been something or could have been nothing. It seemed old but it was worth a shot, and so we'd leapt over the fence and begun to search the thicket: me, Christina, Ali and one or two others, walking in a line, calling his name.

All the while, Christina's face had been set in dejection, staring straight ahead. I remember trying to catch her eye and noticing her hair for the first time: half grown back and hacked in a violent manner that seemed to suggest the blades that had cut it. She was refusing to look at me, peering forward in guilty resolve. I could tell she was admonishing herself – that now, in the stark light of the real world, what we'd done seemed blasphemous. I could sense it: her uncertainty causing her to become mystical, to believe in omens and forebodings, convinced we'd somehow caused Harvey to disappear, that it had occurred by way of our unspeakable offence. I strode beside her, shooting glances at her face, trying to think of something to say, some comfort I could offer, some piece of wisdom so fantastic it would make everything okay.

But I had no wisdom – or at least nothing to combat the dreaded certainty all of us were starting to feel; that no one wanted to give voice to, but that was causing us to head in a particular direction.

Now the air became cool and we heard the sound of rushing water – approaching, becoming suddenly deafening. None of us were calling out anymore. We were trudging in silence, not wanting to think what we couldn't help thinking:

It would have been so easy for it to happen that way, if Harvey truly had dug under the fence. I imagined him racing past the widow makers, the loud music and whirling light all too much; scurrying this way, through slapping branches. The wind had been strong and the trees loud, not to mention the racket from the house. It would have been hard to hear anything. Was he escaping the sound? The lights? I imagined him flying from the bracken, peering backwards and losing his footing, tumbling to the bottom of the hill and into the water. He could swim of course, but not in that kind of current. I tried to shake the image of his antennae bobbing in the water, feeling a dull rise in my chest, seeing the river swirl him away past the rapids and into the rocks–

It was at this point Ali's phone rang.

I remember her fumbling for it, bringing it to her ear; her face becoming white.

It's hard to say exactly what had happened. I doubt Harvey had been looking for a fight though; more likely he'd fled the sound and lights and become disoriented, finding himself in the territory of number four's Rottweiler.

When we arrived he'd been lying under a tree out front, having somehow escaped, but with only a mangled flap for an ear and one of his back legs torn apart. Christina had gasped as she arrived, lifting an absent hand to her brow, suddenly fluttery as though she might collapse; the rest of us standing in shock at the butchery.

Racing down the street, I'd held him in my arms with his head lolling and his torn ear flapping against my chest, the mangled leg useless against my pants. He was hardly breathing, it seemed, as Ali kept a hand on his head, whispering sweet nothings, and Christina shot terrible glances, spearing into Ali's phone: 'Yes, we need the car! No, Mum – the vet. Hurry! What? No – coz I'm on the phone to *you*!' We'd rushed to the house for towels and gauze because it seemed like the right thing to do and then Christina had dabbed at the wounds, apologising as he winced and quivered in my arms. He was already starting to breathe rapidly as the gates opened and dust spilled in a massive cloud and Aunty Carol's Golf flew up the drive. A door opened and Connie splayed onto the gravel, scrambling towards us. 'What were you *thinking*?' she howled, tearing Harvey away and seeing his mangled ear, the mess of torn flesh zigzagging his thigh. 'Oh fucking Jesus!' She had a hand under his back like an infant, lifting him and nuzzling her face to his neck, 'Oh, my man,' as Aunty Carol spun the Golf around and flung open the doors, Christina moving to help. 'I'm sorry, Mum, it was–', and Connie flashing a look so dark the words sliced from her tongue.

Then Aunty Carol was launching us back across the driveway to where the gates had already closed, banging her hand on the steering wheel, yelling 'Fuck it!' and pressing the button a million times until they were swinging open and the car was screaming away – Christina in the front seat snapping directions ('Yes, no – *left!* – straight until the bakery.') and Connie crooning in the back seat with her sickly sweet voice and a hand stroking Mr Harvey as if she were putting him to sleep – him panting and quivering and twitching his wounded leg beside where I sat smushed against Alinta, trying not to meet Aunty Carol's eyes that kept appearing in the rear-vision mirror while she sped and ran lights and cut traffic and took no notice of the B-52's blaring from the speakers – bikinis! and surfboards! and girls rockin' and boys frockin'! – the song going on and on in delirious elation; Connie still crooning, 'My maaan,' slapping Christina's hand as she tried to examine Harvey's ear from the front seat, and Aunty Carol's eyes still flicking back again and again as the car sped along Cranbourne-Frankston Road and I pressed my head against the window and wished to God someone would turn off the radio—

*

—But it's pens down now because I hear Yoav in the hall. Bang crash as usual, as if he needs announcing. He's humming Bowie to himself – but really for everyone, so we can all see that he's been affected by the passing. I could already hear him in the car park.

I suppose I'd better fold this away for the night.

Tuesday, 12 January

TWENTY-FOUR HOURS NOW since I contacted Ali.

No reply.

When Yoav showers, he listens to music. He turns the volume all the way up so he can hear it above the water . . .

I'VE NEVER LOST the image of Connie falling out of the car. Even now, if I want, she hits the gravel and scrambles to her feet, bursting out of the shadow and becoming suddenly radiant; then caressing Mr Harvey in the back seat as the gates took forever to open. She'd said, 'My man, my man,' over and over again, stroking his belly and keeping him awake. It was more than a dog she was cradling, all of us knew; Aunty Carol's eyes in the rear-vision mirror, flicking back at her sister, who seemed to believe her husband was in her arms once again, crooning in an eerie way that suggested a glimpse into their most intimate scenes in the hospital. 'My man, my man,' she'd said again and again as Aunty Carol broke every rule on the road and the car hurtled towards Beach Street Veterinary Clinic.

Then at the clinic: Christina, Ali and I sitting absurdly like butchers in a row with lashings of blood covering our arms and thighs and shirts; sitting beside a portly woman with a snarling Pomeranian who despised my shoes. All about us, owners stood neat and laundered, scanning magazines and peering up at the television babbling in the corner.

181

Connie had exploded into the waiting room, shrieking and howling before disappearing with Aunty Carol, Harvey, and a stunned veterinarian behind an office door. Now all was silent and the three of us strained to make something of the hubbub creeping under the door – frantic, it seemed, though impossible to make out. Were they operating? Perhaps there was no point? Pamphlets had explained that dogs could die within half an hour if not treated. Mr Harvey had not been treated within half an hour. It was only his leg though – how much blood could he have lost? I looked at the TV to take my mind off things: an exposé on hunger strikes in the Woomera detention centre. Asylum seekers had sewn their lips together. A woman was weeping before the camera. Such sorrow in the world – and now Mr Harvey . . .

The door opened and Aunty Carol stepped out gravely. She paused as something was explained behind her, then nodded and made her way to the desk. Connie followed, clutching pamphlets as if they were vital organs. Mr Harvey was nowhere to be seen. The room hushed as everyone craned to hear what had become of the poor dog rushed in so grotesquely. Now appeared the veterinarian – only he was no longer stunned. Instead, he swept the door closed with the grace of a conductor, striding to the desk.

It had been close, he said, quite an ordeal, and Harvey was lucky to have escaped the way he had. They would have to stitch the thigh and there were some concerns about infection – they were going to keep him for twenty-four hours.

'But ultimately, he'll be fine.'

Having saved the day, the vet was suddenly dashing and nonchalant. 'Trust me,' he assured, 'I know a battler when I see one.' Now placing a hand on Connie's shoulder, pleased with himself. 'Just make sure you thank those lucky stars, eh? Unless you want to give me some?'

His grin was the cover of a weekly magazine.

But Connie didn't respond. She was scrunching the pamphlets and staring into the selection of treats and harnesses. The vet's grin faded; he shot the receptionist a look.

'Anyway . . .' tapping Connie's shoulder. 'He'll pull through.'

Connie turned and seemed to realise there was a hand touching her – that she was being spoken to.

'Thanks so much for everything,' Aunty Carol jumped in. 'I can't tell you what he means to us.'

She put her arm around Connie to show the compliment was from everybody.

The trip home was in silence: Aunty Carol driving like a hearse as I leaned against the back window, listening to the air-conditioner trying to blast the smell of Harvey from the car. The horror of the vet was past; one crisis averted. But now, with the landscape flying by, I remembered there were further reasons to dread. Christina was across the back seat, obscured by Alinta peering resolutely forward. I knew she was thinking the same thing I was: we were in terrible trouble. And so, still in my bloodied shirt, I sat freezing under the air-conditioning, not daring to ask anyone to turn it off.

We spent the afternoon raising the house from the previous night's wreckage, Connie hovering about like a ghost, speaking volumes with tremendous silence, then disappearing to her room when she could no longer bear the sight of us. By early evening, the house was in some semblance and Ali left for home, offering grim farewells that suggested she knew we were in for trouble.

After she left, Aunty Carol ordered takeaway and Christina and I ate fish and chips, disgraced in the rumpus room. *Friends* and *Seinfeld* played again and again but neither of us were interested. We were listening to the morose chatter in the kitchen – our fate being decided.

Eventually, the door slid open and Aunty Carol stood with her handbag.

'I'm off, guys,' she said in a tone equal parts sympathy and disappointment.

We smiled weakly and she sighed, shaking her head with a smirk, as though reminded again that life truly *was* the great rollercoaster, and that *she'd* been young and stupid once herself and *God!* weren't we all just so *small* among the *stars!* She disappeared and the Golf's headlights came on, whisking up the driveway.

Then the door slammed and the three of us were finally alone. I remember the sound of Connie's footsteps pattering around the house, pointed and deliberate it seemed, coming close then drifting away. I waited for her to burst in, demanding an explanation, forcing us to hang our heads. But she wouldn't. Instead, she continued to patter, as if the sound was a method of torture. On TV, there was an ad break and everywhere, prices were being slashed and massacred and beheaded; gaudy jingles appearing horribly deformed in the tense atmosphere. Still Connie pattered, prolonging the agony.

Christina didn't share my apprehension though. She was sitting with her eyes on the screen, her face taut and clenched. Somehow, the wait for punishment had defiled her remorse.

Now she was vindictive. I watched her watching intently, the eyebrows set and the tight cheeks, the blonde hair behind her ears raised in sharp hackles.

Connie's footsteps passed the door. Now she was in Christina's bedroom and we could hear the sound of thumping and rummaging against the wall. Christina stood and threw her plate on the armrest, causing a piece of fish to slide on the carpet in a splat of tomato sauce.

'Shit!'

She fell to her knees with a tear of paper towel. I moved to help.

'No no, don't.' She threw up a hand. 'I'll do it.'

I paused, awkwardly half-standing as she scrubbed at the mess, Connie still thumping in the bedroom. The floor wouldn't clean though, and now a bright stain appeared, smudged in the carpet. Christina spat on it, trying again, scratching more and more vigorously until the paper began disintegrating into threads.

'Fucking hell!'

She smashed the fish into the plate and threw it at the couch, chips scattering about the room; pressed her fingers into her eyes. Now the ruckus had stopped in the bedroom and there was silence. I moved to get a cloth.

'Where are you going?' she snapped.

'I'll get a towel.'

'Don't.'

'It's fine – I know where they are.'

'I don't want you to get a cloth.'

'Why not? It's fine, I'll . . .'

'No, it's not fine.' She looked up. 'You're a guest. It's not your problem.'

I hovered as she picked chips off the floor, not daring to help. She sighed.

'You don't need to clean up. It's not your house.'

She was ashamed, I realised. It was a part no one was meant to see, the part they kept hidden. Here I was, witnessing it all – standing helplessly and wondering how everything had capitulated so suddenly, how this could be the same person who'd grinned in a towel only hours before?

Now the door flung open and Connie spilled into the room, pulling my sleeping bag behind like a bridal train. She stopped, confused for a moment by the scatter of chips, then threw the bundle on the floor. It flapped open and my pillow emerged, rolling directly into the crimson puddle of sauce and paper towel.

'What's this?' Christina was standing with her arms crossed, ready to despise all explanations. But Connie swivelled and was gone, returning to the hall.

'What's this!?' Christina yelled again.

No answer. I knelt to rescue my pillow, finding the underside sticky and drawing my fingers away. Christina watched in outrage and disbelief, storming to the door, but was immediately ushered back by Connie re-entering with the blow-up mattress, smushing through the doorframe and nearly falling into the room. She rose and planted it beside her like a surfboard.

'So what,' Christina said, 'he has to sleep in here? Is that what this is?'

The only answer was the babble of the TV. She snatched the remote and turned it off. Heavy silence.

'We have to be separated, do we?'

'There's not enough space.'

'What? My entire room?'

Connie let the mattress fall on the carpet, leaving her arm aloft in second position. 'For two teenagers.' Now turning to me with a mothering smile, her face shiny and swollen: 'Be more comfortable in here anyway, I'd say.'

'What d'you mean?' Christina wasn't backing down. 'It's the same bed – you're not making any sense.'

'Watch your mouth!' Connie suddenly vicious.

'Why though?'

'Why? Because I'm your mother and I don't need to give you an explanation. I want you and Matt in different rooms.'

'I'm sorry I left the gate open – do you know how many times he's got out?'

'I don't care. You're sixteen. You should have your own space.'

She pulled the sleeping bag from under the mattress and draped it on top. Christina watched her, shaking her head.

'Are you worried about what we're going to do?'

'Oh, grow up.'

Christina gave a little laugh, then looked at me.

'She's worried we're going to fuck.'

Connie slammed her hand on the floor.

'Right. Out! Don't you dare use that language in my house. I don't care who you're trying to impress.'

'You didn't buy it.'

There was an awful silence. Christina had said it under her breath. Now Connie's face dropped in a look of astonishment.

'Say that again.'

Christina held a moment – but didn't dare. She turned and slunk away, pausing at the door.

'What if we already have?'

Then she was gone, stomping down the hall and slamming the door.

Connie stood facing the door, still with the expression of disbelief, as though she held a telegram announcing disaster. And me behind with a heaviness in my chest; a dull rising at the notion that last night had somehow devolved to nothing more than muck to fling in an argument. I looked at my shoelaces, listening to Christina thump and stomp, then fall silent. There was an excruciating pause. I wasn't sure if Connie even knew I was still in the room.

Then she turned and smiled, picking up my pillow and examining the underside.

'I'm sorry, Matt,' she said, removing the case. I wasn't sure if she meant the pillow or the last five minutes. 'This'll need a wash – there are more in the lounge room.' She nodded to our dishes. 'Would you mind chucking those in the sink?'

'Of course,' I said. 'Maybe I should wash up?'

'That'd be great – thanks.'

I have no idea how I escaped punishment that evening. I've since wondered if perhaps Christina's argument wasn't a ploy to shift the blame onto herself? Whatever the case, after taking the hint, I retired to the lounge and sat for half an hour, listening to their voices flare in the hall: Connie spitting words like 'respect' and 'discipline' as if they meant a kind of reptile and Christina bellowing so loud you could hear it from the road. 'Aren't you supposed to *earn* respect!?', then Connie: 'something something *dare speak!* something something . . .' Then Christina howling again. I turned up the TV, not wanting to hear, hoping the neighbours were somewhere far away.

Eventually, the door slammed and Connie appeared at the end of the hall, standing for a moment with a warm smile, a remote tranquillity that somehow made me uneasy.

'Christina's gone to bed,' she said. 'Would you like a hot chocolate?'

I leapt to my feet, desperate to offload the weight of injustice and remorse.

'It was my idea.'

'What was?' Her face with fresh innocence.

'Going out into the street,' I said, 'opening the gates. I told her I wanted to leave.'

'Oh?'

'If there's a punishment, I deserve it too.'

'You do?' She smiled again, nodded. Then, after a moment, 'Thanks for your honesty.'

She took a breath, then paused, peering about the room. I waited, feeling again that same uneasiness, as though something was about to happen that I couldn't perceive.

'I wonder,' she said, coming back. 'Have you seen *Planes, Trains and Automobiles*?'

'No.'

'Really? Oh you should. It's the best Steve Martin film.'

'Is it?'

'It's on tonight actually.'

I stood, not knowing what else to say, with my apology capitulated like arrows against a rampart. She grinned to let me know I was in for a treat.

I suppose the film was a kind of punishment – the torture of it: imagining Christina banished in her room, maybe asleep, maybe awake, but betrayed either way – alone and with no hot chocolate. How Connie put it out of mind, I don't know. She was in high spirits though, quoting and laughing before the punchlines, as if it were any other day; looking over to make sure I was laughing, that I was having fun. I couldn't help noticing how she relished our time together.

At the end, it turned out John Candy's wife had been dead for years and he had no home for Thanksgiving. Upon the revelation, I'd shot a glance at Connie; I suppose because her husband was dead and I wanted to see the look on her face – some wistful gaze presumably, recalling the best of times. But instead, I found her looking at me, her eyes piercing and amused, as though she'd been waiting for this exact moment – for the reveal . . .

In the embarrassment of being caught, I'd raised my mug. She raised her glass.

'You know your dad and I went to a festival called Tanelorn,' she said. 'This movie always reminds me. There was a group of us that drove up – it's in New South Wales, Tanelorn. We were there to see Split Enz.'

She chuckled, dragging her thumb around the rim of her glass.

'They were so kooky. I just *loved* them, y'know? They were playing on the third day and so we went up for them. But we had no tent pegs . . . I don't know how we forgot them – or if we just didn't have any or something – but we were trying to hammer these sticks in. They kept breaking. And the tent collapsed in the night. This was a big . . . an eight-person tent. While we were sleeping – it must have been early morning – we woke up and the entire thing had come down around our shoulders. And it was windy, blowing us around inside it. We had to scrape our way through, trying to find the zip. Your dad was saying, "This way! This way!" but I had no idea where I was . . .'

She laughed loudly. Suddenly I was keenly aware of the volume of our voices; of Christina in the bedroom. Was she awake, I wondered, listening to the words floating in the hall?

'. . . your dad was so upset. *So* upset. There was no space in the van so we slept outside. Then it rained and so we were all drenched, our sleeping bags, clothes, your dad . . . we left in the afternoon, missed Split Enz. God, I was so angry. And Alek didn't want to go; I'll never forget – that was the first time they met. And they fought and fought. Alek could be quite . . . I mean, both of them could. Most people were still asleep and they had these drenched clothes – it would have been four or five in the morning – yelling and screaming and suddenly all these torches were on and they were telling us to shut up!'

She twisted the bottle cap off and poured into the glass.

'Y'know, you plan and plan . . .' She leaned back, parting her hands as if something had disappeared in thin air. 'What will you do after school?'

'Me?' I was taken aback at the sudden thrusting of the conversation upon me. 'I don't know – my marks aren't great.'

Connie nodded like she knew the world.

'Maybe I'll travel somewhere.'

I shrugged, imagining my voice floating down the hall. (Was she awake?) The betrayal of it all. Connie leaned forward and put the bottle back.

'Well . . .' She took a sip. 'Maybe you have no plan. That's okay; things go awry anyway. You scramble, flitting around . . .'

She leaned forward over her knees. She was drunk, I realised.

'When Alek . . . we had the funeral. Everything was organised, all the decisions. Then it happened . . . It was like there was no plan, all our preparations, as if nothing had been arranged. And it was just the *worst* thing, the *worst* thing that could possibly happen. The church calling about the pamphlets – God, the *pamphlets;* getting his photograph – I was rifling through the photo albums. But mostly just floating around. It's chaos. The timetable, calendars; everyone off work – you're floating around and it's Tuesday. And I kept thinking, "It's *Tuesday*! And look at us all here, everyone at home." And we had to pick up the flowers . . . it was just so awful.'

She paused and leaned back, shrugged.

'But then it couldn't be worse. That's something. I remember at some point, I felt that nothing worse would happen – at least we were protected from that . . .'

Suddenly she laughed, as if momentarily aware that the situation was absurd.

'How old are you?'

'Fifteen.'

She laughed again, throwing her head back and draining her glass. She looked at me, not laughing anymore.

'You look like him, you know, these days.'

'Who?'

She turned to the screen. Steve Irwin was bending in front of the camera and explaining why he always had his car serviced by Toyota. She screwed her eyes up, trying to see, and took the bottle again.

'I potter round here now. It's a big house. It's a *Big. House.*

The orchard grows faster than I can cut it. Sometimes I cut it right back, the whole thing, until it looks like matchsticks. Do you know how much time I have? I have sooo much time . . .'

She looked at me and saw I was uncomfortable. Or maybe she felt the same way.

'Sorry. Sorry, I'm just . . .'

'No, no; not at all,' I said, wanting to appear relaxed and nonchalant. She knew. But maybe we'd gone too far to stop. She became solemn.

'I loved your dad. Did you know that? I loved him. You can tell him that from me.' And she laughed again, an uncomfortable laugh this time, with more hope than humour. 'All of us were too young though.' She grinned, looking down at the floor. 'Sometimes you wonder . . . sliding doors.'

She looked at the floor for a long time, then shook her head and spoke, almost to herself.

'The heart cannot retreat.'

I wondered if I was supposed to respond. She was elsewhere, looking down, watching something that was happening in the floorboards.

Suddenly, she looked up at me.

'We haven't been to the beach, have we? Tomorrow, we should go to the beach.'

It's been five months since I visited Connie. I used to go every few weeks, though admittedly, it's been less often recently. She makes one uncomfortable, the drooling way she speaks – still with her humour, still chuckling and girlish; only she's not aware of her own decrepitude, the thinning hair and the sultry gaze. I get anxious sometimes, stepping through the doors; a little light-headed.

She confuses me with Dad these days too. The more I look like him – I suppose it's tricky. Last time, she waited until we were alone, then whispered something about a toilet cubicle on an excursion to Parliament House. Happily, I couldn't quite make out the story. I'm very content not knowing what Connie and my father were getting up to at seventeen.

I do owe her a debt though. Much of what I've put in this journal, I only know because of our visits: details and timelines. Of course, I have to be careful. Connie's stories can often be fantastical. She is convinced, for example, that she caused Alek's illness – and this I've heard from her own mouth. Twice. She believes her own actions caused him to

194

fall ill. Such is the power of her guilt. Now whenever she brings him up, she speaks as if he were a prophet. He wasn't a prophet; he was a nice guy. His stories could be a little dull and as I recall, he had a habit of talking over people. Nevertheless, her memories feature a man warped so optimistically that I no longer recognise him.

It's why some days I find Connie so difficult to blame: because everything she ever did was as penance. These days, when I watch her rambling in her chair, I find myself unable to be furious. Instead, I can only marvel at the power of remorse, the way it's twisted her memories – how it can cause someone to genuinely believe in a fantasy.

I realise this is all straying far from *Planes, Trains and Automobiles*.

It's important to say, though; to note. Because when I think of some of her behaviour – allowing everything to collapse about her.

It's important to remember she was eating herself alive.

Not that I thought anything of it at the time . . .

Later that evening – after the film – all thoughts of Connie had fallen from my mind. I had a guilt of my own causing me to toss and turn, lying awake in the rumpus room, my nostrils gripped in the bitter tinge of tomato sauce – imagining Christina pressed against her door, listening to her mother's voice float in the hallway, then my own, how it must have felt like betrayal. She'd taken the fall, after all, while I'd drunk hot chocolate and been exonerated; my only penalty being the loss of a jacket that (it now occurred to me) I'd left bloodied on the roadside after trying to wrap Mr Harvey in it. And so I lay awake, flip-flopping and remorsing, wondering if it would be wrong to creep across the hall, just for a moment, just to apologise . . .

It was 2 am when we ran into each other. Sleep hadn't come and I'd thrown on a pair of tracksuit pants, sneaking out of the room. As it turned out, Christina had had exactly the same idea.

'Matt!'

'Fuck!'

We'd frozen at the same time.

'Is Mum awake?'

'She went to bed ages ago.'

'Was her light off?'

'I don't know. Have you been awake the whole time?'

'Yeah.'

There was a pause; she was a pale blur.

'Did you hear us?'

'Yeah.'

A longer silence.

'Look, I'm–'

'Shh!' Her finger shot to her lips. 'Listen to that.'

I listened. There was nothing.

'What?'

Even in the dark, I could see her grin.

'Harvey's at the vet.'

True enough; had Mr Harvey been home, our rendezvous would have almost certainly been interrupted. As it was, the house remained silent.

'I'm on a mission,' she said, shuffling past to the end of the hall and beckoning me to follow.

The lounge was eerie in the dark, cavernous. The clock on the microwave beamed 2.15 and Connie's uniforms hung suspended on their hangers. Outside, the plane trees were thrashing their branches in a way that made indoors less alive. Christina stood by Connie's room, pale in the light of a streetlamp that reached across the paddock. I approached and she leaned up to my ear.

'Cupboard next to the en suite.' She barely made a sound. 'She'd have no idea if something went missing.'

I looked to Connie's door, feeling anxiety rise. There was no light underneath. Christina leaned away and I saw her eyes shining.

'How do we get it?' I asked.

'Don't worry – she'll be out, definitely.'

She squeezed my shoulder and tiptoed to the door. I took her arm.

'Wait. I want to go.'

'It's okay; I know where to look.'

I stopped her again.

'Please. Let me do it.'

She looked at me a moment. I was a child begging to pay in a supermarket.

'Alright,' she said. 'Cupboard on the left. You'll need a chair.'

I crept to the door, turning the handle as carefully as possible. It swung open and a wave of fetid heat wafted on the breeze of a desk fan. I felt Christina wince behind me and stepped into the room.

It was darker than the lounge; blackout curtains on the windows and only the dull orange of an elemental heater beside the bed. Connie was snoring in the dark, long trembling sounds above the white noise of the fan. I made my way forward, gingerly searching with my hands, the breeze blowing back and forth over me, rippling and disappearing, leaving the smell to settle again. Crossing the room, it became almost palpable. Connie's long snores. She was somewhere to my right now, in the puddle of dark, lying open-mouthed and ready to sit up and howl.

The cupboard stood at the end of the room, hinted in a feeble light from the en suite. Drawing the door ajar, I met with an abundance of objects: clothes and jars, candles perhaps. I felt among them; medicines and toiletries and lightbulbs, aerosols and plastic bags. Then my hand brushed a cold cylinder on the top shelf: four bottles side by side, just out of reach. I scanned back over the room, my eyes adjusted now. Connie was a sack on the bed, rising and falling as her snores rose over the whirring fan. Beside her, a pile of clothes sat on a chair. I slunk over and brought the chair back to the cupboard. Christina was right. There were at least twenty bottles huddled together all the way to the back of the shelf. I reached as far as I could, not wanting to disturb the front, and felt about the lids – oddly shaped for wine, I thought – choosing a random, squattish bottle, holding my breath and drawing it up with the precision of a surgeon.

Then I was closing the door with the bottle in my hand, setting the chair at the bedside and reaching for the clothes on the floor. As I bent down though, my elbow knocked the lampshade, causing it to jolt and rock loudly. At once, Connie gave a deep sputter and fell silent. I froze, holding my breath, looking down at her. She was asleep, lying on her stomach with her head turned to me. One of her legs was disappearing under the sheets, the other bent up, as if she'd tried to crawl from the blankets. I swallowed.

The movement had pulled her slip around her waist. Now, as I stood gaping, the fan swung again, billowing the fabric for a moment. I saw her leg curved into her lower back, and a deep shadow beneath her stomach. In the dark, the skin seemed so much smoother than her face, taut and soft, as though it were someone else's body. I found myself thinking she was beautiful. A strange way to consider an adult, I realise – but in the dark, there was no doubting it. She was. Enough to cause a memory to appear from the previous night: her swaying hips in the lounge, how in that moment she'd been sixteen. Now she seemed that way again; sultry, passionate somehow, with her leg escaping the doona and the deep dark below her belly; all those parts Christina had been desperate to hide. Another breeze and the slip lifted again. I looked, feeling my chest tighten, and my throat, the bottle wet in my fingers.

You look like him, you know.

Suddenly she coughed, jolting from the apnoea and turning her head away. Now the snoring began and both of us could breathe again. I rested the clothes on the chair and made–

FUCKING YOAV AND his podcasts! Not only does he spend every waking moment in this room, he seems to genuinely think I appreciate it. Every time I turn my head, he's there with his feet poking out, grinning like a fool, as if his presence is a gift.

I get nothing done. I have no time. I start to write, I feel him leaning over my shoulder – curious, insufferable, opinionated.

Even Christina won't visit when he's here.

Yesterday, I'm begging him for a moment, just a half-hour so I can finish up.

'Not your room,' he says. 'We share, we share!'

Half an hour – give me a fucking break.

Saturday, 16 January

YOAV ASLEEP – THANK GOD. No interruptions.

Connie was interrupted. That's okay though – she was asleep too, having played her role. Now it was only Christina and I, alone finally, left to gather ourselves after the ordeal at the vet. I'd stolen the liquor from Connie, crept away, leaving her half-wrapped in her sheets. She wouldn't wake until the following lunchtime.

But for me though, the night was far from over.

Christina was waiting in the rumpus room when I arrived, still in her pyjamas, applauding silently as I held my plunder aloft: a bottle of Chivas Regal, twelve years – classier than anything she'd expected. I remember watching her examine the label and feeling my heart sink. I loathed whisky above all spirits – acrid and noxious all the way down. At least the bottles at the front had been wine. Nonetheless, she was impressed, and so I took comfort as we threw on shoes and scampered from the house.

Outside was one of those blustering evenings that seemed like it would rain. Stepping into the porchlight, I watched the trees swirling over the garden, charged and alive – leaves scattering about the lawn. It was still balmy though, even into those late hours, and so I traipsed between the hedges along the path, feeling the warm and watching Christina shoot ahead to the workshed. She ushered me in, closing the garage door behind us. For a moment, we stood in darkness as she fumbled for the switch, the wind hushed into distant surf. Then the room sputtered into light.

Immediately, I was taken aback. Alek's treasureland, once sacred and out of bounds, had become a landfill. I stood scanning the room, catching glimpses of the space I remembered, the workbench covered in power tools and fencing. Over time though, it had slowly become buried in an ocean of the parts you throw away: boxes torn open and ransacked, left to spill books and medical records; countless garbage bags of clothes and photographs – endless photographs there seemed to be – and documents littering the cement. But now other things had appeared: drawers and whitegoods, electrical equipment, vacuum cleaners, fans and bicycles, bookshelves and furniture and filing cabinets, junk and shit; all of it dumped with no attempt at system or arrangement, only left to rot as mould and webbing spread like an adhesive, creating the strange illusion that Alek's possessions, his very memory, festering over time, had grown into a single monstrous entity.

'We don't throw things away.' Christina had moved beside me.

'No kidding,' I said.

'It's a disorder: emotional attachment to random objects. You can't let anything go.' She stepped into the mess and cleared things off what appeared to be a couch. 'See this?' She was holding a vacuum cleaner. 'This isn't the old one; this is the one before that.'

I thought of Connie cradling Mr Harvey in the back seat, crooning, 'My man, my man.' How a similar scene must have played so many times in this room, only with an album of photographs.

'Voila!'

Christina had beaten the daylights out of a pair of scatter cushions and thrown them on the couch. It was a bleak setting for a rendezvous, somehow resembling a frown. But it was private and so we slumped together, uncorking the bottle.

'There's no glasses,' she said.

'That's fine. How do you normally have it? Straight?'

'Usually.'

'Me too.'

'Sometimes I have it with Coke.'

'I prefer it with Coke.'

'Me too.'

A pause.

It was clear neither of us had a palate for whisky. But it was more important not to be exposed, so we agreed it was fine and began to pass the bottle back and forth. As expected, each sip was a unique violation that clawed its way like a cat in a bag. Nonetheless, I maintained a ruse of approving grunts, screwing my eyes up and pretending I supped the ambrosian nectar. If Christina was as repulsed as I, then her bluff was impressive. She seemed to savour the taste, gulping so generously I found myself struggling to keep up.

To begin, we kept to whispers, in respect of Harvey, to whom our meeting was dedicated, and in caution of Connie, who slept nearby. As things took effect, however, and the room began to melt, we forgot how close she slept and our whispers grew to a ruckus. Safe in the knowledge that Harvey was okay, we let our relief spill over and began to view the morning for all its absurdity: the vet and the Pomeranian, Aunty Carol's Siberian air-conditioner, our bloodied clothes and the confusion of the receptionist who'd only been able to find a dog named 'Halfhalf' registered to the Wychwood address. It truly had been a comedy; and now we laughed out loud, though it was clear our laughter stemmed more from gratitude than the events themselves.

Either way, soon the room became hazy and drooped. I'd been swigging huge gulps and now, looking about, things seemed to hang where they were on unsteady hooks; all the trash and boxes set daintily as trinkets in Geppetto's workshop – Christina on the far cushion, blurring and reappearing.

'How now, spirit? Wither wander you?' She was reciting her lines for me – drawling the words and attempting to locate me through a telescope made of the whisky bottle. 'I am that merry wandered of the niiight . . .'

After so many sips, the couch had emerged as fluffy and cocoonlike and I slumped back, giggling at the performance, huddled with her knees on the couch and her hair wiry and displaced.

'Spiriiiit. How noow?'

She watched me giggle a moment, then lowered the bottle, offering it to me. I took another long drink and passed it back. Her smile had dropped now, her gaze grown quizzical. She looked at the label.

'How do you feel about what we did last night?'

The question took me by surprise. I felt inebriation slip at the gravity of her tone, pulling me from my cocoon.

'I feel okay. Why – how do you feel?'

She shrugged. 'Okay.'

Something new had crossed her face though, an uncertainty. I watched her uncork the lid, drink, cork it again.

'I wanted to do it,' she was saying to herself. 'I'm glad.'

But she was disaffected somehow, as though a great hero had been proven a fraud. I shuffled upright, thinking of the previous night: her desperation to pull her shirt down.

'I hope it was okay,' I said.

She nodded. 'Of course. It was.'

There was disappointment though. One she wasn't able to hide; or wasn't trying to. After all, it hadn't been as we'd imagined, amid the swirling neon, the extravaganza. We'd come together only to find, at the deep dark centre of it all, terror and insecurity. We'd found each other's, fumbling in the dark; 'Here they are,' we'd said in whispers. And she'd pulled her shirt down. Now I felt the massive weight of silence, of mirth having abandoned us.

'I left my jacket,' I said.

'Huh?'

'When we got Harvey. It's at number four.'

'Oh. Did you want to get it?'

'Now?'

'We have torches . . .'

But neither of us wanted to get it. We wanted the hysteria of the campfire. We wanted to be able to giggle down the street. The streamers and neon. Where had it all gone? I wondered. Suddenly there was only the rubble of the workshed, and her eyes, which seemed to be asking the same question, with their green and hazel – that searing colour I'd first noticed at the roadside, when I'd discovered she was beautiful.

'Don't worry,' I said, surprised at my voice, suddenly seeming to drift from elsewhere. 'It doesn't matter.'

'Are you sure? We can.' She shuffled upright, tilting her eyebrows in concern. 'I'd hate for you to lose it.'

Only I couldn't remember what I'd lost now, or what we'd even been talking about. Because it occurred to me that I was moving forward. Infinitesimally; moving towards her. And she could see too, watching with her jaw clenched, her voice dropping low ('I'd hate for you . . . to leave it behind . . .'). She was looking at my lips, getting closer, willing them to say something fabulous, some magic line from a film to remind her of the streamers and fireflies, to prove everything was still all around us, peeking through the cracks–

Suddenly I shot forward, stretching my fingers into her hair, pulling her to me in a grandiose manoeuvre from another time. She responded, falling over with her lips wet from the bottle.

–But I was too passionate. All our uncertainty, I think, the moment having swept me away; I'd mistaken everything for a film and crushed into her lips, squeezing her hand intensely. Her knuckles cracked and she let out a yelp.

'Woah! Drunk.'

'I'm sorry,' I said.

Around her mouth was glossy and wet from where I'd smushed. 'Are you okay?'

'Fine.'

She moved back to interrogate me and I immediately shot forward into a hunch, feeling my cheeks burn – all the passion having caused things to stir; my tracksuit pants now bulging at the thigh.

'Sorry,' I said again, pretending to fossick for the bottle.

But she'd seen. Now she gripped my shoulder, slumping me back on the couch, shamefully exposed.

'Uh oh,' she said, looking at the mound.

She passed her hand flatly over, peering in fascination. I realise how bizarre it must have seemed to her; such curious biology. She swiped her hand back over and held it aloft – then slowly pressed, inspecting my face, as if she were conducting an experiment. I felt a reeling pleasure and launched again, gripping her waist and pulling her towards me. She pushed down harder and the pleasure became intense. I slid my hand to her stomach–

'Hey . . . !'

She lurched backwards, pushing me onto the couch. Then a pause as I looked at her in surprise.

'Sorry,' she said, moving my hand onto her shoulder. 'Hands up here.'

But it was too late. I'd already brushed the skin beneath her shirt and felt something else, something against the smoothness – like matchsticks, I'd thought.

'What is it?' I asked.

'Nothing.'

I took my hand away. She tried to put it back.

'It's nothing.'

'Can I see?'

As she hesitated, I remembered Alinta's arms sweeping apart, how the scars had seemed like grass. Then she lifted her top. They were the same little flicks, darker than her skin, speed lines dashing across her stomach; some old, some new – almost like clouds, and her belly button was the sun.

'When did you do it?' I asked.

She shrugged. There was something brutal and hasty, the way they flicked across.

'*Why* though?'

I knew the question was callous, even as I asked it.

She pulled her shirt down, 'Why not?', leaving the image to burn my retinas: a sun with its rays darting away. I thought again of how she'd pulled her shirt down so I couldn't see, how Ali's sister drew tattoos that covered the skin.

'I'm sorry,' I said, as if it could make amends. I put my hands behind her head and kissed her again, hoping to throw everything aside, to show I didn't care – or that I *cared*, but it didn't matter. Something. I leaned in, imitating my earlier passion. But she sensed the imitation. My lips were light and my mind elsewhere: far away in the Kewfield boarding house where she and Alinta were lifting garments to show their patterns.

Christina pushed me away.

'What's wrong?'

'Nothing,' I lied. 'Does anyone know?'

'You do.'

'No one else?'

'Like who?'

I faltered. I didn't know. Teachers? Doctors? Who were you supposed to tell? How were you supposed to help? Where were you supposed to what? Suddenly, the room seemed claustrophobic: junk suffocating and walling us in; the image of Christina's belly projecting somehow, etched in high grass. 'I have to piss,' I heard myself say and felt a vague stab as I stood to escape, excusing myself, knowing that it all seemed fake, that she knew I was fleeing – gripping and stumbling to the door at the back of the shed. Now the room began to swirl, objects swimming as I passed; murky trappings on the

workbench, pickets and hammers and seedling packets, seca-
teurs – Christina behind somewhere, asking if I was okay.
How many sips had I had? Ten? Eleven? I couldn't remember.
A bundle of chicken wire was becoming psychedelic, fanged
and coiled as the flicks on Christina's belly, my head tipping
sideways . . .

–I slumped outside and a breeze rushed up the drive
and hit my face. Everywhere, trees were rocking about and
I staggered over the gravel to hold myself against the fence
of the eastern paddock. I looked into the sky. The moon
fluorescent, beaming high above the widow makers as
they swayed and flapped their arms – the breeze gorgeous,
balmy and alive. I closed my eyes to feel it on my cheeks.
Immediately though, a sugary rush swilled in the back of
my throat and I fell to my knees and hurled into the grass.
The taste was acrid and searing. I hovered over the railing,
spitting strings and brushing my hair as it blew in my face.
Then I stood, unzipped and pissed out into the paddock,
feeling for a moment that I could breathe.

I don't know how long I stood there, peering out, the
grounds eerily visible, as if the moon were a sun. Like
Christina's stomach – the thought returning with the image;
then another: Christina peering in the dark under the bed,
how her belly had been smooth and dry.

Love her, won't you?

I did. Above all, I did.

And at the thought, I was sober again–

*

Just pausing for a moment – as Yoav stirs . . . awake?

Asleep.

I'm thinking of the fluorescent moon, and how I'd run in fear from Christina's belly.

'It's in the past though, isn't it?' I hear her say. 'No point looking back.'

True enough.

—only it isn't the past, is it? No, the past is myself in this story; the boy I no longer recognise, who lunges from the couch to kiss Christina. My dash. My youthful belligerence. I am writing about someone else.

Foolish thinking, I realise. Pointless flagellation – but I can't help myself on nights like these, in the dark with no distraction.

Yoav lies on his back. The moon divides his face. What are you dreaming, little man? Are you dreaming of your friend? Are you holding his stomach together?

There's a tattoo around his middle finger that held the entrails of his best friend, tattooed so he'll never forget. Now he sleeps with a voice jabbering in his ears. He listens so there won't be silence. And I should be asleep too. But I'm not; I'm awake, haunting myself with memories of a boy I no longer recognise.

Is it why we are scared of the dark? These great gaps of silence for things to slip into; for grief to fill. For guilt. Connie spending her nights eating herself alive. Yoav dreaming of his friend. And me: here in a room I am unable to leave without permission, where tribunals determine whether I can take care of myself, whether I'm a danger to myself. Here I am: a man whose mother defends him in a cafe, haunting myself not with the past, but with the present.

*

Christina was in among the junk when I re-entered; clamouring about and tossing things here and there.

'What are you doing?' I asked.

She stood up, holding a wooden ceiling fan.

'Sorting.'

The fan flew over the couch and crash-landed at the door.

'Woah!' I winced at the noise. 'Are you serious – she's *right there*!'

'You think she'll hear?' she asked. Her voice was impersonal; it was punishment. 'Well, I'm already in trouble, aren't I?'

She turned away and began to search in a chest of drawers beside her.

'I'm sorry,' I said. 'It just took me off guard. I wasn't expecting it.'

'Expecting what?'

She stood upright, waiting for me to say. I didn't.

'Don't worry about it,' she said, turning back to the drawer.

'I don't care,' I offered.

'I didn't ask if you did.'

'Yeah, but I just . . .'

'Why don't we forget it? It doesn't matter.'

But obviously it mattered. She'd found a medallion and was inspecting the engraving, tossing it aside so it crashed like an expletive.

'Can't you do this tomorrow?' I pleaded.

'Why?'

'*Why?* Because you're pissed off. Coz we're drunk. Coz it's three-thirty and I don't want to wake your mum.'

'Matt, trust me.' She slammed a drawer. 'She's that fucking drunk, she'd burn to death before she woke up.'

I swore under my breath.

'What?'

Silence.

'No, go on.' She was waiting with her arms crossed.

'Why do you have to be so cruel to her?'

'What, because I'm not being nice?'

'I didn't say that.'

'It's what you mean though, isn't it?'

'It's just . . . you talk like you hate her.'

'I love her. She's an idiot.'

I shook my head with a snigger.

'Sorry – was that cruel?'

'*That?* Yes. That was cruel.'

'What should I do then?' she asked. 'Let her mope around here? Say nice things? Does that make me compassionate? Will you think highly of me then?'

'It's better than running away.'

She faltered for a second, narrowing her eyes.

'Is that what you think? Do you think I'm trying to get away from Mum?'

'Then why go to boarding school?' I said. 'I know you weren't expelled. Why tell everyone you were expelled? Why are you trying to hide everything?'

I crossed my arms, certain of my own righteousness, waiting for her to drop her eyes and confess. But she only shrugged.

'Because I'm tired of explaining what alopecia is.'

She sighed and opened another drawer beside her, took a bundle of papers and started leafing through them. 'Car registration . . . insurance,' holding up a document, 'nineteen-ninety-six.' She threw it across the room, the pages splaying in a flock and littering the furniture. 'I can't be around this house. I hate everything about it, everything in it. If it was up to me, we'd burn it to the ground and get as far away as we could.'

'Then tell her you want to move,' I said. '*Tell* her you hate it. Say – if you said something . . . Could you hear her tonight? She hates it too; she's lonely.'

'Of course she is.'

'Then why not get rid of it? You'd make a fortune.'

'Probably.'

'So . . . ?'

'So what?'

'So why not *sell it?*'

'Isn't it obvious?'

'What?'

'This.' She lifted her hand, sweeping the room to prove the evidence was everywhere. 'Matt – this is punishment.'

'Punishment? For *what?*'

Now she stopped, genuinely puzzled.

'For the divorce.' She spoke simply, with narrowed eyes, as though waiting for me to confess a bluff. 'Did you not know that?'

But any reply I had disappeared with the news. I stood blankly.

'It was just before he was sick,' she said. 'She'd seen a lawyer and everything – I'm sorry; I thought you knew.'

'No.'

I thought of Dad in the kitchen, leering as Mum fussed over the bandaid; his voice quivering on the phone.

'When did they separate?'

She shook her head.

213

'They never did. Dad pretty much got sick straight away – he already was, I think. Mum took it back when she found out.'

'Is that why my dad was coming down here?'

She seemed taken aback.

'What do you mean?'

'Dad was coming here. Wasn't he? Is that when . . . ?'

'*Your* dad? No . . .'

And she gave a half-chuckle, shaking her head, her eyes softening. 'No, he was helping *me* out. He wasn't with Mum; Mum was at the hospital. She didn't like me fending for myself. Sometimes she was there for days. Aunty Carol couldn't always make it so he used to come down. He took me to school and stuff, cooked dinner . . .'

She paused, peering away at something.

'He's a good man, your dad.'

I thought of him slamming the door and leaving the house in silence; flying down the road to fill a space Alek had left.

'–but wait . . . When you guys came to our house . . .'

'I know.'

The thought had taken me to Alek at our dining table, with his bald head, delivering his famous chemotherapy joke, all of us in stitches around the table.

'He didn't seem . . .'

'That was his choice,' Christina said. 'I'm not sure what they said to each other, but one day I got home and everything was the same as it had been before, like he'd never found out. No one ever talked about it again.' She took a half-breath. 'I think he knew he was really sick . . . decided it was better if it had never happened.'

'But it did,' I said.

214

She narrowed her eyes.

'So what should he have done? Left? Thrown Mum out? Started a new life?'

'It's a lie though.'

'What's the point of the truth if it ruins everything? Mum was at the hospital every day. Every single day. It's not like she could take it back.'

I thought of Dad peering forward through excruciating dinners. Mum weeping over *Bladerunner*. Neither of them daring to say a word.

'You must hate her,' I said.

'I don't hate her. I hate that she's still here, trying to prove whatever. She thinks she's doing it for him, but he isn't here, so who's it for? I feel sorry for her; she doesn't have any friends. Aunty Carol and her aren't so close. It's charity. She's been trying to get Mum to find another place – but she won't. It's like she thinks she's paying something off. I don't know, maybe she is. But the whole thing seems so pointless.'

I watched her making her way back through the wreckage, picking up the bottle. Her hair had fallen down now, framing a face that was flushed and weary, as though exhausted from having to carry something enormous.

'I'm sorry if you didn't know any of this,' she said, pulling the cork. She drank a large gulp and held out the bottle to me.

'No thanks.'

She looked at the piles of junk walling us in; memory and refuse, strewn together without discrimination. She shook her head.

'It's a circus, isn't it?'

It was. So utterly pointless.

'Maybe we should run away,' I said. It was a joke, but it wasn't. Christina considered for a moment.

'Where?'

'Oh yeah.'

She nodded and lifted the whisky to her lips, drinking a last gulp and wiping her mouth on her sleeve. She sighed.

'I wanna get your jacket.'

'What?'

But before I knew what was happening, she'd ditched the bottle, taken a torch, and was skipping through the side door.

No, I CAN'T sleep now. My mind's spinning. I'm thinking of that night: Christina flying ahead of me, across the roadside paddock, making for the fence.

–I was chasing an apparition, it seemed, only a feeling; everything flitting around and surreal, my head throbbing; Christina peeling across the grass in her tracksuit, on a mad quest to find my jacket, her torchlight swivelling in the trees along the fence.

I'd caught her climbing over, taken her wrist and pulled her away. It was a fool's errand! I'd said – we could barely see; we could barely stand! And so we'd fallen back onto the piles of horse shit padded along the fencing. She kissed me. Everything was delirious, us clawing at one another until the ground began to stink under the movement. Love in the filth of horses. Corrupt love. Something alive rushing past my elbow. Then Christina was dribbling lips, pulling me away onto the grass where the moon was fluorescent and the paddock almost light.

I can't remember much after that. Only peering down and seeing her belly etched like it was, brilliant in the moonlight, with my hands covering her scars in case they burst at the seams; and with no idea that I was cradling far more. For she was pregnant then, wasn't she? Yes – I'm certain; caused in the quiet of her bedroom, only a night earlier, kneeling before one another as kids laughed around the fire.

Yoav lies behind me now. He's tattooed the finger that held the entrails of his friend, so they wouldn't spill onto the ground. And so was I cradling something – though we had no idea – a new part of her that would have to be torn out. (It seems impossible! That anything could grow in such conditions!)

I remember Christina with her T-shirt pulled up for me to see; her stomach moving forward and back, heavy breathing as I traced the lines – as I told her I loved them; and as she moved my hand away and asked me to say something else. The stink of horse shit, I remember.

*

Still not asleep.

What time is it? Christ.

I'm thinking of corrupt love, the stink of horse shit; thoughts spiralling together – impossible to stop now. And not only Christina and I . . .

–for Connie and Dad loved each other, didn't they? They'd rolled in the same muck as we had. At sixteen; into their forties. Twin stories. Only theirs never amounted to anything. A crescendo of phone calls and flights to Wychwood, but with no climax, no reckoning – and of course I will never ask him; we will never speak of it – but I'm certain, because Mum would never have stayed, surely.

–No, their love amounted to my father driving to Wychwood at night, because there was nothing in the refrigerator, because Christina needed to be taken to school – and because he would have done anything Connie asked in the world. She clutched his heart. And even after she reneged – *still!* – after she stole her promises away with her; still he flew down the highway with his fantasies in a heap, and perhaps wondering what the hell he was doing – as Connie trembled by the hospital bed, superstitious and penitent; clutching Alek and whispering apologies in his ear . . .

–this is corrupt love; is it not?

Sunday, 17 January

CHRIST! YOAV AND his headphones again. What a fake. What a fucking invalid. I ask him if he can't give me the room, just for an hour, because it's impossible to think. Because Christina won't visit if he's here. He swings the curtain around.

'Not your room! Not your room!'

Now I hear the nattering and I honestly don't know what to do.

I've asked politely.

*

–No no no no, I need to rewrite this. It's wrong. I've got to set things straight. Because right now he's getting away with it. Isn't he? And because it's false. He knows, I know, we all know. My father and his famous generosity: driving out to Wychwood; paying for hospital bills – the celebrated philanthropist!

—as if he were a patsy caught in something beyond his control; as if he's the flawed hero of some Grecian tragedy, boffed about at the whim of the gods; as if he's the only person in the world tormented by the inner life . . .

–But we decide our actions, don't we? Thoughts – sure, there's no stopping – but actions we decide; action is calculated.

–And my father is guilty. For he *chose* to slam the door, to drive out to Wychwood; he *chose* to leave Mum and the bandaids, *Bladerunner*, et cetera . . . to rescue a family at the expense of his own – and not just once, not as if it's a whim – it was months, *choosing* to entertain a fantasy, *choosing* to pursue a world that existed only in his imagination. His imagination – yes, in his mind I'm sure it's the greatest tragedy ever told. But in reality – what: sitting at the table, distracted, pretending nothing was awry; hiding secret phone calls; driving Christina to school in some bizarre mockery of fatherhood.

–And then, worst of all: the nerve to ask Mum when *she* became cruel? As if she couldn't see any of it, the manipulation, his use of charity as a foil. As if desire was invisible, and not bursting from him in every direction. Did he not realise that desire, longing, disinterest – these are visible conditions; they are badges we wear, flags we raise, clearest of all to those who love us most.

'When did you become like this?' he says in the kitchen.

–Then turning to the bench cupboards, in case she sees something in his eye. And Mum's eyes wide with terror, because of course she *does* see, because all of us could see.

'Like what?' she says.

'Callous.'

Then snatching the phone with that awful sneer, as though he alone were capable of living beneath the surface of things; while she puddled in her trivial life, keeping house and trying to raise a son.

'Yes – of course Matt'll stay for the weekend,' he'd said. 'And we'd *love* to come – can we bring anything?'

Then slamming the phone down in great defiance and storming from the room, leaving Mum to totter in self-loathing, alone once again, tidying her hair and–

*

If I smash the fucking thing – what would he do?

If I walk across the room right now – What? Cower under sheets? Does he call for help?

–Surely people would understand . . .

*

Silence finally.

Monday, 18 January

CAN ONLY THINK of the clinic, the protesters outside with their signs and pickets. Christina with her head high. The poster on the wall: 'You are stronger than you know . . . Don't forget that.'

This may be my last entry for a while.

*

I did ask politely . . .

Saturday, 13 February

FEBRUARY THIRTEENTH. FOUR weeks. Nearly a month since anything of substance. In that time, I've changed rooms. The incident with Yoav has been sorted, I guess. I've apologised and offered to replace everything; I've been moved into a single room on the opposite side of the building. It's much the same, only the window looks directly into the rendering of the next-door apartments: a sad line of wattles attempting to hide the view – because I assume they want foliage in every direction. Still, it's quiet. I hear nothing.

For the record, Yoav left his iPod playing while he was in the shower, then began singing loudly the moment I switched it off. I suppose something snapped. I kicked in the door and began throwing his possessions at the curtain while he screamed and howled that I was attempting to take his life. I was tackled to the ground; it was very dramatic.

Gloria's been left devastated by the incident. All our progress since November, blown up in her face. I've regressed again.

'How long do you want to be in here?' she says, flushed and raising her voice. 'Have you contacted anyone? Friends? Connections to outside?'

I refrain from asking who she means exactly. Where are these people she speaks of, all so desperate for me to make contact? Does she not realise my old friends are little more than shades now? A collection of fabulous lives shimmering from my computer screen? Does she not realise I am the ghost at the feast? Why the hell would I put any of them through that?

She's becoming restless these days, though; I can see it in her manner. She thinks I'm not telling her the truth.

'Avoidance is a coping mechanism; not a long-term strategy.'

'Avoiding what?' I say, and she falls into aggrieved silence, as though I'm spending our sessions lying through my teeth.

Perhaps I am.

—In any case, to return to the question: I *have* made contact with the outside world, thank you very much; two weeks ago: Alinta finally replying to my message. It turns out that, rather than avoiding me, she'd been trekking in Tasmania, far from the clutches of the internet. She called wanting to meet for coffee, explaining that she lives close by. I explained my own arrangement and we settled on a visit. She was here yesterday.

It was quite enjoyable actually, without friction: she arrived and kissed my cheek; then we spent an hour in the garden, catching up, talking about our lives, the twists and turns. She's had no contact with Christina since high school – moved on, she says, went to medical school, forgot to travel, 'working working'. She's currently at the Centre for Indigenous Health on Nicholson Street, just a few doors from her sister's tattoo parlour. (And at this revelation, she points north-west, revealing a school of angelfish, swimming in bright colours across her wrist. It's beautiful artwork; the scars are gone.)

She asked how I'd spent my twenties and perhaps because there was no trepidation in her voice, I told her the truth: I've been here.

She listened without judgement or concern. Maybe it's true; she has 'seen it all'. Either way, she seemed to understand, nodding and building her miniature fortress of gum leaves. When I finished, she said it was past lunch and she had an afternoon shift, but she would visit again soon – it's only a short walk from her apartment.

I left her in the foyer, watching her trot up the driveway, still with that same bandy walk, her head craning forward. As she disappeared, I recalled how that head had once rested on my shoulder – only then, her hair had been different; not wavy and long, but clipped short. I remembered how coarse it had felt, sitting outside the clinic. How long did we sit for? A half-hour perhaps, me watching the poster through the window, of a woman high-diving off a cliff. Beneath it had said, 'You are stronger than you know ... Don't forget that.' And I'd read those lines over and over until they were meaningless, while Christina lay on a padded bed somewhere and our child was sucked into a tube and turned into medical waste.

Of course, this all happened weeks later ...

Before everything was discovered, that final Sunday at Wychwood was one of the best I can remember.

Mr Harvey had returned from the vet with a bandaged thigh and a cone around his neck, gingerly hopping from Aunty Carol's back seat as she exclaimed that until it was off, she 'weren't goin' nowhere'. It was a decision welcome to Christina and I, who desired only to be alone. Realising the short time, we took no pains to hide affection, walking hand in hand about the grounds and under the widow makers, the trees all seeming to bow in admission, adorned in the fading splendour unique to Sunday afternoons. Then on the neighbouring streets, we finally located my jacket, though so bloodied and morose that we tossed it immediately in a neighbour's bin, cackling all the way home – before retiring to the rumpus room, where we barely watched a film, huddled on the couch, rekindling the sacred hearth we'd discovered in her room only two nights prior.

By early evening, I was on the train in the dark, back to civilisation, my head a mess of pining and logistics. Then at home, I was slamming my bedroom door and throwing myself on the bed – though far from any state of despair. See, bumbling through Carrum Station, my phone had shuddered and come to life:

Mum and AG out. I'm bored. What happens now?

The words had been a shot of adrenaline and I'd read them several times in a giddying rush. Then I'd begun to muse – all the way up the Frankston line as the sun disappeared behind the roofs – so that by the time I'd thrown my bags down and slumped on my bed, I had a plan for navigating a romance in the rough waters of distance and secrecy. It went like this:

Christina, who was back at school the following week, soon developed a mysterious 'feminine illness', which attacked with ferocity every second Tuesday or Thursday afternoon, making it impossible for her to participate in the extracurricular sport programs. Meanwhile, I took the liberty of joining a fictional soccer team which, despite never playing a match, still trained every second Tuesday or Thursday for several hours after school. On these afternoons, I would leave school at lunchtime, citing appointments with an imaginary dentist, then take a train to Kewfield, where I waited in an alley behind the school until Christina found a moment to escape.

Despite its obvious faults, the plan was remarkably successful. Without fail, Christina and I met at least once a week, walking to Fred Smith Reserve and lying under the trees; chatting and watching the people go by; sharing cigarettes and becoming intimate on the swings, and other assorted clichés of abandon.

I suppose that time ought to be one of my most prized memories, not something glossed over in a couple of lines. Unfortunately, recalling it now sparks little more than self-loathing; the most profound disgust at my ignorance. For while they were good days, and the plan was successful, I can't help thinking that it could have remained so – if only I'd noticed the fact that Christina's symptoms were becoming authentic.

She was beginning to feel 'actually sick', she'd said early on, though it was nothing to worry about. It was the season after all: deep into winter, the temperature was next to nothing and everyone was getting it, so we thought little of it – except that she didn't have a cold so much as a kind of nausea. One afternoon, lying in the slide, she'd suddenly put her hand on her chest and rushed to the bin. I'd brought a pack of Marlboro Lights and it struck me that she hadn't taken a drag. She told me that until recently, it had only happened in the mornings. Then there'd been a silence and she'd seemed terrified.

I have no idea why it didn't occur to me then – on numerous occasions, a woman had come to my school with hilarious and embarrassing PowerPoint displays detailing the symptoms of pregnancy and how to avoid it. Yet, nothing had clicked. Instead, I'd put a hand on Christina's back and explained how in Psychology, we'd been learning about the bizarre manifestations of stress – and did she know that a blindfolded man's flesh could actually blister at the touch of an ice cube? She'd leaned into the bin again and that had been the end of the conversation.

Eventually a call came. I'll never forget Dad walking so casually to the phone, picking it up and moving his eyes to me. He'd barely spoken, turning white in surprise – Mum looking up from the sink, imitating his expression.

'Yes, I will,' he'd said and put the phone down. He'd remained staring at the wall a few seconds, then turned and had no idea where to even start.

'For God's *sake*! Do you even *think*!?' Mum had roared in front of the fire. 'How can you be so *stupid* – so *thoughtless*!?' She was pacing back and forth as Dad stood feebly behind. 'Don't they come to schools and *teach* you about this? I thought they gave *lessons* on it. Don't they . . . *Jesus*!' She paused for a moment, newly perplexed. 'When did it even *happen*? I mean . . .'

'They think it's ten weeks,' Dad put in.

'*Ten weeks?*' she shrieked. 'Wh–' and then I could see the clocks spinning as her face became dark.

In the end, everything came out: what happened at the party, where I'd been spending Tuesdays and Thursdays, the fact that the Rippon Lea Red Legs didn't exist; Mr Harvey, the vet, the whisky and the workshed – the whole mess spilling out, fuelling and sparking to set my mother ablaze.

The news was, of course, a meteor for everyone. But unlike Dad, who would inevitably disappear into himself, letting trauma wash like a balm, Mum – usually so quiet, so passive – sparked into a rage like I'd never seen, true fire and brimstone; pacing back and forth and flashing her hands like a wizard conjuring a thunderstorm, reeling punishments that were terrible and comprehensive: our assignations to end, of course, banned from all contact. I was curfewed and my phone was confiscated – not even the landline. No friends, no visits, nowhere by myself. In fact, I was to be chaperoned everywhere, *everywhere*, was she making herself clear? And if I wasn't outside that goddam school by three twenty-five every afternoon then *God* help my soul!

She'd circled like a predator, spitting and hurling words like she wished they were barbs. 'Do you hear me? You don't *see* her. You don't *speak* to her. Anymore. Ever. Got it?' Wanting it to hurt, *desperate* for it to hurt. Wanting me to cry and shriek and brandish my injuries.

–But it came to nothing. That day, all the howling curses, the battery and punishment, all of it was ineffective. That day everything simple washed away. Because of course, the call had been news to me too. I was as stunned as anyone. And Mum's electrical storm was nothing against the thoughts whirlpooling as I stood trying to understand what it meant, trying to make sense of what had happened – going over what I'd seen, what she'd said and what I remembered – all the memories suddenly returning with new significance: recalling the park where Christina had vomited in the bin, where her hormone levels had increased, causing her to feel 'actually sick', refusing cigarettes because – suddenly the PowerPoints were clear! – she had begun the *Mental, Physical & Experiential Journey of Birth*: the fertilised egg had implanted itself in the lining of the uterus and was developing into placentae and embryo. Soon her taste was going to alter. Soon she would urinate frequently and experience tender, swollen breasts and darkening areolae. Her belly would expand, and in the quadrangle she would be called a slut and a whore. People would stand up for her on the train; they would shake their heads. She would be pulled right and pulled left and told to keep it and not to keep it and the experience would be terrifying. Even from the outset, hadn't she looked up from the bin and been terrified? Of course she had; terrified because she'd known all along what it was.

And yet, here was my mother, thundering in the lounge room how we were to be cut off ('You don't *see* her. You don't *speak* to her. Anymore. Ever.'), pacing around and swooping back aggressively – revealing herself to be cruel in a way I'd never suspected.

I'm not sure what I felt more contempt for that day: her savage determination to sweep everything under the rug, or Dad with his impotence; sitting feebly behind, turning to me again and again with that bemused expression that I don't think has ever entirely left his face: stone disbelief that the catastrophe of a boy hunched before him might actually be something he was responsible for.

Either way though, my response wasn't eruptive; nor was it internal and self-indulgent. I didn't shout and slam doors and hurl abuse. I didn't sit shell-shocked at the real-isation of everything collapsed about me; shaking my head in useless bewilderment. No – I was only numb; trying to understand what was happening, the harrowing reality of Christina pulled right and pulled left. Where was she now? Sitting in a room somewhere, terrified and alone as my mother thrashed in front of me.

'Christ!' she was saying now, tossing her hands in appeal to the cosmos. 'What is wrong with that *family!*'

Somehow the line threw me from my reverie, causing me to snap into the moment, leaving Christina trem-bling where she was and returning to the lounge room in fresh resentment. It was Mum's audacity, I think: to fling judgement from the ruins of her own marriage. To assume moral dominion. I felt rage suddenly boil in me. For how often had she knocked on my door this last year, creeping in to rest her head on my shoulder? How many films had she brought home, huddled beside me as Dad flew to Wychwood, pretending it was fun, just us two, spending the night in? Now what – we were discarding Christina in the same fashion?

'I'm sorry – is something *funny?*'

There was a pause. Mum was looking at me wide-eyed, and I realised my lip had curled up in a sneer.

'Is this all a joke to you?' she said, her face awash in dis-belief, flinging her hand out. 'Matt, there's a young girl out there who you've–'

'Don't pretend you care for her.'

The gravity of my tone caused her to falter, her eyes

narrowing as she studied my face, recognising a fury she'd seen before, though never from me; lowering her voice.

'What's happened to you?'

'Nothing's happened,' I said. 'I've just realised that Dad's right, isn't he?'

'What?'

Now she spun around, derailed by the unexpected liaison, finding herself surrounded. But Dad was equally surprised and she turned back.

'What do you mean? What's right? Why is he right?'

I shrugged, hardening my eyes.

'You are callous.'

I admit I enjoyed watching the wound slip across her face, the slow and tragic realisation that she was not a protagonist in my story. For of course, in her mind, up to this moment, we'd been twin conspirators against the world, side by side in the computer room. I'd been the tender oasis she slunk to. Now her voice dropped to a whisper, barely audible.

'Matthew . . .'

It was a plea, an entreaty, beseeching me to recall an alliance. But I didn't relent, I held her eye, the thought of Christina steeling my derision.

'What? I would have thought of all people, you should know what it's like to be thrown away–'

But I barely got to finish because she slapped my face.

There was a crack, followed by an awful pause, Dad shuffling to his feet somewhere beside me.

'Lynette.'

Mum looked around, as though surprised that he was there; then back at me, wide-eyed and scared. I nodded slowly, raising a hand to my cheek, feeling the sting and heat fall away, leaving a cold half-moon. Then I turned and made for my room, not hearing the appeal that followed me down the hall, battering against my door.

I'd lain on the bed with my head hazy in disbelief, picturing Christina in the park, distressed as she looked up from the bin.

Who was there to help her now? I wondered. With Connie so drunk she'd burn to death – who? Ali, with her own mania? Aunty Carol, who was there for charity? School coordinators? Doctors?

No, she was alone, as she'd been at the roadside after her father's funeral. The only person in the world who wasn't fragile: suddenly terrified.

'They're *kids*!' Mum was bellowing now, trying to be definitive but with all the venom disappeared, her voice trembling instead with that unique rage we save only for ourselves.

'. . . *kids, for God's sake!*'

I listened to the words fill the house, paying no attention. I was picturing Christina at the roadside, and wondering who would save her from the rocks? Not that there was much to wonder, though. For I already knew the answer.

THOUGH IT WOULD end up as the making of my parents, our little incident in the lounge room, I will always be ashamed of my behaviour. For my goal that evening was simply to hurt my mother. And I was astoundingly successful. So much so, in fact, that while the sting of her palm faded in a moment, my words are still reverberating across the years – even to this day; words I barely remember – trailing her like a shadow so that no amount of time at my bedside, no amount of love and support will ever rid her of the suspicion that she is responsible for my illness.

See, I believe that no matter how much we as humans understand that events are beyond our control, when it comes to awful things happening to loved ones, it is a most human tendency to later imbue ourselves with the power to avoid them; to secretly believe we caused them. And in Mum's mind, she is the reason I'm in this room. She believes she lost herself a moment, directing me on a terrible path. And she has never forgiven herself.

In this way, I suppose she and Connie are twins, tossed in the same miasma of guilt. Only while Connie lived the dream of Wychwood, Mum visits daily, washes my clothes, bringing food, bringing plants, caring for them, taking me out, walks and cafes, ordering for me, paying for me, raising her voice as my protector.

–Even this afternoon, she flitters at the windowsill, explaining how she's been changing the sheets in my room, still, without me there; still opening the blinds and windows every morning, still vacuuming; still this, still that.

'–Oh! And you know that old desk?' she suddenly warns, as if she's remembered a death in the family. 'The one that was in the back room? Anyway, don't worry – it's in your room at the moment because Dad's been using it for calls – but . . . It'll be gone before you're back. Promise.'

She winks.

'Be like you never left.'

This last part's a joke, of course, but I believe her entirely, watching anxiety return to her face as she studies the control panel on my bedframe, and wondering exactly what she would give to return to that particular time . . .

Either way, she hasn't forgiven herself.

–And already that night, as I was lying in bed with my cheek still tender, you could hear guilt festering: her voice loud and trembling.

'They're *kids*!' she was howling. 'Don't you realise they've got no idea what they're doing?'

I recall listening to her words and burning with indignance, with fury at her assumptions. After all, she was right: Christina and I had made the oldest mistake in the book. We'd been fools, caught up in neon lights and trembling insecurities, forgetting the key message of the PowerPoint display.

But of course, we are at our most judgemental when we blame ourselves; and so that night I lay under the sheets with my loathing focused solely on the voices in the living room, wishing they would tear themselves apart, wishing they would shut up and start throwing punches, wishing they were dead – no – wishing *I* was dead so they could be inconsolable and I could be a spectral wraith, chuckling behind in delicious revenge at their sorrow.

–but mostly though, on that September night in 2002, I was simply wishing they would go to bed. Hoping it would be soon. Waiting and praying with a time in my head: 10.48. Four numbers plastering my brain in bold-face type: 10.48.

See, for all the crashing and banging, a lack of technical understanding had rendered Mum's punishments ineffective. They'd taken my phone and cut me off, but having been banished to my room, I'd immediately been able to jump on the computer and contact Ali via MSN. (xo*AlienTA!*xo) When I logged on, she was already there, waiting to fill me in.

Christina was twelve weeks, she'd said; the nausea beginning a month into term – but she'd been too scared to speak out. Making matters worse, the sickness we'd invented had been 'to do with her cycle', an ironic lie that had made it impossible for her to reveal that actually, there was nothing going on down there at all. And so she'd continued to be sick, hiding the evidence and praying to God it wasn't what she already knew it was. In the end it was her roommate Sophie, of all people, who came to the rescue. Having caught Christina throwing up in the toilets, she'd complained to Head of House that 'if people are being bulimic, could they at least do it in the disabled toilets so it doesn't affect the rest of us?'

Christina was confronted and forced to take a test and the truth had come out. By this time, however, she'd begun to show and so the school decided it best to remove her from all classes until 'the situation resolved itself'. Connie was then notified, and Christina rushed to an appointment at Marie Stopes, where she'd learned it was too late for a medical abortion, and that Thursday was the earliest slot for vacuum aspiration, and that it would all be over in two days . . .

I thanked Ali for the information and asked her to phone Christina, to somehow arrange a meeting that night. I had to see her, I said; she needed me. Ali said she'd try and signed off. Then a half-hour pacing the room before a reply had shot up on my screen:

Midnight.

I'd thanked her and signed off.

Now it was nine-thirty and I lay under the covers with 10.48 in my head. The last train from Highett Station.

It took an hour for the house to finally go quiet. The sound of footsteps and slamming doors. Then darkness. I tried to hear, but couldn't, my parents' voices having drizzled away to harsh, dreaded silence.

I lay still for another few minutes, just to be sure. Then, at twenty to eleven, I couldn't wait anymore and flew out of bed, scurrying to the back door, slipping out and inching it closed behind me. Outside was deeply still, every noise seeming to crash in the silence, and so I snuck lightly by the windows alongside the house, trying to keep low, peering up into empty rooms – all darkness – creeping my way to the front of the house, where I paused, and realised my mistake.

My parents weren't in bed. They were on the balcony. I'd misread the silence, the slamming doors. Now I froze and held my breath. But they hadn't seen me. They were standing side by side with their hands on the railing, having said everything and now fallen into silence. I watched them peering out at separate things; apart, but with an air of serenity far from the wreckage I'd imagined. Now Dad sighed, moving to her, tentative, touching her hand. I watched her not recoil, and let him, as though she couldn't feel. Then his other hand, crossing her back – he was behind her, slipping his arms over her belly. I watched her put her arms over his, still peering away into the dark; both of them peering together. He was humming a tune, something I didn't recognise; lightly at first, just trying it on, with his nose in her hair. I could hear the sound creeping down, only just, floating out and disappearing somewhere between them and the dark road. A tune I couldn't place. Something only Mum seemed to know.

Suddenly, I felt resentment surge again, fresh in the face of their harmony. Their betrayal. I almost yelled out, then thought of Christina, waiting for me. I slipped back around the side of the house, scaling the neighbour's fence and crawling over their lawn. I took a final look – Mum with her head resting into his shoulder now – then flew out into the street.

Winter was well and truly over, but that night, racing for the station, I wished I'd brought a coat. Disembarking at Hastings, I found it had rained and my breath was billowing in foggy plumes. I shot through the barriers and under the streetlamps along Greneila Road, my feet slapping the grimy asphalt, scampering like a rat towards the glow of Kewfield Secondary, the great building looming in the dark as I approached.

The boarding house was over the road and as I arrived, I saw that all the lights were off. I looked at the curtains slumped in the windows and wondered which one was Christina's. Everywhere was silent, deathly; only the sound of cars passing on a highway somewhere far off.

–And then something else. Suddenly there was another noise, a whistling behind a neighbouring fence. I turned and something white billowed and moved. Christina was standing in the next-door garden, a ghost in a dressing gown. I crossed the road and she came to life, rushing to the fence. I leaned across, trying to kiss her, but she threw up a hand.

'Not here,' she said, before I could speak.

'Where?'

'Wait.'

She looked away, as if there'd been a sound. But there was nothing. Then she dashed out of the driveway and into the side street.

I followed, watching her skip across the road like a phantom, her shadow stretching in the orange light, rushing back to her moccasins. Somehow they made no sound. Everything was silent; only my feet slapping the asphalt. Christina took a right into an alley and I followed, between tall fences and trees draping over. Halfway down, she stopped and waited for me to catch up. Then we stood face to face, barely able to see.

'We got in shit this time,' she said.

Her face was a pale blur, her voice unaffected.

'I'm sorry; I didn't know,' I said.

'It's okay.'

'When did you find out?'

She shrugged. 'I knew. Sorry. I should have said.'

There was silence.

'Can I feel it?'

'There's nothing there.'

'At all?'

She put my hand on her stomach. It seemed bloated, taut; but the same. I took it away.

'And it's Thursday?'

'Yes.'

'Okay.'

'Twelve o'clock.'

I nodded.

'Are you coming?' she asked.

'Of course – shouldn't I?'

'Do you want to?'

'Yeah.'

'Then okay.'

'But not if you don't want me to.'

She looked at me in the dark – shadows where her eyes should have been. 'If you're not comfortable, then say . . .'

'I am.'

'Are you wanting me to ask you to come?'

'No.'

She looked at me fixedly. 'I want you to come.'

'I'm not asking for that.'

'Then why ask a question if you won't take the answer? I said I want you to be there.'

'I thought you might need someone to take you in.'

'Oh.' Now she faltered, looking behind up the alley, then at her feet. 'I've got Aunty Carol taking me; Ali's meeting me. Mum too, I think. Sorry, I thought you couldn't–'

'Don't be sorry.'

'Is that why you wanted to meet?'

'Not really.'

Why *had* I come though? Suddenly, it seemed like a mistake.

'I still want you to be there,' she offered.

'I will.'

'It's only fifteen minutes anyway.'

'I'll be there.'

We fell silent then. I wondered what the hell I was doing – all the bravado of daring to meet, the chance to be gallant in a crisis, where had it gone? In every scenario, I'd imagined her wounded, needing me; I'd been her defender. Now here we were in the cold and wet – and I was keeping her awake.

'What happens afterwards?' I asked.

She shrugged. 'I guess I go back to school,' then under her breath, '. . . deal with that.'

'You know this isn't your fault.'

She considered for a moment. 'Yes, it is.'

'No!' I said, and squeezed her hands to show I was a pillar of strength. But it was a gesture too banal and uninspired to mean anything; it became awkward in the dark.

'Well, anyway,' she said, 'I have to deal with it.'

'. . .'

She slid her hands away as I searched the alley for a response. There was nothing but trees hooding us in, wet pavement leading into the dark. It was true: she would have to deal with it.

'We could take to the seas . . . ?'

It was all I could think to say. The joke hung in the air, absurd and incongruous; then fell flat, leaving behind its kernel of truth. I could see her looking through the dark.

'That's a bad joke.'

'I know. I'm sorry.'

She sighed. 'The day after tomorrow, it'll be done. We just have to wait till then – it's not a big deal; it's not like I'm the first person to do it.'

Her smile was brave. She was lying to herself.

'It's okay to be afraid,' I said.

'I'm not. It's a procedure. Thousands of people do it. It's nothing.'

'It's not nothing.'

'Yes, it *is*!'

The hedge behind me shuffled and a possum rushed out along the fence, disappearing in the dark and leaving Christina's words to hang. For a time, she watched where it had gone, a tree shaking further down the alley.

'Don't tell me it isn't nothing,' she said. 'I want it to be nothing. I want it to mean nothing.'

The edge in her voice gave it away. So this was her defence then: annulment.

'What?' She was holding my eye. 'Would it be better if I cried? Should I break down?'

'Shut up.'

She was right though. I'd wanted to grab her and hold her in my arms, to shelter and smother and put all the pieces together again. But the idea was laughable; she was already assembled.

'This is not a hard decision for me,' she said, putting a

hand on my arm, squeezing my shoulder. 'I'm sorry if you thought it would be.'

I scoffed at the insinuation. 'That's not what I'm saying.'

'Then what is it?'

'Nothing. It's good – I'm glad it's . . .'

We paused a long time.

'I'm sorry,' she said finally. 'I have to go back in.'

'I'll be there on Thursday.'

'Okay. I'm glad you're coming. Thanks for asking to meet; it means a lot.'

She leaned in to kiss me. But if there'd been any fire left, her lips put it out. She walked away, becoming a blur and evaporating.

I stood awhile, still seeing her apparition against the fence, wondering why I'd come at all. She'd been right, of course; it hadn't been for her. I'd come to be a hero, to be required, needed.

Love her, won't you?

But what use is a hero without a disaster?

I started down the alley. No need for heroes. She was together already, unfazed – almost indifferent. Yes, that was it: indifferent. As if she was a Replicant.

Monday, 15 February

HORRIBLE DAY. HORRIBLE Wednesday: sitting in a panic through interminable classes; then chained to my desk after school with an essay on *Romeo and Juliet* – Mum having abandoned support and understanding for less traditional displays of maternal upbringing; namely surveillance and dictatorship. I'd been confined to my room, forced to analyse the dramatic function of Mercutio's Queen Mab speech ('Five hundred words by six-thirty!') as Christina quivered alone somewhere at the prospect of tomorrow, cradling a belly swollen beneath a thatchwork of fading incisions. I recall trying to distract myself, trying to concentrate – but concentrating was impossible; the language was stupid and the characters were stupid and I kept drifting off, the Capulet mansion suddenly reassembling as Wychwood; sword-fighting in the driveway – my thoughts swooping around, spiralling and pecking until I returned at the bottom of the page, confused and mouthing the words, 'Love her, won't you?'

Dinner too: sitting in silent protest – because I could be forced to the table but I could not be forced to speak!

Then being sent to bed early and lying awake for hours, tossing and turning – falling asleep only to dream of meeting Christina again; chasing her fluttering spectre through the alley, heavy with child. 'Should I come?' I yelled, the question causing her belly to swell like a balloon, her scars splitting one by one to reveal the same bruised flesh of the plums in Connie's orchard, gaping wider until everything exploded in a shower of snowflakes that sprinkled dreamily across the roadside paddock. Then she was at my side and the procedure was over, deep stains beneath her stomach and gripping the hand of a young girl: 'It's okay,' she crooned, offering my hand to the child. 'It wasn't a hard decision . . .' And the three of us raced out onto the grass, catching snowflakes on our tongues until the early hours of the morning when I suddenly awoke, breathless and tortured.

The morning of, I'd woken at first light; Mum driving me to school in determined silence. She parked outside, pulling the handbrake and turning to me.

'Three twenty-five.'

I'd nodded and looked out the window: students were skipping through the gates, clutching bags and clunky science projects. Somehow they all seemed impossibly young.

'Matty . . .'

I caught the tenderness in Mum's voice and looked around, finding her steely façade crumbled a moment. She was gripping the steering wheel and peering ahead.

'You know I'm . . .' She paused, breathed, looked at me. 'You know we're doing this for you . . .'

It was the same plea of two nights before, as though she wished I could just see that really, at the heart of it all, it was us against the world.

But I could only see her on the balcony with Dad.

'Stop trying to make yourself feel better,' I said, and got out of the car.

'Alright, fine,' she yelled behind me. 'Three twenty-five.'

'Guess so.'

'No, not *guess—*'

But I'd already slammed the door and was walking quickly away, lest I be unable to refrain from blurting the correction that in fact, no, she probably wouldn't see me.

When the recess bell chimed, I was already slipping out the back gate to catch the train into the city. As a precaution, I'd thrown a coat over my uniform, but no one even looked. Swanston Street was a circus of people rushing in every direction who couldn't care less that I wasn't at school – or that I might have been a father. (Strange how the word kept swimming to the surface . . .) Plunging through, I took a right on Collins Street. The clinic was on Victoria Parade and I'd hoped to buy her something on the way, just a little something, just to say . . . What though? Compassion? Were we commiserating? Surely not. Up the hill, Louis Vuitton opened in the windows of the Grand Hyatt, where I paused for a moment before an impossibly expensive designer bag. Further on, there were engagement rings in Tiffany's, then sympathy balloons in the newsagent. The doors opened and a lavish woman emerged, glaring like I'd sneezed in a concerto. She crossed the footpath and I imagined her without her rings, spread on a table with an MVA between her legs.

In dearth and excess, the procedure was terrifying, I thought, and turned for the newsagent. But of course there were no balloons in the newsagent, only a wall of cards expressing a variety of irrelevant sentiments, save: *'It's a boy!'* and *'. . . with deepest sympathies',* both of which seemed equally inappropriate. I settled on a Coke and paid in change, shuffling off towards Victoria Parade.

I found Ali waiting at the corner, smoking rapidly and jittering a kneecap.

'What are you doing out here?' I asked.

'Waiting for you.'

'Is she *in* already?'

'They've pushed it to one-thirty.'

There was an edge in her voice.

'Why, is she alright?'

'She's fine.' She took a drag. 'There's a protest outside.'

'What?'

'I know.'

She exhaled an enormous plume of smoke. 'Want a drag?'

'Please.'

She handed me the butt and we smoked in silence. It was breezy now, the trees on the median strip budding in light green. A tram arrived and the passengers alighted, scuttling in every direction. Ali looked at my face. 'It's not a funeral, yeah?'

'I know.'

'You look like it is.'

'Do I?'

There was a pause. Over the road, the tram dinged and began scooting away. She punched my shoulder.

'Come on.'

*

There were maybe thirty or forty people blocking the alley to the clinic, Ali swearing under her breath as we turned the corner. Clearly, more had arrived and now they stood in a smouldering huddle, waving signs and peddling facts to passers-by. No one was engaging though; pedestrians with their eyes down, striding fast to avoid the mass that seemed to quiver and ripple like something ready for prey.

It was a sharp woman who saw us first, her eyes flicking up and seeming to divine our purpose. At once, a wind swept through the group and they began to mobilise, turning like a phalanx and beginning a chant: 'Abortion stops a beating heart! Abortion stops a beating heart!' They grew louder as we approached, their faces angry, determined, until suddenly the sharp woman reached forward like a proboscis and thrust a pamphlet in our faces. For a moment, I was blinded by the remains of a splattered foetus in a petri dish. 'Abortion stops a beating heart!' Ali slapped her hand away and the woman reared back before shooting in again and calling her a murderer. Then we were pushing through and the chanting fell away to jeery slander, horrible pamphlets appearing in every direction. All I could do was bend forward and raise a forearm, following Ali's heels as she weaved among the protesters. I kept my head low, feeling things swing and flap about me, not daring to look up again until we were halfway down the alley. Then a sharp bleat sounded from the mouth of Victoria Parade and I glanced back.

The crowd were turning away, their jeers subsiding. Something had pulled their attention. It was only as I stepped through the door that I saw the police car pulling up onto the footpath.

*

Finding no one at reception, Ali and I followed into the waiting room. What greeted us was an exact replica of my doctor's practice: clean as an infant's bedroom with threaded chairs and squares of blue carpet. Ringing the walls was a series of encouraging posters, each with a quote and a spectacular view. When we entered, the room was empty, save Connie, who sat against the far wall beneath a huge wave crashing into a promontory. It said: 'Don't let fear choose your destiny.' She was haggard and disoriented, listening to the sounds of the protest drifting in the window.

'Is it already happening?!'

Ali had rushed up to her; Connie seeming to float into reality.

'They've gone in.'

'When?'

'Just now. Where did you go?'

'I thought it's supposed to be one-thirty?'

'They have to close early.'

She looked to the window, the chant swelling up again: 'Abortion stops a beating heart!'

'Please!' Ali said. 'Can't we just see her quickly before?'

'Only allowed one person.'

'Yeah, *me* – I was going to be with her!'

'Carolyn's in there; you'll have to–'

Then she paused, turning to where I was still waiting by the door, life appearing to drain into her face.

At that moment, Aunty Carol appeared beside a doctor who was speaking with her hands ('. . . and she may be groggy for an hour or so . . .'). They stopped in the doorway, frowning and darting their eyes to the windows, to Connie, to us. There was music playing, I realised; something easy and relaxed.

'You need to leave,' Connie said.

'Ah sorry–' the doctor said, having paused mid-sentence. 'Have you seen reception?'

'We'll be two minutes!' Ali was adamant. 'We can duck in.'

But Connie's face was taut now, an arrow drawn towards me. There was a silence; Aunty Carol's eyes growing wide in surprise.

('Abortion stops a beating heart!')

'How dare you be here!' Suddenly Connie lunged towards me, spitting her words. 'How *dare* you . . .'

'Con!' Aunty Carol moved to intercept.

'Are you proud of yourself?'

I was stammering back in surprise.

'I let you into my *house*!'

'Let's remember where we are.' I watched Aunty Carol take her shoulders, the doctor raising her hands. 'I understand we might feel–'

'Twelve *weeks*!' Connie howled. 'What did you think was going to happen? What did you–'

'Con!' Aunty Carol was trying to look in her eyes; Ali sidestepping like a boxer.

'I just want him to say something.' Connie brushing her sister away, glaring at me. 'Here we are, Matt; you're here now, you've come now. *Say* something–'

'I didn't know! I'm s–'

'That's not *good enough*!'

'EXCUSE ME!'

All of us paused. The doctor stood imperiously now, with her hands in the air. She let them drop. 'We *cannot* have this in here.'

Then there was silence, as the receptionist returned from the bathroom.

*

Later, Connie and I stood in the laneway, having been kindly asked to leave. Aunty Carol was inside apologising and Ali had taken the hint and wandered up to look at the commotion. On Victoria Parade, the pro-choicers had arrived and now two factions huddled either side of a police car, baring signs and taunting each other. The lane was no-man's land. Connie watched with her cardigan pulled around against the cold. From behind, she almost seemed to be smiling.

'I just thought you would have got in contact,' she said.

'I wanted to,' I replied, wondering if an excuse had ever sounded as pathetic. 'My parents took my phone . . .'

In the protest, someone had yelled the words, 'Her body; her choice!' and now the phrase began to repeat, floating to us on a tide of angry voices.

('Her body; her choice!')

'You could have though,' she said. 'If you'd wanted.'

I didn't answer and she nodded for me.

The chant was gathering steam. ('Her body; her choice!') And something else too now, growing underneath – a counter muddying the sound.

'God!' Connie sighed. 'You didn't have a clue? No idea?'

'No.'

'I thought they taught it. When *I* was at school, they–'

'They did. We just didn't think.'

Now she laughed, sardonic and disappointed, throwing up her hands. 'Well, that's just stupid then, isn't it?'

('Her body; her choice!' Voices straining, as if they were being overcome.)

'I gotta say, Matt. I thought you were better than that. I mean, you can't . . . People are affected by your actions. You need to *think*.' And I saw her eyes had begun to shine, pools gathering at the bottom. As she blinked them away, I recognised the other sound – it was the Pro-life chant re-emerging ('Abortion stops a beating heart!'), the words bellowing across the laneway.

'We met the other night,' I said.

'Huh?'

'Christina and I.'

The sight of her tears had unnerved me.

'Tuesday night,' I said. 'We met outside the boarding house. She didn't say?'

'No,' Connie whispered, 'she didn't.'

Up the lane, a woman was running across the no-man's land. A swell of voices erupted: chants flung wildly, the words beginning to merge and intertwine.

'I can't see her,' I continued. 'I had to wait till Mum and Dad were asleep . . .'

'On Tuesday?'

'Yes.'

'Right. And what did you hope to achieve by that?'

'Huh?'

The shouting mashed together, becoming so loud. ('Her body . . . stops a beating heart! Her body!') A megaphone barking now; blue light flicking in the windowsills.

'Hmm?' Connie raised her eyebrows, something cold crossing her face.

'What did I want to *achieve*?'

'Yes.' She shrugged. 'The damage is done, Matt. Can you not see that?'

For a moment, we stood looking at each other, Connie defiant; the shouts sailing over her head. ('Abortion stops . . . her choice!')

'But I love her,' I said.

('Her beating heart! Her choice!')

'I love her.'

Connie's head seemed to shake, like there'd been a glitch.

'Don't you know that?'

She was motionless.

'You *know* I do,' I said. 'That's why I'm here, isn't it? There's nothing I can do – I know that. I fucked up. I *know* I fucked up. Right? But I'm not going to sit back and let her be alone in it; I want to know she's okay – I don't want her to be alone. Is that wrong?'

Now Connie nodded absently.

'Well,' she said. 'I did.' Then, blinking back: 'Of course, yes, I knew that. I just didn't think . . .'

('Her choice!')

And here she turned away again, like the news hadn't changed a thing. And I saw she was crying now. For what, though? Who? Her daughter?

'Are you okay?'

'Yes.' She was pressing her eyes. 'Yes, I'm just . . .' Suddenly she shot a finger out. 'I mean, listen to *that*!'

The chants were colliding, megaphones wailing overhead, snapping orders into the crowd.

'Listen to *that*!' Connie bellowed over the noise. 'All I hope is she can't hear *that* in there.' And now she looked with accusation.

But I didn't believe it. She was drawing heaving breaths, trying to make it so I couldn't see. I thought of Alek's boxes ransacked in the workshed.

'Is it even sinking in?' she said. 'What you've done? Because it doesn't *look* like it – *Yes!* You fucked up. *Yes!* And I can't actually see . . . Are you taking it in?'

'I'm sorry,' I said, and she laughed once more, this time because I'd sounded pathetic. And she shook her head and perhaps remembered I was fifteen.

('Her body stops a beating heart!')

'You lied to us, Matt.' She mashed a tear in defiance. 'You lied to me. I thought you were responsible.'

'I know,' I said. 'I'm sorry – but what do you want me to do? Lie down and die?'

She paused as some other thought came to her. 'I'm disappointed,' she said, her voice detached. 'I . . .'

But she trailed off.

('Her beating heart!')

Something had dropped in her, as though she'd suddenly realised that all along she'd been losing.

'I'm sorry Alek was sick,' I said.

For a second, she almost seemed to nod. She was looking out to Victoria Parade, not at the protest, but elsewhere – to middle distance where visions played that only she could see.

'Tell Carolyn I'll be at the car.'

I watched her disappear in the crowd, now spilling into the alley, and turned back to the clinic. Through one of the windows, I could make out a poster of a girl high-diving from a cliff. Beneath, it said: 'You are stronger than you know . . . Don't forget that.'

Only it didn't seem like anyone could survive such a fall.

SO DEPENDING ON the surgery, a patient may be invited to undergo 'conscious sedation' as a more comfortable alternative to general anaesthetic. This is where a patient is induced into a 'twilight state', which, as I understand it, is essentially hovering somewhere between being asleep and awake – a washy half-consciousness where you are able to respond and follow simple instructions. The major benefit is supposedly the recovery time; effects are less hazardous than general anaesthetic, and patients are unlikely to experience nausea or dizziness. Of course, there are always exceptions; headaches, memory loss, et cetera. Some patients have also claimed that, during sedation, they've been aware of things happening around them: people talking, moving about. Others have vivid dreams. Sometimes it's a combination.

To this day, I'm convinced this is what happened to Christina.

She'd had a dream in the procedure; something about a raft and the ocean – but in the lane afterwards, it seemed like it hadn't left her. 'We should take to the seas,' she'd whispered, giggling and pointing to the Pro-life signs as if they were sails flapping on little boats – then leaning close to my ear, 'Don't tell anyone.' She was drugged and groggy but somehow vibrant, leaning away with a secret wink that might have been a joke or a flitter of insanity. Aunty Carol had bolted for the car ('Meet us on the corner!') and left us standing before the throng, Ali on the opposite side, 'You okay, chickadee? Jesus, this is fucked!' Christina hanging off our arms, unsteady on her feet and yet primed and ready, pulling forward like a dog on a leash, 'Let's gooo!'

But by this time, there was no way through. The crowd had sealed the alley mouth and the police were driving them towards us. Cameras and reporters were everywhere; vans blocking passage to the Pro-choice banner. The event had become serious news. Later that evening, I would see myself swinging amid a confusion of protesters and the TV footage would have me expelled. But that was later. Now I was scanning the crowd, searching for a way through to Victoria Parade, Ali tapping furiously at my hand.

'I'm gonna see if I can get help, yeah?' she said, rushing ahead, then calling back, 'Just wait here a second!'

She took off up the lane to where a man held a corner of the Pro-choice banner. I watched her squeeze through and tap his shoulder. He turned and she spoke and he looked to us and to the road. Then the crowd converged and they were gone. A woman was climbing onto the roof of a van, raising her sign in anthemic gestures; all around, people were cheering and swarming as if she were a messiah.

'I woke up when they were doing it.'

Huge words, whispered under everything. I felt a heat on my neck and spun around.

'You *what?*'

Christina's eyes were flared as if the secret was mine now. 'There was a blue cloth on my stomach,' she said. 'They were all looking into it.'

'Who were?'

'Nurses, the doctor. I could see their hairnets.'

'Jesus,' I said. 'Look, we'll get you through in a sec.'

A policeman was shouting at the woman on the van – wild gestures like a silent film. It was her last warning; soon he would climb.

'I think I felt it come out.' Christina was biting her lip. 'Like a kind of surging.'

The woman rushed to the bonnet, hands grasping out like she was being pulled into the underworld. *A surging.* The word turned in my head and I could see it all: stirrups and a wet towel.

'Did it hurt?'

'No.' She grinned. 'They said it would.'

I realised she was shaking. But from the cold or from what, I had no idea – she was only in a T-shirt. I took my coat and draped it over her shoulders.

'That's good then, right?'

I was nodding eagerly, patting her back and praying for Ali to arrive and say something consoling, so I could escape. I hated myself.

'Squeeze my hand,' she said, putting her hand in mine.

I did.

'No. Hard.' She took my hand and crushed it. 'Feel that?'

'Ow.'

'There. Do mine. Harder.'

I squeezed.

'See?' she said.

'See what?'

'I don't feel it.' She was grinning, her fingers white and crushed. 'They said it was supposed to hurt.'

'What did they give you?'

'Nothing!' Her eyes were alight. She grabbed and made me squeeze harder. 'It should be hurting – but it isn't.'

'Hey,' I said, taking her hands. 'This isn't your fault, yeah? None of it.' A cliché – grasped like a life preserver.

'Still,' she said, 'it was supposed to.'

Now the policeman had slipped on the roof; he'd fallen squat and lost his authority, the crowd cheering and laughing.

'They gave me a needle,' she said, watching him writhe up. 'I felt the prick. I went to sleep. The nurse was asking what subjects I was doing and I couldn't say. The doctor was behind the sheet. Then I fell asleep.' She chuckled. 'I had a dream we were on a raft. But there were leeches everywhere and we were pulling them off – but more and more came. And you said, "We have to get out of here!" and you started tearing up the boards so we could use them for oars, but we started sinking.'

The policeman had jumped into the crowd. He was forcing them towards us again like a slow landslide, the megaphone sailing over the top.

'I woke up,' she continued, 'and they were all crowded around the sheet, looking in. And I felt a kind of rush – I think. Maybe; I don't know. But then I woke up later and I couldn't feel anything. I still can't now.'

'Well, that's good, isn't it?' I asked again. 'It's not something you want to feel.'

'Yeah,' she said. 'And look at this.'

She lifted her right hand to show a thick gauze covering the back. I assumed it was from a drip but she peeled it back to reveal the skin torn in deep nail scratches.

'What the fuck is that!?' I snatched at her hand.

'It's nothing,' she said, pulling away. 'See?' And she pressed her finger into the sore.

'Don't – what are you *doing?*'

'I don't feel it. Honestly!' She was becoming exhilarated, grazing the flesh again.

'Stop!' I grabbed for her hand and she clawed it back.

'Why?'

'*Why?*' I flailed for an answer. 'Because – can you just *not?*'

But then she was emotionless, peering in fascination, blood running under the adhesive. 'It's easier than you think,' she said, replacing the gauze. 'You think it's going to hurt but it's mostly the anticipation.'

I was shaking my head. 'Please. I don't want you to do it. Alright?' I turned to the crowd. 'Where the *fuck* is Ali?'

'Shh, hey,' Christina said, as if there was no reason to lose our heads. 'It's okay.'

'What did they give you?' I asked.

She looked at me in surprise.

'You think I'm high? Look at me; I'm not high. I just realised that I'm *scared. You're* scared – but it's the anticipation. Hey . . .' She was jiggling my hands. 'We should take to the seas.'

She was smiling and jiggling, trying to be cute. But the joke was as funny as it had been when I'd said it.

'Listen,' she said. 'I have twenty-five thousand dollars. From Dad. I get it when I'm eighteen. Hey . . .' She was veering down, making me look her in the eye. 'Hey. Look.'

She held up the gauze. 'We're only scared to do it. But if we just *do it—*'

She was gripping my hands like a zealot, her eyes swimming with the fervour of the protest.

'Where would we go?' I asked.

'It doesn't matter!'

All around, the noise was overwhelming, my hands sticky between my fingers. I smiled so she wouldn't be offended, wanting to believe her, but wary of the glazed intensity of her face.

'Hey.' Somehow she sensed it, taking my hands and drawing me in. 'It's alright.'

I let her do it – falling into the skin of her neck, burrowing in; her lips suddenly at my ear again. 'Shh,' she was saying, 'it's alright,' her voice soft and massive, blanketing the screams and cries – drowning the megaphone. 'It's okay.' I buried further in, desperate to believe her, desperate to be persuaded.

–only I was facing the window.

I opened my eyes to see the image of the woman high-diving. The words: 'You are stronger than you know . . . Don't forget that.' Somewhere behind the wall, a mess had been sucked into a bag. They'd told her it would hurt; she'd been terrified. And here I was: the saviour, buried in her neck.

'Shh,' she crooned. 'It's okay.'

I tore myself away, seething and ashamed.

'What is it?'

But I didn't answer, turning to the crowd, hot with self-loathing. Ali was here – thank God! – rushing towards us.

'It's fucked up there!' she yelled.

I strode to take command. 'Can we get through?'

'They can't move the van. What happened to your face?'

'Wha–' I lifted my hand and my cheek was rinsed in blood. I slapped it away. 'We'll have to push through,' I yelled – it was an order. Then to Christina: 'Are you right to walk?'

'I'm fine.'

'Then let's go.'

'It's lighter on that side!' Ali was pointing to the Pro-life crowd.

'Are you serious?' I said. 'No way!'

'It's the only way to get around.'

'But what if–'

'Whatever!' Christina interrupted. 'Let's just fucking goooo!'

Next thing, we were pushing through the crowd, Ali leading the way, ushering people aside and veering us into the Pro-life contingent. The atmosphere was precarious; police scouting nervously like owners in a dog park. No one was paying us attention though, training their eyes on the other side and assuming we were allies. As we neared the mouth of the alley, a path seemed to open and I could see the budding trees on the median strip. I took a step over the threshold, then turned and found myself looking directly into the eyes of the sharp woman.

For a second our eyes locked, her hand held aloft with a pamphlet.

–then it was a mess.

Breaking for Gisborne Street, we were immediately swarmed; in front, behind, beside, people falling upon us: 'Was it a girl!?' A man in a trilby appearing, his breath fetid, 'Abortion stops a beating heart!' Ali swung her arm, 'Piss off!', but he was already gone and a woman was thrusting in her face, 'What was her *name*?'

'Abortion stops a beating heart!' The chant had sprung up again and I threw a hand to Christina, 'Don't listen to them!', but she couldn't hear. People everywhere were turning and realising and approaching; Samaritans, too: 'Get a hobby, dickhead!' This a young woman slapping a Pro-life sign. 'Get a fucking *hobby*!' 'Yeah, reeeal nice!' a man behind – and I watched him turn like a cheerleader and throw his arms up as the chanting swelled. Both sides were mobilising now, like a reaction broken out. ('Racist, sexist, anti-gay! Right-wing bigots, go away!') Police were approaching, wide-eyed; cameras and reporters trying to get something. Ali's phone went off. I saw her reach for it and then she was obscured – an enormous image of nondescript flesh and an umbilical cord. 'Murderer!' ('Racist, sexist, anti-gay!') 'What was her *name*!' A woman shrieking like her dog was run over. Still we forced through, the crowd following like a swarm of locusts, pulling and reaching; everyone seething, wanting to say something, to make their point – to save us or to slander us. 'No, no, we *can't*!' Ali was screaming – Aunty Carol had dumped the car somewhere; she wanted us to wait. I saw police clambering towards us, pushing people aside, helpless; chants still ringing out, colliding again ('Abortion stops a beating heart!'), hands waving, fists waving, the whole crowd with its arms up like a snake pit, trying to grab us and be a part of something.

And there in the very centre, like a prophet entering a city, was Christina, blood dripping from her hand and two police around her as a shield. She strode with her shoulders back, feeling nothing, saying nothing, only peering at the signs and waving limbs – an older lady at her shoulder, mouthing reas-surance; now a T-shirt flung over with a tiny melting hand and the words, '25 without parole!' She flinched at neither;

only walked on, numb and disaffected, as if no one was there but her – or perhaps she herself wasn't there, but floating apart in a deep-sea cage, watching the people spit and bray and flap about. 'Let her through!' 'A boy or a *giiiiiiirl*!?'

All the while, I stumbled behind, losing ground and ducking my head, ashamed. And if I'm being honest, it was shame that caused me to do what I did next – not bravery, not honour. I'd been weak outside the clinic. I'd come to be a hero and I'd buried my face in her neck, usurping her role of victim and taking the sympathy she was due. If I hadn't, I might have kept my head bowed. But as we ploughed on, I felt shame press upon me, watching the gauze on her hand as it dripped. Suddenly, a pamphlet was thrusting into it; a man forcing her to take it, scraping her skin. I watched the gauze peel away, opening the wound. I saw her hand jerk in a shot of pain. Then I saw red.

I rushed at the pamphlet man, pushing people aside, throwing myself headlong and hearing him yelp as pamphlets flew in a plume and scattered over the crowd. People tried to grab me but I flung my arms about. They were screaming, toppling over; someone taking my wrists and me forcing them away, swinging a fist and connecting with something – a shriek – then people were prising at my face. But I didn't care; Christina was gone – freed! And I was a hero, with enemies on all sides, pushing them away, flailing and swinging; my hand catching a cheek, a thigh – Christina was free! – and as I flailed, I glanced around, thinking of the high-diver, and hoping that she could see. But there was no way. People were piling from every side now, taking my wrists, taking my ankles; limbs and fingers pulling my hair; police arriving, 'It's a peaceful march!', pinning my arms and dragging me until a woman held my knees and all of us toppled in a heap.

I became lucid then.

Someone flipped me onto my belly and pressed a knee in my spine, twisting my hand excruciatingly. I peered up, panting and exhausted, into a ring of shocked faces hovering above. A camera bearing down. I looked into the lens. The jeers had gone now, the chanting silenced. 'It's a peaceful march,' someone repeated, and someone agreed. I closed my eyes and heard a bell chime, the trams passing on the median strip.

How OFTEN IN life it's the insignificant actions, the after-thoughts we don't even consider, that end up truly affecting the course of things. And the effects of my performance outside the clinic did end up being far wider reaching than I could have ever imagined. It was almost as if, from that moment – peering out the window of the police car – an aperture had narrowed somewhere. I'd felt it then, hadn't I? – watching the crowd disperse and fall away: a sense of the world becoming somehow unmagical, as though enclosing itself and choosing to no longer reveal its wild possibility.

I don't think the school would have cared had I not offered Christina my coat. As it was, that evening I appeared on channels 7 and 9, flailing about with the emblem proudly displayed on my shirtfront. A meeting was called the next day: Mum, Dad, principal, vice-principal, chaplain – all of them shaking their heads that a boy could fall so far. It was decided best for all parties if we separated. The school couldn't accept the possibility of more violence. I was escorted to my locker, Ms Andrews' biology class ogling as I cleared it out. On Monday there would be words in assembly, a reminder that we were representing the school at all times. But what did it matter? We drove home in silence.

Then the pamphlet man wanting to press charges: a letter arriving the next day, followed by an emergency summons – the presiding magistrate visibly disinterested, asking what I thought of my actions? I said I thought they were bad and she rolled her eyes and handed me sixty hours community service and a corrections officer. I was ordered to cover medical bills, which the man's sling, trauma and whiplash had raised to over fifteen hundred dollars. My parents remained silent throughout the hearing, and again on the way home.

But where I might have expected fire and brimstone, I found none. There was no famous stoush in the living room. No – somehow my behaviour at the protest seemed to wring the house of vitriol, to bring us all together. After the hearing, I'd slumped on my bed only for the door to creak open a moment later, Mum creeping in to sit beside the pillow.

'Matty . . .' she'd whispered, searching for my hand, taking it – I'd been rolled away, facing the wall. 'What are we going to do with you?'

She'd kissed my hair and I'd felt the flooding sense of returning home after all these years. I remember gritting my teeth as hard as I could, yet unable to stop the desk and wall dissolving in a mist. 'Matty,' Mum crooning, her chin finding my shoulder, 'you don't have to live your whole life right now . . .' and I'd blinked everything away, desperate to keep my breath even – unable though – wanting only for her to stay exactly where she was, saying other things just like that . . .

Home was different then, since leaving them on the balcony with Dad whispering in her ear, humming his tune;

his incantation perhaps. I don't know what words they spoke, but it was clear he'd felt her slap as keenly as I. Now they were, if not entirely at peace, then at least settled on a truce. They floated about the house, peering frail looks into my bedroom window: warm smiles and glancing anxiety – softly closing the door in case the force caused me to shatter. Both of them felt responsible, I knew; as though I'd been a civilian swept into their war. Now they turned themselves inwards, taking time from work and spending it on family bonding, on beach days and movie nights and games of Monopoly so wholesome that no one ever won or lost because the bankrupt were given property windfalls and allowed to roll themselves from gaol. Mum spent entire afternoons in the computer room, examining school websites or simply sitting to be near me. 'But let's wait for Term Four, yeah?' her iron fist having disappeared, 'take a bit of time and start afresh.'

Dad, for his part, seemed to become a sort of glazed man, chortling about the house in an almost mock homage to the Kodak father; cheerful and automated. It was as though, having witnessed the tremor of his actions, he'd made the decision to retreat from a part of himself; swimming up from the deep dark where emotions are only desperate, and choosing instead to live life at the surface of things – where I believe he remains to this day – with food and exercise and views out the window. He started calling me 'mate' and bought me a bicycle, raising me early to show all the tracks around the bayside area. He raided my CD collection in an effort to realign our musical tastes. Then in the evenings, he flurried about the kitchen, conjuring spectacular meals that Mum had forgotten all about, grinning with genuine relish as she enjoyed them. Both of them began using sprightly voices at the table, trying their best at first, but then I think simply enjoying it: lowering their eyes now and then to chuckle at a reference significant only to them. In these moments I would sit quietly at the head of the table, watching them disappear to their little bubble of solitude, where despite all history there were jokes and experiences binding them eternally, and feeling snug in the harmonies of my childhood, grateful at their efforts, and enjoying a warmth I'd not realised had been missing for so long.

–Except it was a false harmony.

On the third day, Dad had crept into my room, returning my phone to the bedside table.

'Thought you might want to call Christina,' he'd said, 'see how she is and everything . . .'

I'd thanked him and he'd made to leave, striding to the door, then turning around.

'Oh . . .' there was a pause as he shuffled his feet, '–and if you get a chance, say hi from me, won't you?'

It was a heartbreaking attempt at nonchalance.

I said I would and he smiled.

'Thanks.'

'No problem.'

–But of course, he didn't know that I'd already tried to call Christina, that I'd tried and tried and heard nothing. Not a word since I'd slumped in the police car and caught her expression through the windshield – stunned it had been. Afraid, even.

As it turned out, she'd stopped going to school as well – though for other reasons. While her face never made the news, word had spread like wildfire around Kewfield and a few days later, she'd returned to the boarding house to find her sheets torn and splattered in red dye, then voices jeering over the toilet stalls as she'd scrubbed at the stains. She'd left the following day.

But I never heard any of this from her.

They were bleak months. Three of them; the geography of my world having condensed to the short route from home to work. Without school, I took more shifts at Safeway, moving to produce and slicing watermelon four days a week, standing at the display fridge and watching kids enter after school to buy lollies and cigarettes, rushing away in boisterous huddles. Another two days, I spent removing great swathes of graffiti with a seventeen-year-old felon named either Marissa or Melissa, who would pause to throw her sponge at passing trains. The rest of the time I spent leaving messages on Christina's voicemail; despairing at her words casually affected: 'Hi, it's me. You know what to do . . .' pouring lamentations into the receiver; or else writing letters in homage to our earlier correspondence, letters that seemed to vanish from existence upon entering the letterbox.

Twice, I took the train out to Kewfield – unaware that she'd left and hoping to catch her eye in the boarding house window – loitering in the shadow of the high building, unable to decide which room was hers, then giving up and watching the Under 18s skittle soccer balls across the oval – the remote slap of the ball echoing the distance I felt from these students who all seemed to literally effervesce with the infinite possibility of their own futures.

I recall taking the train home, passing walls of graffiti and peering in derision at the faint outlines of my own amateur scrawl: my once-grand gestures of love now peeking childishly as I wondered how they could have ever seemed so grandiose; how the world had ever seemed so grandiose.

–For there had been a wild moment, hadn't there? When I'd entertained a possibility. A moment of insanity when the world had suddenly enlarged and I'd imagined it. A child. Yes. For a split second – between dismay at the impossible biology and buffoon attempts at heroism – it had fluttered into consideration: a strange image of the three of us, alone somewhere in a room. A portrait perhaps; facing the camera with a bassinet. It had only been a moment, a split second, but I'd felt that same liquid harmony of the morning Christina and I had seen each other at our most exposed, the same pure innocence, grinning nervously in our underwear.

–but the image had extinguished as quickly as it arrived, sucked into a bag, stealing with it all the world's enchantment so that now when I looked around, I found a landscape mysteriously drained of splendour. I'd not yet learned that external things are neither beautiful nor ugly, but merely adorned at the whim of the inner life – and so I gazed in confusion at the vast bleakness that seemed to have descended upon the world like a season.

They were morbid, fugueish days – a calm before the final storm, I suppose – spent strolling footpaths in the enchanting weeks of new daylight savings, seeing the gardens explode with mid-spring bloom and yet being unable to appreciate anything. Nights at Sam's listening to music and smoking weed in the hope of witnessing fabulous images on the fence. But there was never any magic. The closest I came was a work colleague offering a half box of whipped cream canisters for forty-five dollars – spending the evening on the verge of a transcendental experience, inhaling canister after canister and seeing a vague impression of Christina's face in the leaves, believing I was one step away from some enormous under-standing. I never understood, though. Instead, I approached the co-worker again, who suggested I try pouring house paint in a sandwich bag and huffing the contents; then subsequent evenings I recall only as a vague breeze of euphoria, and some of the most searing headaches I've ever experienced.

In the end it was Ali who pulled me out.

It had been three months when she suddenly appeared on MSN under the pseudonym *psychosweetie16*. I'd leapt from my despair and started hammering questions into the keys, feeling optimism rise for the first time in weeks. Christina was at home, she told me, but couldn't be contacted. Why? I asked, and she explained the bloodied sheets and the jeering in the cubicle and the boys stuffing her pencil case with fistfuls of wet tampons. I asked her why she'd changed her username and there was nothing for a minute. Then she told me to meet her in Frankston.

I took a train in, fidgeting up the line as my chest tightened, and my throat – did it occur to me then how much of myself I'd waged on this connection with Christina? How much I'd invested in a desire completely beyond my control? Either way, I found Ali pacing the platform, flighty and jittering as she'd been outside the clinic – though with some difference in her manner now; something guarded, serpentine perhaps. She greeted me with a glass kiss and I paid for Gloria Jean's. Then to the park where I rent my clothes, pacing back and forth and issuing a detestable monologue about how I was in the dark and how it was torture and how all I wanted to do was understand!

The whole time, Ali watched from a swing, emotionless, dragging a foot and saying nothing, still with that curious manner. Then when I was finally exhausted, she stepped down and took a breath.

'You have to leave her alone,' she said. 'She doesn't want to see you. I'm sorry.'

She sighed, holding my eye with a simplicity that made my torrent of words seem embarrassing and ridiculous.

'Why do you think she hasn't answered your messages?'

'So she's been getting them?'

Ali couldn't help a small laugh escaping.

'Are you serious?' she said. 'How could she not – you've left a hundred of them. If she hasn't replied, it's coz she doesn't want to.'

'Why can't *she* tell me that?'

Now she paused and crossed her arms, eyes narrowing. 'Vikki said she saw you outside the school. What were you doing?'

I didn't answer and she raised her eyebrows. There was a derision I hadn't seen before, something sticky and delicious.

'Well anyway,' she said, 'I wouldn't go back, yeah? Vikki told the office – they've all seen the news.'

It was satisfaction, I realised. She shrugged as if to say things were shit but hey, that's the world, isn't it?

I shook my head. 'No – if Christina wants to say something, she's got my number.' (Ali sighing again.) 'I just want to apologise. What, I'm not allowed–'

'She knows you're sorry!' she yelled now, suddenly irritable. 'God – give her some credit.' Then, catching herself, curling a lip, 'I mean, what could you possibly say that she hasn't heard on voicemail?'

I felt my hatred burn then, imagining her on the phone to Christina, giggling into the receiver with her stupid birdish neck craning back and forward. I wanted to spit on her.

'When did you speak to her?'

'Yesterday.'

'So she's home then?'

'She's with her mum.'

'What, and she's told you to say all of this?'

'She doesn't have to tell me anything. It's . . .'

But she trailed off. A boy was passing with an ice-cream, stopping at the bin beside us, tearing at the wrapper. I lowered my voice.

'What does that mean – she doesn't have to?'

'It's time for you to leave her alone,' Ali said, crossing her arms in triumph. 'Okay? Simple as that.'

But as she spoke, something in her seemed to falter a moment, her weight shifting right to left. I narrowed my eyes.

'Did she ask you to say this?'

The kid was taking forever with his ice-cream, trying to jiggle it off his thumb. Ali didn't answer, her eyes hardening, as though trying to glare through uncertainty.

'Did she?'

Still no answer; she only shifted again. Suddenly I understood everything. I chuckled to myself.

'*What?*' she snapped.

But the boy was between us again, stomping merrily with his ice-cream free. I watched him disappear up the road.

'You love her, don't you?'

'Ex*cuse* me?'

I raised my eyebrows and she scoffed. 'You're so full of shit.'

'So you don't then?'

'I'm trying to help her.'

'That's not what I asked.'

I could feel her tense. 'That doesn't even . . .' She was shaking her head.

'You do, then . . . ?'

'I *don't*.'

There was a long silence. I shrugged. 'You're not trying to help her; you want something else.'

'Oh, and you don't?'

But all of a sudden she seemed defenceless; her words not quite as barbed. I made her wait as I finished my coffee.

'If you knew her at all,' I said, 'then you'd know she needs to be away from that house. You'd know that she hates it. Did she tell you *that*? She told *me* that. She said if it was up to her, she'd burn it to the ground.'

Ali was glaring like she wished me dead.

'So while you're on the phone with her,' I continued, 'giggling at my messages—'

'You're pathetic.'

'—fingering yourself over her voice—'

Ali exploded: 'Have you ever thought she doesn't want to see you coz you're a fucking nutcase!?' She threw her cup. 'Huh? Coz you're deranged? Has that ever crossed your mind – that she's scared? That she doesn't want to call you coz you're waiting outside her school – turning up at her house!' Her chest was heaving. 'No one wants your help. Yeah? No one needs it! Get that in your head. Go home. She doesn't want to see you! How hard is it to understand!?'

I nodded, holding my tongue, waiting to see if she had anything else to say. But she was exhausted, chest still heaving. I'd cracked her spirit.

'*I'm* deranged, am I?' I said, walking over and picking up her cup, taking it to the bin. 'Well . . .'

I dropped it in, peering for a moment at the trash, then coming back to her:

'At least I didn't teach her to cut herself.'

It was like a punch to the stomach, all her fight suddenly disappearing as the air flew out of her. She became dark.

I sighed. 'Sorry – that was out of line.'

But I knew something was true for her. She was trying to hold herself together, lips curling – desperate not to cry.

'I didn't even mean it,' I said.

She turned to pick up her bag.

'I'm gonna go.'

'Let me walk you.'

'Really, Matt, I'm *fine*.'

And at these last words, like a final thrust, she managed to sweep humiliation aside – so there was only contempt. For a moment, we stood glaring at each other, both seeing horrible sides that couldn't be unseen.

'Alright,' I said. 'Well, piss off then.'

It was the last thing I would say to her for twelve years. She shook her head like I was a heathen. But I could see in her expression some other part that told me the heathens had won – and now the world was godless.

THAT LAST PART'S not exactly true. Ali and I spoke once afterwards.

Can I say where? Do I dare?

Reading back, 'where' is pretty clear though, isn't it? It comes as no surprise.

Still though – to actually *say* it.

*

–And today, Ali speaking about it with such clarity . . .

Yesterday morning, Ali called to apologise. 'For rushing away last time,' she said – and was I free? She sounded nervous.

Thursday's her day off and we took coffee to the gardens behind Chapel Theatre. The sun was gorgeous and it felt a little like betrayal, the two of us a second time – Ali arriving sleeveless, showing off her angelfish. We shared a blanket and sat watching the basketballers.

But talk wasn't easy like it had been last time; she was anxious and fidgety, as though she wanted to leave. I kept waiting for an excuse, but it never came. Instead, she became solemn – we'd been chatting maybe a half-hour:

'It's lucky you contacted me when you did,' she said out of the blue, 'and not a few years back.'

It was her tone of voice that made it clear. I felt my fingers go pins and needles, knowing exactly where she was headed, and thinking: 'Here we are.'

'I hated you for a very long time.' She was watching the game, so she didn't have to look me in the eye. 'I want you to know so it's out there – if we're going to be hanging out.

278

I blamed you for a long time . . .' Now laughing because she was uncomfortable. 'Obviously I don't anymore . . .' Becoming serious again. 'I've wanted to get in touch – I've looked you up before; I knew you were at the clinic. I wasn't sure if you'd want to meet.'

She kept turning to see my expression – or because she wanted me to respond. I don't know; either way it doesn't matter because I wasn't listening. I could only think: 'Here we are.'

And obviously, I'd been expecting it – it's the entire reason for contacting her in the first place. Isn't it? The whole reason I'm keeping a journal. Still though; the suddenness yesterday took me completely by surprise. And arriving at the topic, I realised I was no readier to discuss it than I have been during any appointment with Gloria, no readier than at any point sitting at this desk with a pen, knowing I should probably be including it.

She died, of course – Christina.

And I did see Ali once more afterwards: at the Kewfield Memorial Hall for that awful service where the principal mispronounced her last name. We'd shared a few words out in the cold, both of us blaming the other.

'It doesn't heal,' she was saying yesterday – she'd wanted to tell me this one thing: 'The biggest mistake is to think it will, to think it just takes a long time. It doesn't. Y'know? . . . then you wait and wait; people lose interest – you're ashamed because it didn't happen to you. I mean, I wasn't her sister; I'm not her mum. I'm a friend. Everyone wants you to move on – but you still grieve, don't you? You can't help it . . .'

She was telling her story because she thought it applied to me.

'It's the most liberating feeling – to realise something won't heal, to learn you can't be the same person, that it's impossible. If you accept that, then you think: Right, I'm trying another way – you're in a different lane. Yeah? You can't get back, but you can go *this* way . . . it's the relief. You think: I can *do* that.'

I let her roll on, listing wisdoms she understood so comprehensively they merely required a dot point. To me, they were only words.

'But . . .' Now she paused – because here was the point, here was the key that was going to unlock everything for me: 'You have to be honest,' she said. 'You can't avoid it. You've got to look it in the eye.'

It was wisdom from the handbook of Gloria, spoken as she looked into *my* eyes, as though in demonstration. I wondered how much she'd rehearsed it beforehand – it was clearly what she'd come to tell me, the reason she'd called. Now, with a sense of justice done, she nodded, parting her hands in a final affidavit.

'The heart cannot retreat.'

I almost laughed then, at Connie's old phrase rearing its head again; one she'd used primarily as an excuse for another handful of Maltesers. How it's lived on all these years, with its meaning grotesquely warped.

But of course, Ali wasn't finished with me yet. She'd said what she came to say and now, flinging her hands as if it was all just chitchat anyhow, she turned to me, fresh from confessional:

'And you?'

'. . .'

*

And me? What *about* me?

Am I looking things in the eye? as everyone keeps telling me to do?

It's not that simple though, is it? There are sides to truth. And sometimes, those sides are of use to no one.

Still. I'm here, turning up to the page – when I could just as easily not – with my pen ready.

Can I though? This last part. Do I even *want* to?

Today, all I can see is Ali parting her hands. 'The heart cannot retreat,' she says, as if everything's clear as day.

But things are never simple.

The heart cannot retreat – true enough.

It can, however, be annihilated.

*

I remember the weather first – rain streaming down the windows as my parents dressed in their bedroom: 'a little Italian place on Lygon Street, then afterwards, perhaps a film.' I watched them, hovering in the doorway as they made themselves up, putting attention into themselves, remembering how it could be fun, all this stuff – Dad turning with an unmade tie: 'You be right on your own, buddy?' 'Of course,' I'd said, smiling back, feeling guilt rise up – because at that point, I'd already packed my bag, and as soon as they left, so would I – Dad winking and returning to the mirror. I watched the headlights reverse out of the driveway.

Two days earlier, Ali had left me in the park with a fire rekindled. Now the rain was sweeping the road in sheets as cars sluiced by and I skipped from tree to tree, avoiding the torrent. At the station, I'd missed a train and had to sit twenty minutes with a rail worker eyeing me across the platform. He peered through the white rain; orange globes hovering about him. I dialled Christina and she said, 'Hi, it's me. You know what to do,' her voice reedy and faraway as the awning hammered above. I thought of calling the house – thought against it. Then the boom gates rang and the train was screeching to a stop. I chose a carriage that was empty, save an older couple in the far corner. As we flew along, I watched them delight in one another, his arm on the back of her seat, leaning in and leaning out – her shrill laughter all down the Frankston line – thinking of my parents at their little place on Lygon Street. When we terminated, neither of them moved. It was pissing down. *Good luck to them*, I thought.

Over the road, a line of taxis was waiting for passengers.

'Where to, moit?' A cabbie with his window down and a drenched cigarette. I told him where and he frowned. 'Jesus, you gonna wet my seats?'

All the way, he chattered: Brisbane winning a threepeat – fucking interstate teams. I paid no attention, letting him bubble away as the houses began to disappear. Then it was bushland and the church made of triangles. Not a soul was about; everyone indoors, watching television snug in the covers. I told him to drop me at the corner of Hartley Drive and he pulled over at the bus shelter, peering up the road.

'You be right, kid? You don't want me to go down?'

'I'm good,' I said.

I paid and got out and his window came down again.

'You runnin' away or something?'

I didn't answer. He frowned.

'You got somewhere to stay?'

'Not really your business, is it?'

He scoffed, 'Fuckin' punk,' spun the cab around and left me at the shelter.

The rain still poured in curtains and I sat, waiting for it to break. It didn't – and in five minutes, I was frozen through. I began trudging towards the estate, pulling my jacket over. With only the dim streetlights, I kept to the lines, watching the bushland thrash either side of me, rivulets pouring into my jeans – wondering what the fuck I was doing. I thought of turning around and going home. But there were no cabs anymore. Not out here. Only the dim light of the shelter – far behind now – and somewhere ahead, the gates to Wychwood.

They were closed when I arrived. I imagined Connie looking up from the TV and seeing them bend apart, her eyes narrowing – stepping out to find me drenched. I threw my bag and it sploshed on the driveway; a horse spooking somewhere at the noise. Then I was climbing the railing, avoiding the livewire, and swinging myself over. My feet slopped in God knows what – a sludge burying the driveway. There were horses watching from the roadside paddock and I could see the entire thing had been trodden into a morass. The rain had swept it onto the driveway, I realised. Now my feet sank in and I doubt the gates could have opened if I'd wanted. I picked up my bag and crept forward.

Light was flickering in the lounge room; TV patter under the rain. I paused at the verandah, behind a rosebush that clung to the parapet, sagged and ravaged by the weight of the downpour. I sank lower, squinting in the window. There was someone on the couch, an elbow in a dressing gown. I heard the laughter of a studio audience, then a cackle, loud and sharp, as the elbow shifted – Connie. I peered further around, shielding my eyes, the rain turning everything into static. She was on the couch, her face blue and fluttering like she was in a pool. A man's voice burbled and she cackled again, cords pulling tight on her neck.

But she wasn't alone, I realised. Because here was Christina, entering the picture with a cup of tea. I watched her move in – a silent film: Connie looking around, warm smile, taking the cup. A man's voice burbling. Laughter from the studio audience. I stood up – wiping away the rain, trying to see: Christina on the armrest now, Connie fossicking for her hand, taking it. Laughter from the studio audience. I watched the scene, no longer trying to hide: mother and daughter, Connie resting her head. And it occurred then why Christina might not have been at school. They were laughing at something the man had said; impossible to hear in the clamour of the rain. Was I wrong? All this . . . And I looked back into the dark of the driveway with second thoughts, wondering if maybe the cabbie . . . If I apologised, perhaps . . .

But a sharp noise caused me to jump. I lost my grip and fell back on the grass, my hand sinking in the muck. There was a shape circling at the door, leaping and snapping at the handle: Mr Harvey. I pulled myself up again, praying for him to be calm. But he knew it was me; he'd seen – he whirled in a stupor. Now Connie was on her feet, confused and startled. Christina disappeared around the couch. I was going to be exposed; there was no way around it. And for what? I thought. Some idiot plan? To be smeared and filthy and lose feeling in my fingers? Christina had come to the door now, standing in a dressing gown with her brow furrowed, the hair wiry and lifeless in her eyes. She bent to stroke Mr Harvey as he wheeled in desperation, whimpering at the door. She squinted out and lifted her hand.

Suddenly, I was bathed in light. I dropped behind the verandah as the door slid open and Mr Harvey scuttled along the decking. He howled and launched into the rain as I flipped over, crawling towards the darkness.

'What is it, Harvey?' Christina called.

She was outside now, wrapping her gown against the rain, peering forward and trying to see. Mr Harvey had arrived and was bristling my neck, crooning an anguished whine. 'Shshshsh,' I told him, but he wouldn't relent. He sploshed in ecstasy.

'Harvey?'

Now Connie was behind her, squinting blindly in my direction, surprised at the rain. She tottered forward and Christina turned and spoke. They argued; she ushered her inside. Mr Harvey was prodding me with his nose. He'd realised he was drenched and began to whimper.

'I know,' I said, stroking his ear. 'I know.'

Now Christina was crossing the deck with an umbrella and a torch. 'Harvey!' She leaned over the railing like a figurehead. 'Misteeeer!'

Harvey's tail began to spin and he shook himself dry.

'Harvey! Come here!' Connie at the doorway again.

Christina spun around. 'Go inside!'

'Harvey!'

But he wouldn't come; his tail dipped. Christina lifted the torch and began to swivel the beam about the garden.

'Harvey! C'mon mister!' His tail helicoptering again. 'Good boy Harvey!'

Now he raced forward, leaping onto the deck.

'What are you *doing*, Mister?'

He clomped merrily about her, explaining that I'd arrived.

She kissed his neck and brushed him away, lifting the torch again. I watched it fly about, darting in the trees like something alive. Then I was blinded.

'What is it?' Connie croaked.

The light burned for a second, then shot away and began to search again.

'I don't know,' Christina said. 'Fox, I guess.' I didn't dare move – the beam examining everywhere else around me. 'I think it went under the fence.'

Connie took a half-step, squinting as if she could see. I looked into her eyes, heavy and sightless.

'Well, don't let him in, will you?' she said. 'He's filthy.'

She turned and tottered back into the house. Christina waited for the door to close, then swung the torch and blinded me again. Still, I didn't move. She held the beam a second or two, then switched it off and went inside.

Strange night it was; the rain never relenting. I have no idea how long I sat, jittering by the workshed, soaked to the skin, not daring to approach the house – Mr Harvey disappearing and returning, standing sentry. An hour, maybe more? I watched the shadows move across the walls of the living room, waiting for darkness. Finally, the lights went dead. A moment later, the door creaked on the far side and Christina was on the verandah, striding up and down, peering into the blackness. I stood and the light flicked on.

'What are you doing?' she said, rushing forward and leaning into the rain, her hair flushed across her face. 'You could've gone inside!'

I could barely hear though, tottering towards her. She saw my clothes, saw me shivering, flew into the house and returned with a towel. I clenched it between my fingers, feeling nothing at all.

'You're insane,' she said.

Silently, she led me inside and to the hall. I held my shoes and walked on the towel, still leaving a trail. In the laundry, I shivered and was unable to stop – trying to work my fingers. Somehow, I threw off my clothes and slopped them in the basket. Then a knock came and the door cracked open with a fresh towel and a set of clothes: blue pants and a collared shirt. I held them beside me. In the mirror, I was corpselike and hunched. But I recognised the outfit: Aleksei's. I saw him sweeping his backhand across the table-tennis net – we'd been to La Porchetta and then home for *The Princess Bride*. 'How 'bout a match?' he'd asked, 'two versus one,' dispatching us with ease, then becoming gallant and letting us win. I'd thought him superhuman, sweeping his backhand. Now I watched myself buttoning the collar and was surprised at how perfectly it all fit. I pushed the towel into my face again, drew my hair across like he used to wear it, thought how old I looked these days.

I found Christina in her room, sitting on the bed. I stood in the doorway as she turned to examine me – the shirt and the pants.

'You can't keep turning up,' she said.

I came over to her and we lay back together, listening to the rain pelting overhead, hammering the roof and turning the grounds into sludge. Still, she wore the dressing gown, wrapped like a wedding dress and flared over the edge as if she were drifting away; me in Alek's clothes. Weirdly, like some portrait of bride and groom, we lay peering at the ceiling.

'I saw you on the news,' she said.

'I was expelled.'

'I'm sorry.'

'Don't be.'

Above our heads, the stars washed across – for miles and miles, it seemed; tiny and meaningless.

'Were you ever going to call?'

'I don't know.'

The rain crashing the roof, swathing the paddocks in sheets – all the mush and muck covering the estate, bending the orchard. Tomorrow it would be destroyed.

'You shouldn't have come,' she said.

'I'm glad I did.'

I found her hand and she slid her fingers into mine. We lay like the dead. Then a sound crashed in the kitchen – a cupboard slamming, shattering glass on the tiles – and Christina shot up like someone pulled out of a dream.

'Does she ever *stop*!'

She snatched her hand away and stood, pulling her gown around her. I made to follow.

'Stay here,' she said, rushing from the room before I could reply.

Then there were voices, the two of them sparring in the kitchen, a rummaging in the cupboards. I crept up the hall to see, hearing deep sobs under the rain. I peeked in. Christina was on her knees, brushing glass into a dustpan. Connie, red-eyed and bewildered, standing aside like an invalid, apologising again and again with strings of drool. She was the remains of a woman, hunched and repulsive. I watched her heave and tremble, realising I felt no pity; only disgust. Then thunder cracked so loud it seemed directly above me, and I fell away.

Back in the room, I paced for God knows how long, straining to hear, hearing nothing but the storm. Suddenly, the door flew open and Christina was holding my clothes in a bundle.

'We have to go!' she yelled – she was irascible.

'What, where?'

But she was already gone and I was chasing after her again, rushing down the hall. In the lounge, the side door hung open and leaves were swirling in the house. I watched them rise in strange patterns, sweeping away like a spirit departed. The room was still – Connie's doorway a mouth gaping into utter blackness. I heard a toilet flush somewhere and scampered across, slamming the door behind me.

Then outside, torrents were falling in great sheets from the guttering and as I stepped out, I saw Christina disappearing behind them. I heard feet splashing and the grinding shriek of the workshed door and made after her, wind and rain slapping at my collar; throwing an arm against the barrage as trees and hedging thrashed about me; keeping my head down until I was under the garage door. I stepped inside, pulling it behind me with a clatter as Christina spun around.

'You can't be here,' she said. 'You need to go.'

She threw my clothes on the couch and was taking out her phone.

'What's going on?' I stammered back.

'I'll call you a cab – you can wait here but then . . .'

'I don't want a cab.'

'You can't just turn up somewhere unannounced!' she yelled, the rain hammering the roof like applause.

'*What?* I want to help you – I'm . . .'

'I didn't ask for your help.' She was dialling, 'I'm sorry,' raising the phone to her ear. It rang forever and she waited, staring me down. She was a Replicant. 'Yes, hi.' She whirled around. 'I'd like a cab please. For now. Yes – it is. Hartley Drive. Yep. To Highett. Yes. Okay. Okay, thanks.'

She hung up and turned to face me like it was my move.

'What's happened to you?' I asked.

'You can't just come here whenever you want – expect everyone to drop everything all the time.' She had her arms crossed in defiance.

'What, so you just stay here then?' I said. 'Screen me completely and shut yourself away – is that the plan?'

'I'm not shutting myself away.'

'Really? Then what's *this*?' And I threw my hands apart to show that she was. 'How many times have you been out? Where have you been – which places? You're not at school, what have you been doing?'

A sheet of rain blew over and was deafening. I waited for it to pass, watching her pull her arms tight against the cold.

'How many days have you been wearing that dressing gown?'

She shivered and was silent.

'You don't have to stay here,' I said. 'Take a cab with me. You can stay at mine – Mum and Dad won't care. We'll work it out tomorrow.'

'Work what out?'

'I don't know, things – what to do next; where to go.'

'. . . where to go.' She repeated the words to herself like an incantation.

Now a gust blew again, tearing a pane of sheeting that began to flap against the roof, water drizzling in from the rafters.

'Is that why you came?' she asked.

'You said it yourself – we just have to go. There's no right time; we have to see what happens. And you're right: it's just the anticipation.'

She held my eyes for a moment.

'What?' I asked.

But I knew already. She sighed and raised the hand she'd scratched in the clinic, the wound flaking and weirdly iridescent.

'I did this to myself,' she said.

'I know – I was there.'

'Then you know I was out of it.'

'You weren't.'

'Matt.' She was shaking it in front of me, a puddle on the back of her hand. 'You're putting stock into something I said when I was off my head.'

'Doesn't mean it's not right.'

'I was off my head.'

'So you don't mean it then?'

'Whether I meant it doesn't matter – I was *manic*.'

'How does it not matter? Of course it matters. What else matters?'

'It's a fantasy.'

'No, it's not! We can go right now. Think about it, we just–'

'Matt. Be realistic.'

'I'm realistic. Put some clothes in a bag–'

'It's a fantasy.'

'It's *not*!' I yelled, and kicked a table that was sitting beside me, the leg snapping and collapsing in a crash of books and candles. 'I've got money,' I said, paying no attention. 'Yeah?

I've got eight grand. Right now. *Eight*. I have it. Not in a trust fund. Not in some place I can't get to. Now. I *have* it. I just go to an ATM – whenever I want. Alright? Don't tell me what's realistic. I've been working. I'm not going back to school, not to some other school. Fuck it, right – it doesn't matter. Don't tell me to be realistic. If we want, we can go. There's nothing stopping us. I've got nothing stopping me – nothing that . . .'

But as the words tumbled out, I'd been struck by their truth: I had nothing. Nothing at all. How had I ever thought of myself as her saviour?

We stood looking at each other, the sheet slapping against the roof, as though to emphasise the silence.

'We can go if we want,' I said. 'You just have to say.'

Beside me, the table lurched under the weight of itself. I tried to pull it upright, but the leg was snapped entirely and collapsed again, sending boxes and piano manuscript crashing between us. I scrambled to pick them up.

'Leave it,' Christina said.

I tried to wipe the pages, but it was useless.

'Look,' I sighed, 'I'm not saying to run away. I know that's stupid. I just want to get you out of here. Somewhere else. Go stay at Aunty Carol's even – or I'll pay for a hotel; whatever, I don't care. I just . . .'

'What about Mum?' she said.

Now thunder cut us off, a swell rolling above us, going on and on. Christina looked at the junk piled all around. 'Ali told me you met,' she said. 'She called me after. I had a feeling you were going to come.'

'Are you afraid of me?' I asked.

'Of *you*?'

'That's what she said. That you were scared because I was deranged. That I should stay away. Was she right?'

No answer.

'Look, I don't know what happened at the protest. I was a fucking idiot; that's all I can say. I fucked up. I'm sorry – I can't take it back.'

'It's not that.'

'What is it then? What – did you think I was going to give up? Just go home and forget about it?'

'No.'

'Then why not say; I wouldn't have come if–'

'Coz I didn't want to speak to you. Alright? I didn't want to see you.'

'*Why?*'

Now the rain slammed back again, rattling the door on its hinges; strings of rain swinging between the cracks.

'Fucking hell,' I said, 'you can at least say now.'

But she didn't want to. She dropped her gaze, her eyes almost tender, as though she couldn't bear to watch.

'Look at us,' she said. 'Look at you. Look at me. Can you not see how we're sick? We keep coming back – something keeps pulling us back. I didn't want you to come tonight, but I *did* – like I was addicted. And maybe we are. Think about what's happened – look at your life. It's like you don't even care. We're *sick*. And now you're here and I *want* you to be here. I don't think you even see it – you just see the bits you want. And it seems impossible because . . . I mean, *look!*'

And she threw her arms apart to show that everything was fucked, and that if I needed proof then I only needed to look around. And I knew in that moment, raising her arms, that she was including herself, that she was a part of it, standing in her robe like something strung together, as though pulling the knot would cause her to dismember and collapse.

'I didn't want you to persuade me,' she said, looking at her hand. 'If you came, I knew you would.'

'And have I?'

The door rattled again, the pane slapping the roof. She moved a finger over the scar without answering.

'It's not us,' I said. 'It's just everything else.'

She smirked to herself, shaking her head as if I were nothing but a dreamer.

–And who knows? Maybe I was. But if I was a dreamer, then she was the opposite: in her dressing gown with stains on the collar. She was ill, of course, caught once again in her affliction – that gift from her mother's side – and perhaps for the first time, I was able to see it clearly, watching her pick at the wound and wondering how in the history of the world, there'd never been discovered an elixir for self-loathing.

The rain swept again in shattering applause. But she didn't seem to hear, working at a flake on the wound. It fell into the trickle from the rafters and was swept away.

'Do you love me?' I asked.

Now she looked up in surprise; the question simple and devastating, as if I'd sung a tune from a time she barely remembered.

'Because I love you.'

'Do you?' she asked.

'Course I do.'

She dropped her hands and looked into the rafters, searching for an answer somewhere in the sound of the rain pouring on the roof, pouring across the grounds, in the trees and in the weeds, all bending and being swept away. I waited, watching the trickles fall around her. There was something in the way they fell, cascading down. She almost seemed to be ascending.

'Do you?' I asked again. 'I just want to know.'

Now she dropped her head and I could see her eyes were puddles.

'Yep.'

I shrugged. 'Then what . . . ?'

There was a long silence as she studied my face, the pane slapping relentlessly above us. Suddenly it went quiet, the slaps pausing a moment as the wind died and the rains fell away.

Christina seemed to teeter on her feet – towards me and away – and dissolve somehow, fading in a bleed of colour and light. She was a mess, it was true, strung together by a dressing gown; teetering one more time away.

Then she fell into my chest.

Thunder crashed again with the rain, and I realised now it was my eyes that had gone. The bleeding colours. Everything had become a puddle and I could only feel – Christina's lips creeping up my chin. I tasted the salt humidity of tears. They were my own. She was holding my wrists as if they were the thing causing her to stand. And I couldn't see at all. The world was a mist now, and she was somewhere in the middle, gorgeous and light, kissing my cheek.

But it was only for a second.

A grinding sound caused us to jolt away from each other. The clamour on the roof meant that we'd heard no footsteps – Connie twisting the handle on the garage door. I spun at the shriek of the door, saw her appearing in a night slip, thin rivers splashing at her feet. Christina pulled away and stood, frozen.

'Mum.'

Connie squinted forward, moving out of the rain, steadying herself against the wall. She hacked something in her throat and Christina moved to help.

'Weren't you going to bed?'

'Nurofen.'

'Is there none? What about the laundry?'

Connie shook her head. She was peering about the room.

'I might have to get some tomorrow,' Christina said. 'Why don't you have a lie-down?'

But she wasn't listening. I watched her scanning the wreckage, as if it had appeared overnight. Her eyes passed through me without noticing; then suddenly came back, transfixed.

'Matt was soaked. We didn't want to wake you.'

I gave a half-wave and Connie tottered forward, reaching out for the shirt. She ran her fingers up the seam, remembering the fabric. At the collar, she paused and frowned.

'I called a cab . . .' Christina's voice was meek and faraway.

Connie fastened the top button, shuffled the neck even.

'Yep,' she said, giving a soft chuckle as she picked a thread, wisping it away between her fingers. She took everything in, beaming. She patted my chest.

'. . . it's on its way.'

Now Connie spun around, as if Christina had arrived and we were interrupted. She scanned the room, bewildered again – came back to me with a fixed glare.

'When are you gonna clean this place up?'

Christina moved over, touching her wrist.

'Why don't you lie down, Mum?'

'Is there Nurofen?'

'I don't think we've got any. I'll have to go out tomorrow.'

Connie nodded, turned back to me. Her eyes were grey and empty.

'It's a mess though, really,' she said. 'We're gonna get one of those . . .' She motioned into the corner, lost interest. Her eyes narrowed.

'Mum.'

Christina was holding her arm. Connie turned to see, nodded thanks, then pushed away and began towards the door. She paused at the threshold.

'Night, Mum,' Christina said.

Connie stepped into the downpour, wind smattering the slip against her figure. She disappeared into the white rain. When she was gone, we stood watching where she'd been. A car horn sounded at the gates.

'It's the cab,' I said.

Neither of us moved.

'Am I getting it?'

'Leave it,' she said.

The horn blared again, far away.

'Let me put her to bed.'

She followed Connie into the house.

Then I went to the couch.

WHY DO I feel the need to defend myself?

(How could we have known!? How could we have foreseen!?)

It's what people do though, isn't it? Horrible useless thoughts: If I'd not turned up, it wouldn't have happened – et cetera, et cetera.

Was it wrong then?

–But the answer's irrelevant. Why? Because thoughts like these are self-flagellation and there's nothing more indulgent than self-flagellation. And because it's easy to criticise something when you know the end. And because what could be more flawed than pinpointing an arbitrary decision and crowning it as *the* definitive error causing a downfall?

Did things happen because I showed up? Sure. Would they have happened in every permutation of events that included me showing up . . . ?

There were worse things than me appearing unannounced. For example: Christina choosing to rot with her mother in the workshed – worse, because it was no choice at all. Because who else was there to rot with her?

When I was in trouble my parents turned inwards – it's not lost on me and I'm grateful for that.

Who ever turned in for Christina?

And to think I curse myself for trying to get her out . . .

Either way, that night I lay in the rumpus room with an ear steeled, straining for any sound. There was a noise in the hall and I sat up to see: the door opening and Christina creeping in, stealthily, desperately. It was time to go, she hissed, and I wondered about Connie – where was she?

'It's okay,' Christina whispered in my ear. 'It's alright.'

I looked past her shoulder, to the doorway. Was it a shadow I could see? No. Impossible. We were alone.

Then Christina was gone and I lay for a second.

–or perhaps it was longer? I don't know; strange . . .

Anyway, time seemed to pass and then the room was brighter. Out the window, the paddocks were grey but visible, the light patter of rain. I threw on Alek's shirt and pants and found Christina's door ajar. The room was empty, clothes trashed in a bundle, drawers open – the pair of fairy wings still hanging from the bedside. It wasn't morning though; in the lounge, the microwave read 4.48. Everything asleep. Only the door outside swung on its hinges, rapping the wall again and again. I watched it swing and took a final look around the lounge. Clinical and desolate; flickering blue – she'd left the television on, a weather presenter in a dark dress explaining the rains. I stepped out into it and began up the path.

Christina was standing under the raised door of the shed; in the white drizzle she seemed to be disappearing. She grinned as I approached. *Far too cold for a dress like that,* I thought. Her dress? No. She was wearing one of Connie's – yellow and covered in those winding flowers we'd all admired. How it fit perfectly now, drenched and delicate. She was her mother – one and the same. And I supposed I was my father – but as they'd been at Tanelorn: young and saturated. In love. And like it was some bizarre omen, a gust of wind sailed in the shed and I watched an ancient stroller somehow wheel itself across the floor and topple over the couch where I'd once sat, drunk and cocooned. There was a crash and a shower of papers flew in the air, landing all around Christina. She turned to look inside.

'Are you going to take anything?' I called out in the rain.

But there was only junk; there seemed to be nothing of Alek.

She shook her head. And for the last time in both of our lives, we looked at each other, me trembling in the cold, grinning and trying to think of something cool to say, some fantastic line to herald the beginning of our Hail Mary.

But there was no time. Something flashed over Christina's face, and suddenly she broke for the eastern paddock, leaving me stranded and confused. I turned to where she'd looked and a movement caught my eye, a flutter at Connie's window. Curtains settling inside. And something – what was it? Now a howl came from in the house, long and drawn, and I saw Connie's face, white in the glow of the bed lamp, peering between the curtains, seeing us by the shed, drenched in the rain. The face disappeared and I turned to Christina, already halfway down the paddock.

For a moment, I stood torn, watching her disappear and wondering where she was going – far from the road and the buses and taxis waiting to take us anywhere but here. The road was *that* way! And as I looked back, I noticed suddenly that the house seemed to have changed, to have mutated and disarranged; the paint flaking and the windows cracked. Had it always looked like this? I wondered. How had I never noticed? As though rot issuing from the workshed had finally reached the house and was slowly encompassing it, just like the graffiti all over the—

And with that thought, suddenly I knew where she was going. I turned and ran, tracing her footprints across the paddock, my feet sploshing and sinking and an arm thrown up against rain that seemed to fall in every direction, as if all the rain had been saved up in case we ever tried to make our escape; and far ahead, I could just make her out – maybe – sprinting and shielding just as I was, and I called forward, 'Christina!' knowing she couldn't hear, but shouting anyway, again and again as she leapt over Davies' fence and scrambled into the thicket. I reached the wire as she disappeared, pausing a second to look back, squinting; impossible to make out anything in the sheets of rain, only the murkiness of the workshed – and something wraithlike, a white phantom, fluttering and blown to the side, still bent forward: Connie – climbing the fence, wailing like a tribal dance; her howls floating back on the rain.

I gripped the fence and vaulted over, feeling my ankle catch on the way down. There was a tear and a shot of pain and I looked to see the wire twisted where I'd slung my foot, a string of flesh – then another shot as I tried to walk, and now something was flapping and there was a warm trickle and I didn't want to look. Instead, I hobbled forward, breaking into the thorns and tangles, squinting barely ahead – *she's there!* I thought, branches clawing at her dress; now disappearing, now reappearing – and all the boughs swinging and swiping as if they were alive with some terrible premonition, flinging their arms and screaming not to go that way! To turn back while there's still time! Take a train! Take a bus, taxi, anything other than where you're going! And as I plunged further, slicing my cheeks and my wrists, my ankle excruciating, I wondered if we shouldn't just listen to them? Turn back the other way, wait for another time, a time where we could see – after all; it was madness, wasn't it? A fool's errand – *There!* – My ankle seared again, tearing against something as I caught a glimpse of her dress, disappearing in the static; and Connie's long howl some-where behind me – all of it telling me it wasn't a dream, that I was awake and still lunging on, thrashing at the brambles, still exhausted and stumbling downhill; bracken and trunks either side now, darkness ahead, footprints vanishing and the sound of rushing water – *Was it?* – and high overhead, swamp gums that were black and invisible and rain that seemed to fall from nowhere. I lifted my head to wash the grazes clean, feeling the cool on my face, the blood pooling between my toes; then pushed on again, hobbling through the trees, my ankle thick and misshapen but numb at least as I made my way blindly towards the footprints, straining for the sound of rushing water and hoping it was the right direction, stumbling and clutching at the foliage and tearing it aside–

Suddenly it was light. Out of the canopy, I could see the sky; clouds and the moon behind – and the rain pelting so hard it would have caused any river to break its banks and throw itself over. And I felt something boiling in me now, as the rain crashed and shattered around me, a rising injus-tice – and I wondered if it was really possible for everything to have been for this moment; all our decisions, our deceits, every smile and conversation, every plan and kiss and every corruption – all of it unfolding so perfectly that we might be drawn to a body of water in which no one could swim. Was this as it had been foretold? Our Hail Mary? Had we been calves grazing before a slaughterhouse? And as if the thought had caused her to appear, suddenly I could see light on the bridge – *There!* – that strange wooden bridge, looming tall over the water. I could see her torch swivelling back and forth, whizzing in the dark sky as she ran across. She was making for the shack, I knew, for the stash she'd been nursing all this time in case we ever needed to escape. But as I leapt forward, staggering towards the swivelling light, thunder crashed loud above me and I lost my footing, slipping and tumbling to the ground.

For a strange few seconds there was peace, sound falling dull and globular as if I'd slipped under the water, catastrophe suspending a moment. I lifted my hand to where my head had slammed the ground, feeling a warm trickle from my temple, mixing with the torrents of rain and getting in my eyes. I blinked it away, seeing my ankle too: a dark rivulet gushing from a chunk of loose flesh. I stared in fascination at the blood diluted with rain, like cordial almost, and at the dark stain of my sock.

–But a shriek pulled my attention, and I flung my head to the bridge; now only a vague batwing shadow, completely deserted, where Christina had been only seconds ago scampering with her torch. Then another shriek – this one cut horribly short – and I leapt to my feet, hobbling to the bridge, not wanting to think what I'd seen, what I'd heard, grasping at the railing and hauling myself up onto the steps, falling again as my ankle collapsed – then pulling myself up as lightning flashed once more and for a horrible moment I could see below me.

She was in the water – I saw for a second – caught in a strange half-dive from her fall and trying to swim, trying to keep her head above the surface – then everything was dark and I could see nothing of her struggle against the current, I could only make out her cries, billowing under the rain, the weirdest scream. And I yelled her name as if in reply, staggering up the stairs and bracing as my ankle made a slippery slide of the wood; my head becoming dizzy too, light-headed and pins and needles – and the vague sense of someone taking my arm. Was it? *Yes* – someone was grabbing my wrist. Who *was* that? Strong hands bruising my wrist, wrenching me away. It was too dangerous! they were yelling now, in my ear, and trying to haul me back down onto the grass – and I yanked as hard as I could, hearing Christina scream again in that strange, muffled voice, scrambling in the water – *There! On her back!* – a light flashing across for a second; torchlight, I realised, swivelling across the water. And it occurred to me then that we weren't alone; that Connie was wailing somewhere behind; that she'd seen us running away and phoned the police and now there were lights swizzling across the sky; and across the trees and grass and down to Christina – *There! In the water!* – For a moment I could see: backstroking with her left arm over her head – But too slow! All of it, too slow! Couldn't they see she needed help?! And at the thought I surged forward again, lurching from hands clutching my wrists and my chest – It was too dangerous! – tearing them away and bellowing, 'I don't want to *go* that way!' flailing my arms, 'She's *that* way!' For I could see clearly now: Christina in a strobe of torches, still trying to paddle; but with the strangest look on her face, the look of an idea gone horribly wrong. And it occurred to me that she must be trying to find me, because I'd been calling her name, over and over – only there was no way she could hear because of the rain and the noise around us. And even if she could, what was she meant to answer? Here I am? 'Yes, Matt. Here I am, in the water.' And what would I say? That I was here too? That I was coming to save her? That I'd followed and don't worry because I was right behind? Only it wouldn't be the truth, would it? Because I still wasn't in the water; I was on the bank. And I was being pulled in the other direction now, lifted by strong hands because it was too dangerous. And if I'm being totally honest, I wasn't even trying to break free anymore. I was exhausted, enjoying the arms around me, cradling me, as Christina drifted further and further away, appearing and disappearing. And for one second, as she was disappearing, we almost caught eyes – we would have actually. But not quite though, because she went under. And then I could only see her hand. She was raising her left hand, and her middle finger was touching her ring finger, as though she was trying to communicate something.

Then I couldn't see her in the water.

*

I was on a bed with wheels. And there were phone calls and people to wrap me in blankets; a green whistle in the ambulance as a young paramedic covered my ankle and told me to inhale slowly for the pain. The sun rising against the light of the police cars.

*

Then halfway to the hospital; someone handing me a phone – Mum screaming on the other end.

*

Then three days I barely remember: stitching my ankle and apparently some complication with hypothermia. Doctors and nurses and the sympathy of relatives; balloons from the newsagent downstairs.

THERE WAS NEVER anything in the papers; nothing on the news. I don't know what I expected – a column in the obituaries? Something. But there was nothing. At home too, there seemed to be a code of silence, my parents tender and sympathetic, but not daring to mention anything. On the Tuesday, Dad creaking open the door to explain they'd opted for a private funeral.

'Family only,' he'd said with immense pity, then rushed to close the door in case I had a question.

For nine days, I crutched to the newsagents, scanning the papers and wondering how it wasn't newsworthy; wondering if I was insane, or if it simply hadn't happened. Then on the twelfth morning, we dressed for the public service at Kewfield Memorial; the entire school turning out to hear the principal speak about Christina as if he knew her. And three times, he mispronounced her last name; three times and no one stirred. They only clapped politely and agreed that it was tragic.

The service ended with a slideshow accompanied by the chamber orchestra. And I'll never forget the rapturous applause as the final shot appeared across the wall: Christina centre among the Q-PATT, posing in their *Midsummer* make-up, turning and laughing at one another. All around, people were cheering and whistling, as if there'd been a great triumph and they demanded a curtain call. Only I remained silent, sitting at the back of the hall with my crutches, unable to fathom how there could be applause, that it could somehow be warped into a celebration.

Afterwards, leaving the hall, there'd been that line of children dressed in towels and goggles; the crowd pausing at the entrance, waiting for them like ducks over the road. As they passed, I'd wondered how it was possible for someone to have scheduled a swimming lesson now? Today. Ever again. The idea was monstrous and cruel. And yet, here they were: the Kewfield Tadpoles, making for the indoor pool, just as Alek's coffin had drifted silently down the road and people had begun to speak and to laugh. And watching them pad away, I realised it was because the world hadn't changed. The service was over; Christina had been put to rest and now children were learning to swim. And tomorrow, bins would be filled with service programs, and there would be chamber rehearsal in the Memorial Hall.

My blood had risen at the thought – the young swimmers plodding one after the other, as if no one was gone forever. Something had snapped. Suddenly I was pushing my way through the mourners, screaming at the kids to 'Go somewhere else!' and 'Could they not see there was a service!?'. A moment of anarchy: people gasping in disbelief; the Tadpoles scattering, all except a tiny girl in a swimming cap who stood bawling. Dad had caught my arm and I'd slipped on my crutches and fallen backwards, still yelling incoherently – onlookers watching in dismay from the entrance hall; me on the ground, the howling child, the service in tatters.

It was guilt, of course: my outrage at the audience and the swimmers, at the disinterest of the universe – causing me to fling rebukes in every direction; just as I'd launched at the Pro-lifers, and blamed Ali for the scars on Christina's belly.

And strangely enough, it was Ali who had appeared then – our final meeting – as everyone else stood back, not daring to intervene, embarrassed by my crutches and the performance as a whole. Only Ali was brave enough to do what needed to be done: bursting from the crowd and wrenching me to my feet. We hadn't spoken since she'd raged in the park. Now she stared me down, her face glossed and expressionless.

'Today's not about you,' she'd said. 'Don't you dare make this about you.'

People were turning away; the tiny girl no longer sobbing. And Ali looking me in the eyes – as she does so well – with the vacancy of a death mask.

'We're not here for you; we're here because of you.'

*

I've always admired Alinta for that moment.

To this day, she remains the only person to speak her mind, to be honest, while everyone else stands about my bed with flowers and balloons, ensuring that I'm comfortable, that I'm an object of pity. As though everything happened to me, and not to Christina.

It is a mulish compassion that began in the hospital room: people surrounding me with advice and concern, refusing to listen when I revealed my culpability, forgiving me, telling me it was perfectly understandable . . . that they could imagine how under the circumstances, one might . . . how I could want to . . . Choosing instead to blame Christina. For where was she to defend herself?

'How cruel it was,' I began to hear, 'such a selfish act – awful – but selfish . . .' Whispers behind the door when people figured I wasn't listening: 'Look what it's bloody done to him – just *terrible* – and her poor mother . . .' Relatives and friends tensing at the mention of her name, glazing over and changing the subject.

Then one day – it might have been three months after my ankle was healed – Christina's letters suddenly disappeared from my desk drawer: Mum and Dad deciding that enough was enough, that it was essential for all of us to start moving forward again, that we needed to take control of our lives and look to the future. And I'd had to break eight of my neighbour's windows before they would give them back.

That night, Mum had sobbed on the lounge room floor, wailing that she 'couldn't bear to see me wasting away!'. I remember swooping in to demand where all her tears had been when there was dye on the sheets? Mum sitting in a mess, confused and blubbering. 'What dyyeee!?' And I explained that of *course* she didn't know, because she hadn't lifted Christina's pyjamas, had she? She hadn't seen her belly was a sun! Well, I *had*, hadn't I? And what had I done? Nothing! That's right – nothing! And if she didn't know *that*, then how could she possibly have any idea about anything *else*?!

'Listen to what you're saying,' she'd shrieked. And then I was swatting her hair and yelling over and over that she had No fucking idea! No fucking idea! and Dad had wrestled me out of the house and the CATT team had arrived and it was the first time I visited this clinic.

Since that day, people have done their best to regress Christina. From my first appointment, she was no longer a person, no longer a human being, not even a memory – but an idea, a crux every counsellor was desperate to unpack and examine. And when I refused to unpack, she regressed further still. She was simply a hurdle to my recovery, a hurdle that must be overcome if I ever hoped to 'love myself again'. If I ever hoped to 'be the best version of myself', to 'be on my own team' – and other such slogans of positivity and self-esteem.

See, these are the words spoken by people standing at the bedside. The people urging me to get on with it, who are frustrated when I don't, as if there's some fundamental piece of information that's escaped only me. People neither listening, nor wanting to understand; they are the words written on their cards and flowers.

–Just as that afternoon I defaced every photo of myself in the house, scribbling over my face with permanent marker in an act of self-loathing. And Mum had seen what I'd done and immediately wrapped me in her arms, clutching me tight until I couldn't breathe. '*Yes*, Matt . . .' she'd said, with tears at my furious scrawl, 'you *are* stronger than you know . . . Don't forget that!' The phrase somehow twisting in meaning to become, from that very moment, the catchphrase of my recovery; Mum repeating it again and again, rocking back and forth as we wept for completely different reasons; and as the ghost of Christina flitted dimly between us, no longer able to haunt, but quashed instead beneath the perspective that life must go on.

How quick people are to betray the dead.

Well, I will not. I refuse to let go of Christina's memory. I talk about her; I think about her. I speak to her; I write her letters. I keep her memory alive. And some days, I swear to God, she seems more alive than anyone, that if I look around, there are traces everywhere: an ashed cigarette in the park; spinning around just as the swing becomes still, as if I've missed her by a second. Or in the cafe, when that woman smiled and there was something so familiar that for a second, I almost . . . Surely not. Or standing by the fence of the Kewfield Oval, squinting in the mist of the sprinklers and seeing something rushing about – *was it?* Perhaps. In these moments, suddenly she's everywhere. And I'm able to feel her. And I swear to God she's alive – just behind the door maybe, about to turn the handle.

But I'm told this is unhealthy. The kind of talk that causes people to glaze over and grow weary; friends losing interest; Dad's brisk visits: arriving with chocolate and asking for developments, keen for signs that I'm moving on – as if *I'm* the one who can't bear to look things in the eye . . .

And now that I've been reminded, I think I might finish with this one last memory: (getting late now anyway; time to turn in) the morning Christina left – sitting in the ambulance.

At that point, it was still dark and torches were flashing everywhere, people rushing about: police and firefighters, neighbours ushering their children away, wary of the boy in the ambulance, wary of the sirens and the tape and Connie moaning her long, terrible moans from somewhere. All of us could hear it, even with everything going on: Connie moaning like a home birth, asking awful questions that no one wanted to think about.

Then suddenly the paramedic was handing me a green whistle. She had a kind face, smiling and telling me to inhale for the pain; sensing my distress and realising I had no guardian – asking if I could remember a phone number. I gave Mum's and she smiled again, putting a hand on my shoulder.

'It's going to be okay,' she'd said.

It was like the words had been a cue in a play. I remember everything suddenly going quiet as Connie's moaning fell away. For an eerie moment, there was silence; everyone uncertain, waiting for her to start again. But she was finished, sedated I think. Then, out of the silence, a bird had started singing in one of the trees. Tentative at first, chipping and chirping; then singing – a happy song piercing the silence. Soon after, another bird joined, then another and another; until suddenly there seemed to be hundreds of them, all singing from the trees and heralding the daylight. And sure enough, the sun was lancing out of the trees now, lifting the fog in blues and oranges – a gorgeous morning. And people were stopping to look, the first responders forgetting their work, neighbours and children, the paramedic, everyone turning to look at the shadows peeling across the grass. And it struck me then that Christina was gone. She was gone and here was the most spectacular morning. And it was as if the world itself was repeating the words of the paramedic: the birds and the sun, telling me it was going to be okay. After all, they said, Christina was gone and here was this beautiful morning – perhaps more beautiful than ever before. And looking around, everyone was glad to see it.

The neighbours and first responders, glad to be reminded that it was a new day, that the horrible noise had stopped and whatever had happened was over – for here was the sun, rising again. They were standing with the tragedy behind them. And I could feel their relief.

At some point, Christina has become a horrible noise. And everyone wants me to turn away because they can't bear to look themselves. My crime is that I refuse. This is the truth. I refuse to turn away, when others can't bear to look.

I am the only person in the world who isn't fragile.

*

Anyway, that's all I've got.

Tomorrow, I suppose I'll tell Gloria that I've finished. We'll discuss. And then afterwards, perhaps we'll both sit in our separate places, wondering what the point of all this was.

Just as I am now.

Tuesday, 23 February

'BUT YOU'RE NOT telling the truth, are you? Matt? You know you're not. I'm sorry – but we can't keep doing this.'
   –Gloria

Wednesday, 24 February

TODAY I AM numb.

Yesterday, Gloria asked to transfer me to another clinician. Because she 'can't see any way to move forward'. Blindsiding me with a heavy heart, because: 'How can we possibly move forward if you're not telling the truth?'

She was agitated, red-faced like I haven't seen before, talking talking: 'People thrive in different environments . . . It isn't uncommon.' Telling me about some fabulous contemporary in Armadale, very good, very experienced – she thinks I'd make strides:

'Relationships are the things that determine whether people are comfortable to express . . .'

Was she ashamed? She was speaking faster than usual, reciting from a book, wishing it wasn't the case but not looking me in the eye, consulting her notes as I babbled a denial – I don't even remember what, so taken was I by surprise.

'See, people feel comfortable,' she explained again, 'in different environments . . .' explaining explaining – ashamed – throwing up her hands as if it simply couldn't be helped.

'I just don't see any way around it . . .'

Finally looking me in the eye. An expression of immense pity. Was there anything I wanted to say?

I thanked her for her time.

Afterwards, in my room, I had an overwhelming desire to speak to someone. Who though? My mother, so she could coddle me and tell me I'm wounded? My father, so he could veer the conversation to things less vital?

In the end, I could only think of Ali. I dialled her number with shaking hands. She heard my voice and said she'd 'be right there!'.

I wonder when was the last time I had a friend who'd be right there?

We met in the foyer and she took me for coffee, paid and listened as I explained the whole thing to her, everything I've told Gloria: about the journal and about my indiscretions – about all the times before that; waiting rooms, corridors, plastic bed frames . . . Did I like Gloria? Not particularly – I mean, I *did*; I'm sad to see her go, but we had no special connection. Do I feel betrayed – sure I do – but it's not that.

Then what? Ali asks.

–And I find myself asking too: Why this numbness today? Why not other times? When it's happened before? Because it has, after all; hasn't it? Yes. Again and again. It . . .

(Ali looks up from the paper napkin tower she's been building.)

But I've gone silent now, my words catching and falling away as a reason suddenly presents itself, hung right there in vivid clarity:

I am headed nowhere.

*

I am on a wheel. All my appointments and sessions and classes. I always imagined I was heading somewhere. But I'm not, am I? I am going around and around. I am on a wheel and it only seems like I'm going somewhere. But I'm not. I'm stationary – always running, of course, running running. But to nowhere. Only to different corridors and hospital wings, to different people asking the same questions: ('Do you *often* have thoughts like that about yourself?') Where did I think I was going? I thought I had a destination in mind . . . a light at the end. How close did I think I was? Three-quarters? Halfway? Irrelevant. ('And would you say this is a *common* experience for you?') I can't be halfway or nearly there because I am on a wheel, telling the same story: starting with a funeral, ending with a river. And things are passing by – people are passing, friends, relatives, standing at the bedside – an invitation to a wedding. I stand at the back with my hands clasped, wondering if it will ever be me. *Laughter from the studio audience.* But I am running around instead, to another office, another bright room with another person asking me questions. ('And how often would you say you think about these things?') Telling the same story; from the funeral to the river. Telling the whole thing, so they can read their notes and suggest I transfer to someone else – their fabulous contemporary in Armadale – as the world keeps passing by, making love and buying houses: 'What have you been up to?' an old friend asks now, cradling a brand-new baby girl. I've been here, I say – oops! She's crying; sorry, she needs a change. Quick quick! – rushing away . . . I've been watching my twenties, I say now, to no one; watching them slip away, gone in the blink of an eye as I told my story to different people in different rooms. Over and over again. Down to the river. As I refused to turn away.

And so I ramble and blather – Ali sitting the whole time; sympathetic, listening. She doesn't judge, she builds her napkin fortress.

When I'm finished, she looks up, and I can see she feels sorry for me.

It feels good, I think – sympathy – like a balm. Only she's a little confused, she says. Her arms are crossed now. She has a question; uncertain though.

'Why do you keep talking about a river?' she says.

Yes, it's definitely sympathy. Bemusement – but sympathy. She wants to help. She's waiting for an answer.

Only the question has silenced me.

Why do I keep talking about a river? It's an interesting question, one I'm not sure I can quite answer.

I think of Gloria's frustration.

Now Ali takes my hand – still tender – she wants to help, leaning in.

'Matt, there's no river behind Wychwood.'

Thursday, 25 February

I'M TWELVE YEARS old and I sit on a hill beside Christina. We're throwing bottles across the tracks at the decrepit junction house, where she's hidden her stash. The house is half covered in graffiti. A horn blares and she asks me if I want to see her game. Her favourite game, she says, have I ever played? She's skipping down the hill.

'What are you doing?' I yell.

She grins and steps onto the tracks, turns her gaze to the train. She waits.

'What are you doing?!'

But she's not listening anymore. The train has appeared and she keeps her eyes focused. The horn sounds and it brakes. But it's going too fast. It won't be able to stop in time. She watches it approach. And at the last second, when it's right there, she jumps out of the way. My heart drops and she runs laughing back up onto the grass. She takes a stone and throws it. It bounces off a window and the horn blares one final time.

We race back into the thicket.

Friday, 26 February

'WHAT WAS BEHIND the farm?' Ali looking me in the eye, curious, warm. 'I know,' she says. 'You know. What was it?' She wants to help. 'Say out loud, now – to me.'

But I have nothing to say.

CONNIE KISSED MY cheek when I was thirteen. When she'd tucked Christina in. She knelt down and I felt her breath on my neck, a cold half-moon on my cheek.

I thought to myself: Who the hell kisses someone else's kid?

ALI, ALI.
  Do I dare, though?
  You pull one thread and the thing unravels.

March . . .

CHRISTINA AND I in the workshed; Connie at the garage door; she wants Nurofen; she disappears in the white rain. Then the taxi.

'Am I getting it?' I ask.

'Leave it,' Christina says.

The horn blares again, far away.

'Let me put Mum to bed,' she says. 'Wait for me.'

I watch her follow her mother down the path.

And then I go to the couch . . .

What happened on the couch?

March ...

IN THE AMBULANCE, I watch the sun rise. No one can believe it. People aghast everywhere. They're being told to wait for replacement buses.

And I will never see Christina again.

March . . .

WHO THE HELL kisses someone else's kid?

March . . .

I NEED TO say something.

I haven't said it yet because I've forgotten. Well, not entirely. I don't know. Either way, it's something I've not said – about why Christina ran away.

What do I remember?

The kiss. The garage door. Nurofen. The white rain. The taxi.

Then Christina leaves the workshed to put Connie to bed – and I go to the rumpus room.

Then it's fragments.

I lie awake listening for sounds, my head spinning with fantasies (the door opening, taking Christina's hand, a train somewhere far away, 'Wait for me!' she says).

Outside, the rain is pummelling the grounds; I peek through the blinds at everything thrashing about, wondering if it's morning yet, not knowing the time and sitting up to see.

It happens in the moment I sit up to see – the door opens. I look out into the dark and think: Here she is!

Here she is.

But it isn't – I realise immediately. There's a figure crossing like they don't know the room. The cushions collapse and I see fingers and swollen knuckles. And I think: how do those fingers play the piano? But I don't move. The smell is sweet and rancid, and I feel a mouth on my cheek – open, so when it pulls away, it leaves a cold half-moon. I focus on it; I feel how it's still wet. She's telling me things, begging me. But she's too heavy for herself; the skin on her arm is caulied and doesn't fit her bicep. She trembles. And I think: If I wanted, I could send her flying. But I don't move – and I wonder what that means. I think: She is older than me. Is that why I'm not throwing her aside? I could; there's nothing of her. And just as I look to where she'd go flying, I see something shift in the doorway. *Did it?* Just now – is something there? A figure. Was that shadow always there? I don't remember. But now I'm being raised and propped uncomfortably; a finger strokes my cheek. 'Please,' she says. Or was it her wedding ring? Either way, here she is: Connie. Greedy and kind. She's bruising my wrist, pushing herself into my neck and taking long trembling breaths. And I think: Here I am, doing this now, as she shudders up to my ear. And I could throw her away, if I really wanted, I could throw her right past Christina in the doorway. Right past Christina watching. But I don't throw her away, because I want her to be okay. I feel sorry for her. I touch her face and I listen – for she's at my ear now, leaning forward, sweet and rancid. She's whimpering.

'It's okay,' she says, softly, in my ear. 'It's alright.'

*

How long do I lie awake afterwards? Not daring to move, in case I'm not paralysed.

*

And things will happen later, won't they?

When there's time to consider. With space for thoughts to intrude. Lots of things will happen then, won't they?

Later I will be violent. I will be irrational. I will assault my mother and cause her to fear me – and a girl in a Safeway cool room, who approaches quietly from behind to touch my hand. I will sleep with the light on. I will become nauseous in a class discussion about visions of a hag that manifest during sleep paralysis, and cry in the sick bay for no reason in the world. I will run screaming down the street as my father tries to apologise to neighbours in the windows. And of course I will feel that deep nausea again, an asphyxiation, rising in waves at the sight of a van door opening outside Sable aged care, when a woman steps down who I recognise; that unexpected meeting in my second year of teaching – my final year.

Yes, it will return, this evening. And I will do many things. But all much later . . .

For right now, in this moment, I don't think about it. Right now, I lie awake, peering at the paddock out the window, becoming a chalky grey. The horses stepping like clay figures. The act hasn't quite solidified. It still wavers as something undefined and phosphorescent. I feel vaguely that tomorrow it will not exist. That perhaps in the morning, Christina will open the door wrapped in a towel. And we will grin. Yes – tomorrow. I push away the flutter in my chest. Fluttering away. Past the shadow in the door, that's no longer there. It had been though, hadn't it? Seeing me lie still. Seeing me let it happen.

But anyway, silly thoughts. Because nothing might have happened yet.

And so I lie still – in case I'm not paralysed – waiting for the sun.

*

Do I sleep?

Yes.

I must, because something jolts me awake: a banging that enters my dreams, causing me to rise in confusion, oddly propped in my underwear. I dress and fly out of the room.

In the lounge, the outside door is flapping against the wall and the clock says 4.48. Leaves are rising and blowing away in strange patterns. And I think: Am I awake? as a toilet flushes somewhere. I rush out into the rain, up the path. And then there she is: Christina – at the garage door, standing in a dress with a backpack. She's looking at me though in some new way; she wants me to speak. She's waiting for me. But what? I yell through the rain. That I'm sorry? That I saw her in the doorway? That I could have thrown her mother away?

And does she reply?

No – because I've made all this up, haven't I? Somehow I've made it up out of nothing.

Christina's not really there. I'm standing in her father's clothes, before a shed full of awful memories. And I am alone. There's no one else, only rain tumbling everywhere. And a set of footprints in the mud, running away from the house, from her mother, from me. And I know where they're going.

I sprint through the paddock, under the widow makers and over the fence, feeling nothing as I mangle my foot on the barbed wire – No, I can't have – because the fence was electric, not barbed wire. My foot is fine as I run through Davies' paddock. I just can't see anything for the rain. I'm stumbling along, pulling myself forward, blindly thrashing at plants – until finally I come out the other side, to the river.

Only there's no river.

I am on a hill. And below are lights and confusion; bells and sirens and people unable to believe it – they're being told to wait for replacement buses. I run forward and slip, cracking my head open and slicing my ankle on a broken bottle. I become groggy watching blood drizzle in a fountain, as a woman's voice floats nearby. She says: 'Oh my God, it's a girl,' and I look and see someone on the bridge. I see their torch flailing as they scamper across. Then the woman screams and I raise myself up, hobbling to the steps. I slip again, but not before I see – for a second as the torches swivel around – Christina doing backstroke. Only she isn't. Now strong hands are pulling me away. I'm screaming her name and everyone's looking at me. People are telling me to calm down. They're bruising my wrist. I'm calling out, trying to see her between the carriages. But she's disappearing, appearing, disappearing, held mid stroke with her head turned my way. And for a moment, I swear, we almost catch eyes. I try to catch her eye. But not quite because I'm being pulled away. And because she's disappeared again. For good this time. And now I can only see her hand, still raised. And I notice that her middle finger is touching her ring finger. And I wonder if she's trying to communicate something.

But I can't see her under the blanket.

MY PARENTS' HOUSE seems foreign. The garden is unrecognisable, the furniture rearranged. I am in the spare room – my old room – on the black-framed bed of my adolescence, and the kitchen is stocked with the same food as it always was. But somehow the house remains foreign, in a way I can't place.

How to describe this last month?

It was two Saturdays ago that I stood in the clinic car park with my suitcase, peering into my old room, the curtains and bedding creating an illusion of sepia against the bright lemon trees.

On the drive home, I felt that first unmooredness of freedom, passing people shopping and dining and aware that if I so desired, I could eat at those restaurants, walk on those streets – anywhere I liked – out over the St Kilda pier, with all the tiny figures being tossed in the wind.

Instead, after an early dinner, I retired to my room; my first night home spent as a lifer released, terrified of an unfamiliar world. I lay in the shelter of my room, listening to Dad's restrained disappointment at Melbourne losing to Essendon; Mum typing emails in the computer room just outside.

A serene imitation of domestic life – only Mum's tapping was overtly loud, reminding me of her presence.

Four times she entered my room, ostensibly with bits to do: bringing my clothes, bringing the case, placing the ficus by the window, fussing and fretting at the wardrobe – a champion of the staunch philosophy that love is something one does rather than feels. She hangs about the doorway as I wait patiently, looking up from my novel; she smiles and doesn't want to leave.

At night she's been walking by my room, as I lie awake, her footsteps on the tiles, treading an anxious vigil. I hear her approach and drift away; the beam of light appearing across the carpet as she peers in and I pretend to be asleep.

I understand her impulse to tread lightly. She has cause, after all; she only follows precedent, stripping the house of sharp objects, et cetera . . . Except I maintain that something's different this time. I'm not exactly sure what; but something feels adjusted.

–And *yes,* I'm fragile, I understand that; and I realise it's only two weeks – but I don't know . . . There's a togetherness that feels different from other times. I move with the ginger mannerisms of a convalescent; my limbs ache, but with healing.

I am certainly supported: with Mum behind every door and Ali here all the time. I suspected her friendship was merely the kind of waning charity I've become accustomed to. But we've grown close. We've started meeting several times a week, after her shifts. We go to Carlton Gardens and walk around the Exhibition Centre, the neighbouring streets.

It's here that I've been feeling it most: with Ali in the gardens, among the trees; when I feel almost – dare

I say – in control. Together, at least. We sit on the benches, watching the riders enjoy the last of the weather, and I am held in that way only nature makes you feel. And fragile, of course; but cradled, sitting in the pale sun as the trees swish over there. It is an intimate harmony. Thoughts arriving and leaving. They are tempered. They do not fling me about and turn me upside down. And I don't know – in these moments, I feel that maybe, almost, perhaps, I am turning a corner.

So why am I writing this down then?

What finds me here with a pen once again?

Gloria's suggestion, of course – even though our sessions seem to run so well these days: her sitting forward in her chair, almost with budding excitement; mapping future goals, consolidating positive behaviours, practising defusion. I have been going to bed early, getting up early, swimming with Dad. I have contacted friends who have greeted me with open arms.

So what then? What's that thing Gloria detects at the end of our sessions, when I fall silent and she shuffles upright in her chair?

I visited Connie yesterday.

What can I say about it?

Ali offered to accompany me but I wanted to go alone – I suppose to face things.

She was there of course, as always, in the tearoom with her blanket and her bag of fluids, flinging up her hand as though from a cafe across the road, rising to greet me – not rising, obviously, but raising her hands to my cheeks.

'Well, look what just dragged in.'

She remains the same, as though the world hasn't spun since I left: noodling her hair with the grace of an heiress; leaning forward and dropping her voice in liaison against a decrepit woman asleep in an armchair; doing all the talking, as she always does:

'I mean, with the council and everything, who knows these days?' peering out through glossy eyes, '–But I'll *definitely* be getting a few things done. All this'll be reupholstered, of course.' Her finger scanning the plastic chairs in the waiting room. 'Then here: I'm thinking of opening this up, getting a bit more light, maybe a bay window or something.'

She was indicating the reception desk, half-dropping her finger; then suddenly coming back: 'But enough about *me* . . .' slapping my shoulder and pushing away with a beachball laugh. 'How are *you*? How's the house? How's . . .'

'Matt?'

'Matt.' Her eyes shimmering a moment. 'God, he must be . . . He'd be almost out of school now, wouldn't he?'

He was, I said. Several years now.

I left her in the hall, with her blanket; her voice twittering behind me, chatting on to no one: 'Oh yeah, but then he's always just that same old thing, isn't he?'

Then a final girlish laugh as the doors closed behind me.

Connie is ill.

What else can I say?

She's ill. As we always knew she was.

And while I had been warned – by Gloria and Ali both – that I may not receive the closure I was after, still, there was a heaviness in my chest, striding home from Sable Road, through the park, and feeling so much loss.

I know what I was after, of course. The very same thing I've been after all these years; the reason I've continued to see her. I am seeking a connection, some link to the past.

It's what I'm waiting for, isn't it? Even now. Even still. For Christina to appear, to somehow present herself. Even at this very moment – sitting in a cafe, as I am – looking over the road at a woman walking with her daughter, the child clutching a bright blue envelope; the mother having to lift her up because the letterbox is too high. I am watching her being lifted now – though not exactly. I am seeing something else instead. I am watching myself – I am lifting the child up. And there are three of us now, walking away from the letterbox, to somewhere else, home perhaps; walking in a line with the child clutching our hands–

–I've just smiled and the mother's smiled back; only her smile didn't reach her eyes. Because of course, I'm some weird guy smiling at her child for no reason.

She has no idea what she is to me.

I hoped there would be some link, something clean and uncorrupted. Because the truth is, Christina is nowhere. It's as though I lost myself a minute, disappeared into my own head where she was swirling and imperious and now, when I look about, I realise none of it exists. Everything has gone; the streets are repaved and the buildings have disappeared.

Christina exists only in my head, buried deep in a tangle of memories. And sometimes she'll flutter to the surface, tossing stones at the window or appearing wrapped in a towel, grinning in her doorway – but then I am taken with that sick feeling and suddenly she mutates. She is debased: a shadow in the doorway; a ghost in a dressing gown. The memory is corrupted, as was Alek's, as is the woman at Sable Road – whom I will never visit again. Even in my dreams, I stand at the track side and watch her become engulfed. So where is she then? What is she? A vague shape, forever running away, just out of sight.

Then Ali clings to my arm as we sit in the gardens–

'It gets easier,' she says, 'from here . . .'

And who am I to say otherwise?

–But perhaps this is what I fear most of all: that resolution has arrived. That I have won. That this is winning. For I am seeing clearly, am I not? I am together, am I not? I have stepped back and I see my entire life strung to a memory. And just as Alek lay withering, so the memory had grown to something monstrous. The images I defined as happiness – to which all things were compared – were themselves corrupted. When the curtain is stripped back, they were my very illness. This is a story of corruption.

And so I rid myself of illusion then. I see the memory for what it is, a smokescreen, a cancer causing me to wither.

And then what – I am healed? I am winning?

Maybe it's all true.

Then why can't I shake this gnawing thought, as Ali peers at the trees swaying in yellows and oranges – rich autumn colours that I suspect don't quite shimmer the same for me; for though leaves may colour with the season, their lustre is determined by the heart.

Why can't I shake the thought that in the end, I've vanquished an ally?

ALI ARRIVED TODAY at twelve for our excursion – our 'expo-
sure therapy' as she chucklingly terms it – leaving my parents
to the VFL and toasted cheese sandwiches and making our
way to the station, the weather blustering but still balmy.

I've been trying to think of the last time I took a train.
Years, at least – but is it possible I've managed to avoid them
this entire time?

Either way, standing out on the platform, I feel that
light-headedness again, scanning right and left at the tracks
bending away and disappearing; feeling my fingers numb
and become disembodied.

On the way, Ali natters about her job and her patients,
talking talking above the loud beat of my heart, keeping
the conversation running without being hamstrung by my
hurdles of silence. She's a good friend.

Then from the station, we take an Uber to 'Fairby Estate',
as it's called now – the driver nattering all the way about how
they run a shuttle to and from Frankston, these days.

I barely listen though, peering out the window across the
road.

339

Everything's gone, of course: the plane trees, the house, the paddocks. Only the workshed remains, gutted and refitted as an indoor dining area; picnic tables dotting out onto the grass. As we're led to our table, I catch myself trying to work out exactly where I would have been. The verandah? The rumpus room?

But today we don't talk about Christina, perhaps deliberately. We simply share a platter of cheese and wine and talk about other things. At one point, it even strikes me that we're sitting where the couch would have been, right where Christina once told me her mother would burn to death before she ever awoke. But the thought causes nothing to stir; just as there was no great catharsis upon arrival. I simply drink my wine, peering at the grapevines beginning to colour: the rows of lime-green and yellow strung away down the hill through what was once Davies' paddock, and on further until a high Colorbond fence marks the beginning of a housing estate: grey roofs sprawling back to the railway line.

On the train home, I'm quiet again. I suppose I'd hoped for one last glimmer, a little nod from somewhere; a secret wink. But there's nothing left to fall into place. She is simply gone; Wychwood is gone.

And perhaps Ali understands, because as we near Highett, she says there's something she'd like to show me before I go home, if I've got a moment? I tell her I've got all day and we stay on to South Yarra.

As usual, Chapel Street is teeming with people out and about. But today we make a left, away from the thoroughfare, and follow a side street up to a sleek apartment complex with jutting rows of glass balconies. We enter with a key card and take the elevator.

Inside, Ali shows me around: bright furniture and dark carpets, walls of such crisp white that the whole place seems impervious to shadow – though not quite home yet, I deduce, spying a line of boxes half-ransacked against the living-room wall.

'It's only been a couple of months,' she says. 'Still settling in.'

It's nice, I say, and we go to the balcony for coffee, neat in the afternoon sun, peering down onto Chapel Street: at the corner cafe I've visited I don't know how many times with Mum; at the bazaar and the fish 'n' chip shop, the chemist and the pho place, and then, of course – if you take a left and walk down a bit: Yarra Clinic, sitting somewhere to my left.

'Thanks for coming today,' Ali says, as though I've done her a favour. She grins. 'Y'know, I actually hadn't been out there yet.' Then she looks away and for a split second, I see the grains of a story as long and difficult as my own.

Before I leave, she tells me there's one more room she wants to show me. Peeking inside, it seems just like the rest, bright and crisp with neat carpet; an orange couch to one side and a desk on the other. On top sits a lamp, craning over a series of reference books I'm confident I'll never be able to read. But my eye only scans these things. I don't even really see them. Because it's what's above the desk that catches my eye – and I realise why she's saved the room for last. Hanging above the books is a framed board full of photos. I feel my breath catch and I step into the room.

They are of Christina, scores of pictures I've never seen: sitting on her bed in the Kewfield dormitory; squealing with excitement backstage in her Puck costume; dangling her feet from the roof – now with Ali, peace signing in yellow face paint at a sports carnival.

'It's kind of my shrine,' Ali chuckles from the doorway.

I scan picture after picture. None of them are my memories; they are all moments that happened in my absence. But I recognise the expressions; the expressions I have seen many times. And in each photo, her face is clear and bright.

'I've sort of been using it as a study,' Ali says, still cradling her mug. 'I was planning on letting it out but work's been a little crazy . . .'

I peer at the room again, noting the crisp walls, freshly white. The bright couch.

'Unless—' she says, 'I was thinking on the way home . . . Maybe you were looking for somewhere?'

I look back at the photos. Bright memories in this bright room.

There are no ghosts here.

2017

2018

Sunday, 11 November

I'M SITTING AT a table in the kitchen. It's armistice day and I'm surrounded by a flurry of pages. Ali was going through the cupboard last week and found them in a box: my old journal. These last few hours, I've been reading back. I thought I'd jot one more entry, just explaining a couple of things, in case I or anyone else ever happens to read it again – God forbid.

What is this journal exactly? It's hard to say. A memoir? Fiction? Catharsis? Pages of rambling blame? rambling vindication?

All of the above, I guess.

I suppose the overriding thing to remember is that I was ill. It's clear in the entries, I think: the anger and frustration. Reading back, I had to keep reminding myself that when I wrote this, I was stuck. I hadn't moved forward yet, hadn't faced certain things. I remember sitting at the desk in the clinic; 'Write what you remember,' Gloria had said. And I would sit at the desk, thinking of a time, and there would be nothing. Blank. As if my mind simply refused. Other times, I could remember all too clearly – and I would be ashamed,

347

scared of anyone reading it. I would bend the truth, painting myself in less harsh a light.

The result is that not everything in this journal is true.

—not that I ever told a lie; I didn't set out to be deceitful. But there are things left out of this journal, things that are altered, some that never happened at all.

There was no river behind Wychwood. There was a train line; a clearing on the other side of Davies' paddock, trees hacked away and a steep hill going down to the tracks. From inside the thicket, the trains would sound like rushing water. But Christina never drowned. She was never trying to escape – there was no great plan, years in the making. Nor do I think she witnessed what Connie and I did and was driven into a frenzy. No, the truth is, Christina just had a tendency to wake some days in that fervour of hers, completely ecstatic and able to seize a pulse no one else could even feel. And then other days: waking to a world more desolate than any of us could understand.

So why change the story then? I guess the simple answer is self-preservation; to have something to understand. A reason gives us something to come to terms with. It's easier to digest; the same way it's easier to imagine her drowning – easier at least than imagining the real story, if that's what you want to call it. Because real stories are awful, aren't they? They have no moral and no purpose; there are no lessons to learn. And in this case, the real story is simply that before her seventeenth birthday, Christina stepped in front of a train. Because to her, there seemed no other way out.

There's comfort in reinventing the truth, because some-times the truth makes no sense – almost as little sense as her illness.

In the years after, I've come to understand it. Avoidance is a most human thing – a strictly human ability. We have no claws and we have no shell, right? But we have the gift of illusion. Our defence is to warp things that can't be borne, so that we can bear them, to change awful realities into something else; we make sense of them, we accept them, repaint them. Like angelfish tattooed over a scar. And when life has a tendency to inflict tragedies that are ruthless and completely without meaning, then comes illusion, parading as a gift.

But it's a mistake, isn't it?

See, for so long, I was muddled – all through my twenties; earlier – incident after incident appearing so unhinged and erratic, until you step back and see the thing as a whole and suddenly there's logic:

The intimate moment with Anna Blakey in the Safeway coolroom, when she'd leaned up to my ear and I'd flinched and knocked her to the ground.

At that point, I'd already begun sleeping with the light on – waking endlessly from awful dreams. Trains and tidal waves; waiting for the headlights to come from behind the trees. How many times have I had that dream? Countless – watching Christina on the tracks, the water lifting the train and sweeping over her; she raises her hand . . .

Then later, when I'd returned to school, Ms Cavanaugh describing 'sleep paralysis': the hag creeping towards you in the middle of the night, climbing on top and strangling you until you awaken. Year 12 Psychology. 'The mind making sense of apnoea,' she'd said, and her voice had become piercing. I'd looked out to see the oval bright and overexposed; then stumbled out of the whirling classroom. 'There's always support here if you need,' she'd told me later in the sick bay, having detected something sinister.

God, and then the rage – flung every which way, because of course I couldn't fling it at myself. Enormous rage, at anyone trying to help, at anyone suggesting I move forward and try to live, at any suggestion other than complete isolation. Because I desired only emptiness, space to fill with dreams of Christina, with thoughts; infinite space so her memory could become huge and then I could be crushed as I so deserved. How many years spent in self-flagellation? isolating myself as Connie had done – unable to see the world as it was for the cataract of my own self-loathing.

Yes, I was sick. Unable to look things in the eye. Unable to face that after Christina was gone, I'd sat in the back of the ambulance, watching the most spectacular sunrise. And knowing that she'd seen what Connie and I . . . what Connie had done. And knowing I would never be able to tell her that I wished it hadn't happened – that I wish I'd never gone to the house, never defied my mother, who knew somehow in her dismantled way that I ought to stay away from Wychwood.

Instead, I spent ten years confirming how I was to blame; running fine-tooth combs for any moment that might have changed the course of things – as I suppose one does.

But honestly, is there anything more pointless? To confirm my own guilt? Of *course* I was guilty. But wasn't I fifteen and self-centred? Wasn't I desperately unequipped? and with no ability to see into the future?

'Yes, but still I might have . . . If I'd only realised . . . Then perhaps . . .'

Ad nauseam.

Perhaps what's more self-centred is to believe I was involved at all, to insert myself as tragic hero of her story. Christina was ill. Isn't that the story?

Anyway, it wasn't long after this journal that things began to turn.

Ali and I were meeting regularly. We became close – finding camaraderie in our shared grief, finding we were eternally fused.

Not long after the clinic, she suggested I move in.

It was strange at first: Christina seeming to permeate everything, to sit in the silence between words. We stayed up long evenings, talking on the balcony, getting to the heart of things. Perhaps we talked so much that there was nothing more to say? Perhaps we simply understood it was terrible and that was enough? Either way though, eventually we began to talk about other things, deliberately not mentioning her name, then sometimes forgetting to.

Slowly, infinitesimally, I found Christina's memory starting to recede – not far away, never far away – but little by little, enough that everything wasn't crushed beneath it.

–And perhaps I was merely letting myself mourn, something I'd never done before; I don't know. But either way, that's when something unexpected happened. One day there was a change, and I found I was suddenly able to look things in the eye. I turned and looked, expecting to be dazzled. But instead, I found that Christina's memory had become something else. Not something massive and destructive, no longer a cataract; but a lens, delicate and uncorrupted, transforming everything that passed through. And when I looked then, for the first time in I don't know how long, I discovered life around me. Though not life as I'd known it – not the blazing fever of colour and sound, but something intimate, glowing in my palm, delicate and enchanting.

Christina sits beneath everything. She shines out, as though I've discovered the secret magic of things, and now I see it between the cracks. I can see it glimmering. The inner life adorning the outer. And I see that life is rich. That the oceans are filled with angelfish, and the swish of the trees is enchanting. And I thank God to be alive. To remember clearly. Because the memory is a gift – learned through terrible lessons, yes, but a gift all the same. And every so often, I'll take my keys and drive the car far out of my way to the Kewfield gates. And I'll stand at the fence and wait for the sprinklers, the oval becoming white with mist. And I've found that if you squint, you sometimes catch things rushing about.

Here I am, washed to the side.

I've been living with Ali for a year and a half now. We have separate lives and separate schedules, but we support each other. I've taken a six-month contract at Stonnington Primary. I still think about Christina most days – every day, really – but the memory enriches life. It does not prevent it.

We cannot let ourselves be defined by tragedy – something I've learned. And in these last two and a half years, I have relearned and relearned.

But anyway . . . I just wanted to note. Ali's arrived home; I hear her pottering in the next room. We're going to Shukah for her birthday, then maybe Yellow Bird.

I can fold this now and shovel it away somewhere. Perhaps to read sometime as a reminder. Or perhaps not.

M. Lacey, 11/11/18

Acknowledgements

THERE ARE SO many people to thank for making this book possible, far more than I'm able to list here. But I'll do my best.

Firstly, to my publisher, Cate Blake, for championing me and, with the help of Rebecca Lay and the excellent team at Pan Macmillan, bringing this story to life.

To Pippa Masson, who first saw something in this manuscript. Without her tireless work, as well as that of Caitlan Cooper-Trent and Benjamin Paz at Curtis Brown, this story would still be a ramshackle document on my laptop.

To my wonderful friends, in particular Giuliano Ferla, Tom Whitty and Phil Rouse, whose discussion, honest feedback and ideas helped turn my ramblings into something coherent and defined.

Also to my friends from AtticErratic, especially Celeste Cody and Steph Speirs, who were there in that underground car park all those years ago, when this story was in its infancy.

To Kerry Armstrong, who first told me I was a writer, and whose mentorship across the years has given me the confidence to stick at a work of this magnitude.

To Beth Shelton and Arie De Bruyn, whose ideas and advice, particularly in the field of mental health, were invaluable throughout the writing process.

Then to family: my parents, Julie and Graeme Pitts, for a lifetime of encouragement and opportunities in all areas I have chosen to pursue.

To my dog Polly, who really is the best company, currently asleep beside me at my desk.

And finally, to my partner Kate Monger. Writing this book has been, if nothing else, a gruelling process, and without her endless patience, her keen character insights, her ready conversation and unwavering support, I am certain there's no way I would have been able to finish it.